SPACE RUNNERS

THE COSMIC ALLIANCE

SPACE
RUNNERS
THE COSMIC ALLIANCE

JERAMEY KRAATZ

HARPER
An Imprint of HarperCollinsPublishers

For anyone who has ever felt lost in space

My Dearest 2085 EW-SCAB Winners:

Welcome aboard the Alpha Maraudi ship! I know you have many, many questions, likely beginning with "Why am I on some kind of alien spacecraft and when can I go back to Earth?"

As soon as most of you were evacuated to the city carved out far beneath the Lunar Taj, the Grand Dome was shattered by an Alpha Maraudi assault. Shortly after, a group of American forces—code-named Project New Apollo—arrived, and a battle between them and the Alpha Maraudi broke out. From what we can tell, the fight is now winding down, with the humans victorious.

So, if the Alpha Maraudi destroyed the dome, tried to take the Taj, and fought against forces from Earth, then why are we on their ship now? Simple: in order to save both our species, we're going to have to learn to work together. Let me be the first to say that the Alpha Maraudi on this ship, led by Commander Vala, have not been hostile toward us (thanks, in part, to a spirited speech by the Moon Platoon's own Benny Love, who assured them that we want only peace). Remember that their world—their entire population—is in the path of an exploding star that threatens to completely obliterate it. The lives of their people are on the line as well. Together, we'll try to find a solution that will save both the aliens and our own species. That, I think you'll agree, is the right thing to do.

Given the delicate nature of our relationship with the extraterrestrials, though, it would be advisable to take communications *slowly*. Since this mother ship has more than enough space for all of us, I'd ask that those of you arriving from the Lunar Taj remain in the hangar for now. The Pit Crew will lead you through the ship and help get you settled in once everyone has arrived.

I know many of you are frightened. I understand that, and as soon as we've put more distance between us and the Moon, we'll be organizing a caravan home. Also, for those of you worried about Elijah West: never fear! We've received word that he is alive and well! Unfortunately, he will not be joining us for the time being. (Hopefully soon, though!)

Please also keep in mind that my presence on this ship is in a much more limited capacity than what you were used to back at the resort. In fact, I'm currently restricted to a single swarm of nanotech projectors with a reduced ability to communicate with those outside my immediate vicinity. As such, if you need assistance, I urge you to please contact one of the members of the Pit Crew.

Finally, I'd like to thank all of you for your patience, your bravery, and your commitment to remaining calm during these stressful times. The Elijah West Scholarship for Courage, Ambition, and Brains has attracted the most exceptional youths from Earth for five years running now, and I believe with all my programming that the 2085 winners truly do represent the best of humanity.

Here's to saving a few worlds.

Pinky Weyve
Lunar Taj intelligence and executive
assistant to Mr. West

1.

Benny Love stared at the Moon, a small satellite covered with mares and pocked with craters. For thousands upon thousands of years humans had gazed at it, dreamed of it, and even worshiped it. He himself had spent many nights lying on top of his family's RV in the Drylands—the desert that had once been the western United States—unable to tear his eyes away from the glowing orb, wondering what secrets and marvels might be hidden across its rocky landscapes. What *possibilities*. He'd often fallen asleep imagining what it might be like to visit the little gray ball's most famous attraction, the Lunar Taj, humanity's first off-world resort. In his mind, the place was all chrome and dazzling lights and luxuries he'd never be able to afford on Earth: a shining beacon among the drab, seemingly endless sea of dust and rock that made up the Moon's surface. The most spectacular human achievement ever built. A place where anything

1

was imaginable, designed by the smartest, most incredible human who ever lived—Elijah West.

At least, that's what he'd thought several weeks ago, before he'd actually landed on the Moon and everything had gone so wrong. It had started with the asteroid assault on the resort that sent him and his new friends racing across the dark side in a stolen car. Soon after, they'd realized that an alien species called the Alpha Maraudi was planning to take Earth, and that Elijah West was going to let that happen. It had been left up to the newly formed Moon Platoon to attack the mother ship of Commander Tull, a fearsome alien leader, in order to stop a deadly asteroid storm speeding toward Earth. Before anyone had much time to celebrate, though, the Lunar Taj was invaded first by alien forces and then by human ones. Benny and the rest of the scholarship winners fled to Commander Vala's ship—but only after they discovered that hidden somewhere on the dark side of the Moon was a superweapon the humans had created, one that could apparently annihilate the Alpha Maraudi completely.

Now, the resort was in shambles, and all the sense of wonder he'd once felt for it was gone, replaced by a knot in his stomach that seemed to throb every time he thought about how what was supposed to be a fun-filled two-week trip to the Moon had turned into a mission to save his home planet and everyone on it—including his brothers, grandmother, and the caravan family he'd left behind.

Benny took a deep breath as the hologram of the Moon being projected in front of him flickered and zoomed in, giving him a better view of the Taj as it currently looked. He could just make out the human and Alpha Maraudi ships fighting above the resort. Below them, the courtyard that had been perfectly manicured earlier that day was now a cratered battlefield. He watched an alien ship crash near the mangled remains of the fountain that had once welcomed elite guests from Earth. Human soldiers charged past the wreckage and through a gaping hole in the front of the resort where giant chrome doors had previously stood, before the aliens had blown them away. Nearby, a cloud of smoke was visible above the garage, where Elijah West had promised Benny and a hundred other EW-SCAB winners the vacation of a lifetime their first day on the Moon.

Benny was so consumed by the vision of the Taj that for a moment it was easy to forget where he was. But then the accordion wheeze of an Alpha Maraudi rang out from somewhere behind him, echoing through the big rock chamber that served as the bridge of Commander Vala's ship, reminding him just how far from home he and his friends were. A few seconds later, Drue Bob Lincoln the Third walked through the lifelike hologram of the Moon, pausing in the middle of it. The image rippled, distorting around him.

"Dude," Drue said, putting his hands on his hips and sticking out his chest. "Look at me. I'm like some kind of planet-destroying giant. Do you have your HoloTek on you? Take a pic." He sucked in a breath through his teeth and nodded to the other end of the room. "Uh, quick warning, by the way: Those aliens are *not* cool with being in the background of holo-selfies. One of them yelled at me when I tried to snap a few." He paused. "At least, I *think* it was yelling."

"Seriously?" Hot Dog Wilkinson asked, shaking her blond curls as she stepped up beside Benny. "*That's* what you're worried about right now? Not, like, the fate of Earth and all of humanity?" She got quiet, leaning in. "Not these aliens turning on us?"

"Please," Drue said. He raised a hand and made a fist, showing off one of the silver gloves he and Benny's small group of refugees from the Taj had used to fight the Alpha Maraudi. The aliens had metal bones, and the electromagnetic gloves had turned out to be incredibly effective at neutralizing them.

Drue brought the glove to his lips and blew across his knuckles. "Don't you worry. I've totally got us covered."

As the two of them started squabbling over who was better equipped to protect the EW-SCABers if something went wrong, Benny took a deep breath and looked around the bridge, the reality of their situation sinking back into him.

On the other side of the room, Jasmine Wu and Ramona Robinson—the brains among his friends when it came to strategy and technology, respectively—were hunched over what looked like a control panel. Beside them, inspecting the glowing strands of lights floating above the terminal, was the hologram of Pinky Weyve, the disembodied AI from the Lunar Taj. An alien wearing long red metallic robes, the fibers of which seemed to be alive and constantly in motion, approached her. It stared at Pinky, the tentacles on the back of its head flicking in the air, until she noticed.

"Oh," the AI said. "Don't let me get in your way."

Pinky walked right through the alien, who shuddered, though Benny couldn't tell if it was out of fear or annoyance. Possibly both.

At the far end of the room, the giant mother ship's commander, Vala, sat on an egg-shaped throne made of gold and deep purple rock and pored over what looked to Benny like holographic readouts floating in the air. A guard stood beside the Maraudi leader. Benny couldn't see its eyes behind the metal mask that the aliens all seemed to wear, but he could feel that the guard was watching him and his friends closely, ready to protect Vala if necessary. Tentacles tipped with blades hung down to its waist, and Benny took a deep breath as he watched them swing back and forth.

Earlier that day as they'd tried to sneak through the Taj while the Maraudi invaded, he would have been terrified to stand in the same room as these aliens. And deep down, he was still uneasy—not just about being there but about the looming fate of his home planet and his family. Even though he and Vala were working together to find a way for both their peoples to live, they were just two groups among their species. Plus, they didn't really have a plan yet.

They had so much work to do, and fast. But Benny knew that if he let fear get the better of him, everything they'd fought for so far would be for nothing.

Benny's dad had been the one to teach him that fear only holds you back. And though he couldn't imagine what his father would say if he could see Benny now, he was determined to live by the man's words. For the past few days Benny had denied that he was the leader of the Moon Platoon—it had seemed like too much to take on, given everything that was at stake. But now, despite how scared he was and all the pressure that came along with people looking to him for answers and guidance, he was ready to at least step up to the plate and try his best. It felt like the right thing to do. And so he took a deep breath, trying to steel himself, and turned his attention to his friends.

"You should have seen the way I worked this electro glove back in the courtyard when Benny and I were after those stealth drives," Drue continued, taking fake shots at Hot Dog as he walked out of the hologram. "I was unstoppable! There were aliens flying left and right! Not to mention, the way I handled the Galaxicle was—"

"Guys," Benny said, glancing at the guard again and then back at his friends. "Maybe now's not the time?"

Drue let out an exaggerated sigh as Hot Dog shrugged.

"I know I can't blame him," she said, nodding to Drue, "but he really does bring out the worst in me."

Drue rolled his eyes and turned back to the hologram, where the few remaining alien ships above the resort continued to fight, despite being obviously outgunned. "Uh, so, should we be worried that my dad's forces are gonna come after this ship once all the little ones are taken down? Because he definitely does not know I'm here and that he shouldn't try to blast us out of the sky."

"We're far enough from the Taj that we should be safe for now, but we can't get going until all the Space Runners from underground are on board," Benny said. "Actually, can you guys go to the hangar and see how we're doing with that? Most of the EW-SCABers have got to be here by now." He looked back at the hologram. "And I'm guessing it's kind of a long flight to Jupiter."

Vala had told them that the moons of the gaseous planet were their next destination. There, more Alpha Maraudi—mostly scholars and researchers, according to the commander—were collecting samples and running tests, though what those tests were Benny couldn't imagine. All he knew was that the faster they got on the move, the sooner they could start talking and figuring out their next step.

"Maybe it'll be a short trip," Hot Dog said, a glimmer of light in her eyes. "A mother ship like this has probably got insane engines, right?"

Drue's mouth dropped open. "Light speed!" he half shouted as the two of them started toward the bridge's exit. "Like a Star Runner times a million!"

A few steps away, Hot Dog paused and turned back. She looked at Vala and the guard, then at Benny. "You sure you're okay here without us?"

"Positive," Benny said. He reflexively clenched both fists. On one hand was the same silver electromagnetic glove that his friends had. On the other, he wore a gold glove he'd swiped from another Maraudi mother ship, one that somehow gave him the ability to manipulate certain alien rocks. Without the two gloves, they never would have made it off the Moon or been able to infiltrate Vala's vessel.

Hot Dog nodded. "Aye, aye, cap'n." Her eyes lingered on the Maraudi guard a few seconds more, and then she hurried to catch up with Drue.

Benny took one last long look at the hologram of the Moon before walking across the bridge. "Pinky," he said as he approached the AI. "How are we doing?"

"Do you have any idea how frustrating it is to go from being the all-seeing, all-knowing central intelligence of the

Lunar Taj to being tethered to a handful of projectors from your hologram bracelet and the processing power of a data-pad?" she asked, her voice piping through the speakers in his space suit collar. She didn't wait for him to answer. "I don't even have the power to get in contact with the Taj servers from here," she continued. "But I'm getting used to it." She nodded to the nearby alien in red. "I've been watching Griida here operate the ship's controls. The Alpha Maraudi technology is . . . well, it's far different from anything we ever conceptualized on Earth." She leaned closer to Benny, her voice quieter. "Honestly, it's not just in another language, it's built on an entirely different realm of thinking."

"Great." He sighed.

Pinky gave him a little smile. "Don't look so down, Benny Love. I *am* still the most sophisticated program humanity ever created. Even without the full resources of the Taj, I have no doubt this is something I'll become accustomed to." She cracked her knuckles silently. "You know, this ship could *really* use some sort of artificial intelligence running it."

Griida let out what sounded to Benny like a groan. The two dark brown tentacles hanging from the back of the alien's head swung to one side before twisting around each other. Each was as thick as Benny's wrist and almost touched the blue stone floor.

"Once everyone's on board, Griida will kick us into high

gear. Jasmine and I have already double-checked the plotted course." Pinky hesitated, adjusting her black-rimmed glasses. "Speaking of the new arrivals, I think it would be best if you addressed them. They believe in you. Half of them followed you out into space to blow up an asteroid storm a few days ago. They'll want to hear from you again. Or at least see your face."

"Sure," Benny said, nodding. The idea made it feel like he had an engine sputtering in his chest—he'd discovered recently that public speaking was *not* something he particularly enjoyed—but he told himself he'd power through. He didn't have time to worry about it: there was too much at stake.

"It's all so *fascinating*," Jasmine said, not taking her eyes off the thin ribbons of light filling the air above the alien controls, looping and weaving around each other. She frowned. "I just wish I could read it."

"You and me both, Jasmine," Pinky said. "I'm dedicating much of my limited computing power to analyzing both this and the complexities of the spoken language of the Alpha Maraudi."

Beside them, Ramona shrugged, her face buried in the datapad strapped to her left wrist. "Letters. Numbers. ET scribbles. It's all just patterns and coding, hologhost."

"I find it hard to believe that you're not interested in all this," Jasmine said, eyeing their tech wiz.

Ramona looked up at her, grinning. "Don't be a troll, J. I'm doing max research here."

Movement from the other side of the room caught Benny's eye. Vala descended the few stairs that led down from the throne and walked to the hologram of the Taj battlefield in the center of the bridge, as if entranced by the image.

Jasmine noticed, too. "Vala's people are being defeated. Left behind so this mother ship can escape. I know we thought they were the bad guys, but, well . . . This is all really complicated. Maybe . . ." She bit her lip for a second. "Should we say something?"

"Like, 'I'm sorry the humans are shooting your people out of the sky, but you *did* attack the Taj'?" Benny asked. He paused. "Did I sound like Drue just then?"

"A little," Jasmine said. "But it's not like you're wrong, exactly."

"If open communication is your intention," Pinky said, "perhaps it would be a good idea to offer your condolences. It would further show that you are not of the same minds as those who are destroying the alien soldiers."

"Right." Benny said. "Okay. No problem. I'll just . . ." He took a few steps forward and then turned back to the others. "Uh, Jazz. Would you mind backing me up?"

She smiled and nodded. "Of course."

They walked toward the central hologram slowly, finally standing beside Vala. The alien's arms were at the commander's sides, the four slender fingers on each hand twitching slightly. Under the glowing stalactites that hung from the ceiling, the gemlike pieces of armor that studded Vala's body gleamed.

"Hi," Benny said, and then he paused. It suddenly dawned on him that not only was he talking to an alien—which, oddly enough, was something he was kind of getting used to—he was talking to someone who was likely much, much older than him. He had no concept of how long the Alpha Maraudi lived. All he knew was that both Vala and Tull had mentioned something about the aliens having been around far before humans were and that they lived much longer.

Benny took a deep breath and held his head up a little higher, trying to at least make it look like he was sure of himself. In fact, now that he thought about it, putting on a brave face when he was scared or feeling helpless was probably the only way he'd survived all the fights and space battles he'd found himself in lately.

"Hi," he said again. "I just wanted to say that I'm sorry . . . *we're* sorry for the ships that went down."

Vala didn't react. Benny opened his mouth, ready to say more, only to find that he had no idea how to continue. He looked at Jasmine, who must have recognized that he was at a bit of a loss for words.

"As the commander, I'm sure it was a really difficult decision to leave your people behind," Jasmine said, speaking carefully.

"We have a word for them that does not translate," Vala eventually said. "Not fighters, necessarily, but ones who protect. Those who . . ." The commander paused, standing so still that for a second Benny thought something was wrong. "Those who give themselves up for the whole," Vala continued.

"Right." Benny nodded. And then, without knowing what else to say, he found himself apologizing again.

One of the dozens of slender tentacles piled high on the commander's head reached out. It grazed a ribbon of green light floating above the image of the Moon. The hologram shifted, until it was Earth in front of them, spinning almost imperceptibly.

"One world," Vala said in a voice that sounded like a dozen people of different ages speaking at once. "Out of all the planets in all the galaxies, it had to be yours that we need."

Benny stared at Earth, a ball of water and sand and trees and people all kept alive by a glowing star millions of miles away. It was strange to see the planet look so peaceful and small, despite knowing that two species depended on it for their survival. He spotted the Drylands, which had always seemed so enormous to him when he was growing up, nothing but desert and cloudless skies as far as the eye could take in.

It seemed so foolish to have thought the Drylands were big, now that he'd learned of the Alpha Maraudi and realized how tiny his planet was in the grand scheme of the cosmos. In the last few weeks, he'd discovered that his perceptions of the universe were hopelessly limited. Space, it turned out, was a treacherous place. Full of wonder, yes, but also danger. There was much more out there than he had ever imagined.

Bathed in the glow of the hologram, a new thought entered his mind.

"You've never been to Earth before, have you?" he asked.

"No," Vala responded. "I know it only through our research and observations. I've never felt its soil myself. We have been very restricted in terms of visiting the planet."

The commander was silent for a moment as Benny tried to wrap his head around how it must feel to put so much importance on a place you knew only from holograms and research. But, then, that's how he'd lived in the Drylands. His caravan had survived by putting its faith in the idea that whatever their destination—even if it was a place they'd never been—it held the promise of a better life.

"What is it like?" Vala asked.

"It's . . ." Benny started, memories of his home filling

his head. The heat of the sun. The smell of a campfire on cold desert nights. The sound of his grandmother snoring, which he now missed, though he'd always thought it was so annoying back on Earth. "It's beautiful. Well, parts of it are. Even in the Drylands. I don't think I realized that until I got to the Moon, though."

"You miss it."

"Yeah," Benny said. "I mean, I miss my family. A lot. And . . . you know. Earth in general, too."

Vala nodded. "I understand. It is a long time since I've been on my world."

"We ruined parts of ours, that's for sure," Jasmine said. "But I always thought we'd make it better." She shook her head. "That's one of the reasons I got into science in the first place. I think a lot of EW-SCABers felt that way." She paused. "*Feel* that way, I mean."

And then they stood there, side by side, staring at the hologram together.

Benny wasn't sure what Vala and Jasmine were thinking about, but his focus drifted to the blip of the Moon in the background. He took a deep breath and tried to calm his nerves as his mind wandered to the dark side. There, an insane genius named Dr. Austin Bale had hidden a super-weapon capable of utterly destroying the Alpha Maraudi. One they knew virtually nothing about.

In a faraway galaxy, an expanding star threatened the

existence of the Maraudi planet, but it was possible that their annihilation would be orchestrated by humans.

Two worlds were at stake. Two species. And somehow, it felt to Benny as though it had fallen to him and his friends to try to save them all from extinction.

2.

The sound of boots on the stone floor broke the momentary stillness on the bridge. Benny turned to see Ricardo Rocha, the oldest member of the Pit Crew, walking toward them.

Ricardo looked at Vala and nodded cautiously, then at Benny and Jasmine. "The last of the SRs from the Taj are here," he said as he came to a stop in front of them. "The hangar is already closed up and everything."

Vala called something out to Griida across the bridge, and then turned back to Benny and the others. "Our power cells are being prepped," Vala said. "In a few minutes, we'll enter accelerated travel."

"A few of your people showed us around the mother ship," Ricardo said to the commander. He looked at Benny. "There's plenty of room for all of us. We're trying to help get everyone oriented. As much as we can. But the new arrivals are pretty . . . weirded out. A lot of them are upset."

"Yeah, I'm sure," Benny said. "Hiding out on an alien mother ship wasn't in the EW-SCAB brochure."

"It was the smartest thing we could do, given the way things were at the Taj," Jasmine said. "*I* definitely didn't want to get sent back to Earth so Dr. Bale and Drue's dad could try to destroy the Alpha Maraudi."

As Jasmine spoke, Vala's tentacles constricted around the glowing red ball they held. Before the commander could respond, though, Drue swaggered in, a half-eaten apple in one hand.

"Good news, guys," Drue said through a mouthful of fruit. "Our friends brought food with them. You'd better grab some now, though, because there's a *lot* of stress eating going on in there already."

Across the bridge, Ramona looked up from her HoloTek and zoned in on Drue's apple. "Snacks?" Her eyes went wide. "Is there soda? Energy drinks? My battery is depleted."

"Oh, yeah. But we'll def be running on sustenance squares soon if we're not careful." He came to a stop in front of Benny and scrunched his eyebrows together. "As the core members of the Moon Platoon, maybe we should stash some of the good stuff for ourselves?"

Benny blinked. "You're not serious, right?"

"Ehhhh," Drue said, shrugging.

"We will look at our own food reserves and try to discern what you might be able to eat without harm," Vala said. The commander looked to Griida and said something in their musical language.

Griida barked back.

"What did he say?" Drue asked. Then, after a beat: "Um . . . or is it she?"

"We do not classify our people as you do," Vala said. "There are many subtleties and nuances to our pronouns. They are not as restrictive as yours."

"Okay, sure, that's cool." Drue paused. "Uh, but, before I was kind of calling all aliens 'it' and that sounds a little harsh, right?"

Vala stared at him for a moment. "*He* would be the closest word you have for Griida. A female pronoun would be acceptable for me."

Drue nodded and bit into his apple. "So, what did our dude Griida say?"

"That you should eat whatever you like, and if it kills you, it will be a lesson to the others," the commander said.

"Seriously?" Drue asked, his face scrunching in disdain. Then he grinned a little. "Oh! I get it. It's a joke."

But Vala didn't laugh. Instead, she reached a tentacle down and removed the mask covering the top half of her face, revealing two diamond-shaped eyes that burned with red pupils and a third one in the center of her forehead that glowed a vibrant blue. She turned her shining gaze to Benny. "I believe now would be an opportune time for us to discuss what we're going to do next. You said you want us to work together. We must figure out what that will entail."

"Heck, yeah," Drue said. He took a final bite of fruit and then looked at the core. "Uh. You guys have trash cans up here or what?"

"It is customary for the Maraudi commanders to speak alone before small councils are brought in to advise. This helps to build trust."

Ricardo clenched his jaw, and Benny was sure he was about to protest. But then he just crossed his arms. "That makes sense."

"Come on. I'm the charmer!" Drue protested. "I should be in on this."

"Go back and help with the new arrivals," Ricardo said to him. "Like I asked you to earlier."

"What if I'm absolutely quiet and just listen?" he asked.

"Drue," Benny said.

He sighed. "*Fine.*"

"I'll join you in a moment," Ricardo said. Then he hesitated. His eyes fell to the floor, and then to the hologram of Earth spinning slowly beside them. "I'd like to see him again."

Without a word, Vala tapped a tentacle against one of the ribbons of light that floated on the fringes of the hologram.

In an instant the planet was gone. Instead, standing before them was the person responsible for the Lunar Taj and the very existence of Space Runners. The world's first trillionaire. A man who had raced cars across the Milky Way galaxy and who, despite having lost his faith in humanity for a while, had seemingly sacrificed himself to stop an asteroid storm from destroying Earth.

Elijah West.

It was only a recording of the call they'd received earlier, but it looked so real that the hairs on the back of Benny's neck stood on end. A gold mask covered Elijah West's eyes. Oddly enough, it matched the gold studs on his driving gloves, as well as the accents on his maroon space suit. It was almost as if the whole thing had been planned, like Elijah was dressed up for some costume party at the Taj. Were that the case, the hulking alien standing beside him might have been slightly less terrifying to Benny. It was Tull, the Alpha Maraudi commander who'd led the asteroid storm against Earth—and who Benny and Hot Dog had faced days before when they'd been sucked aboard a different mother ship. The commander's two slick black tentacles curved into the air like horns, and his menacing grin showed off rows of shiny gray teeth.

Ricardo was silent for a moment, unblinking as he looked at the hologram of his mentor. "I wish I'd been here when the call came in," he said quietly, "to see this for myself and tell him that we're trying to find him. To let him know the Pit Crew is still fighting."

"I'm sure he's never doubted that," Jasmine said. Her eyebrows drew together as she looked at Ricardo. Then she grabbed the sleeve of Drue's expensive-looking space suit and half dragged him toward the door. "Come on. Show me and Ramona where the snacks are."

"Mmmm," Ramona said, looking up from her HoloTek. "Take me to the foods."

Drue groaned, but led the girls out anyway. "Just for the record, Jazz, I am well aware that you're trying to distract me." He shrugged. "I just happen to know there's a stash of cookies in one of those boxes with my name on it."

When they were gone, Benny took a deep breath, swallowed hard, and then turned to Vala. "Okay. Lead the way."

Vala pointed a long finger at a pulsing dot of light on the edge of the hologram. "When you're ready, this will play the communication," she said to Ricardo.

She then motioned to a jagged hole in the wall. Benny had actually made it when he'd infiltrated her ship. It led into a gigantic chamber full of alien plants and flowers. "Walk with me, Benny Love of Earth."

He nodded, following her. He was almost to the garden when Elijah's voice filled the bridge.

"Benny," Elijah said. "What in the name of the Milky Way galaxy have you done with my resort?"

Benny stopped short when he heard his name, turning to see the recording that Ricardo had begun. By this point in the video, Commander Tull had removed the mask that had hidden much of Elijah's face. He flashed a wide smile and spoke in an upbeat voice, but even from across the room Benny could see that his eyes were rimmed in red, and that bruises were beginning to form around his hairline. Elijah may have been pretending that everything was okay, but Benny was pretty sure that was just an act for their sake. When he'd met Tull, the commander had threatened to take him and Hot Dog hostage as the last remaining humans, to set them up in some sort of lab or zoo so that the Alpha Maraudi could learn from them. They were to serve as examples of a species that had ruined itself—a warning to future generations of aliens. But that was before Elijah had blown away part of the asteroid ship with an overloaded hyperdrive. Now Tull was undoubtedly very angry. Who knew what he was capable of?

Benny had been on the bridge when the call came in— had talked to Elijah himself. He'd watched the recording afterward several times, too. He *knew* what happened next. Tull would question Vala's loyalty and warn that he'd already sent word to their home world that she was conspiring with humans. He would grill Benny and his friends about the superweapon they knew hardly anything about. And, finally, he would assure Benny and the others that the only way they'd see Elijah alive again was if Dr. Bale's weapon was destroyed.

Still, Benny stood there, part of him wishing that, impossibly, things would turn out different this time. He might have watched the entire recording again had Vala not made a harmonic noise behind him and, letting out a long breath, he turned to join the commander and discuss the fate of their peoples.

3.

The rock that Benny had melted earlier in order for
him and his friends to get to the bridge had hardened into
blobby pools on the floor. Benny felt a little embarrassed as
he stepped over them and into the garden.

"Uh," he said. "Sorry about the wall."

Vala nodded as a thin tendril tipped in gold moved
through the air, obviously intent on fixing the mess. Then
the commander paused.

"Can *you* rebuild it?" she asked Benny. "With the glove
that I assume came from Tull's ship? It is not of a design
that my crew members use."

"Well . . ." he started. He'd managed to close the hole
in the hangar that he'd created when they first boarded,
but that was about it as far his experience went with fixing things. Mostly, he'd used the glove to punch away alien
rock, which had worked out pretty well for him and his

friends, even if it wasn't the most delicate way to get things done. "I'm not sure if I can," he admitted.

"Why don't you try," Vala urged.

Benny hesitated. Was this some kind of test? And if so, to what end? Did the commander just want to know how adept he was at using the alien tech? He could almost feel her gaze on his face as she stared at him. Then he reminded himself that he was there to talk to Vala, to work with her—and in order to do that, they needed to start trying to trust each other.

"Sure," Benny said.

He stepped to the break in the wall, placing the golden palm of the alien glove against it. He concentrated, imagining the stone reforming, sealing them into the garden. Slowly, the rock began to move and grow, as though it were a thick liquid expanding under his touch. He slid his hand across it, hoping that plugging up the hole would be as easy as closing a sliding door. For a moment, it actually *felt* that simple.

And then the rock was stretched too thin and could no longer hold itself up. Chunks of it fell to the floor, crumbling, breaking Benny's concentration. He let out a breath and stepped back.

"Huh," he said. "I did it back in the hangar, no problem."

"What was different?" Vala asked.

Benny shrugged. "I dunno. I guess then I was mostly working on adrenaline. I didn't really have time to think. We had to seal the hole before we could move forward."

"Curious. As far as we know humans have never used this sort of science before. I admit it is a bit of a shock to me that it yields to your will at all." Vala flicked her gold-tipped tentacle in the air. Almost instantaneously, the wall was whole again, the melted stone rising and re-forming into a solid mass.

"Whoa," Benny said.

Vala extended a hand ahead of her, beckoning Benny to start down a trail covered in purple gravel.

The cavernous space was teaming with life, housing plants like Benny had never before seen on Earth or even in the Taj. Flowering pods in every possible color dotted yellow soil, thriving amid vines bearing metallic fruits, trees that looked as though they were topped with gossamer streamers, and bushes full of blooms that opened and closed every few seconds, a different shade of the rainbow each time.

The coiled, furry frond of a plant three times Benny's height grazed the side of his cheek. "Uh, so, should I be worried that one of these plants is going to kill me?"

Vala's lips curved into what might have been a smile. It was difficult for Benny to tell, since the Alpha Maraudi mouths were somewhat unsettling to him in the way they stretched all the way back to where a human's ears would be.

"I don't believe so," she said. "Though I would advise you not to touch anything in here until we know for certain. Definitely not the thorns in the back corner."

"Sure," Benny said. "I wasn't really planning on exploring."

They walked side by side, past bronze tree trunks and bushes covered in cotton candy–like puffs. Benny didn't know where to begin—there was so much on his mind, so many questions all fighting for his attention, that he was left overwhelmed as the gravel crunched under his boots. Finally, Vala stopped near the center of the garden in front of a mushroom cap taller than Benny and made of milky opals. A viscous, shimmering gold liquid dripped from its rim, forming a gleaming pool beneath it, surrounded by huge chunks of black quartz. Vala turned to Benny, her eyes still uncovered, burning into him.

"We each know how grave this situation is, do we not?" the commander asked. "My people are threatened not only by our expanding star but by this 'superweapon' that you warned me about."

"And your people want to take my planet, destroying humanity to do so," Benny said. "It's just the survival of both our species that we're dealing with. Nothing big."

They stared at each other.

"That was kind of a joke," Benny said.

"I have heard that your people use humor to mask their anxieties and true feelings," Vala said. "That is unnecessary here. We will find it easier to communicate if truth is prioritized."

Benny shifted his weight, his feet digging into the purple gravel. "Yeah. Of course. You're right. I know what's at stake. So do my friends."

"Then let us not waste time. You are the one who broke into my ship. Where would you like to start?"

He wondered for a second if he should apologize for that but worried that doing so would make him look weak, which was probably not the best way to begin this talk. Plus, he *had* apologized for the hole in the wall. That was something, at least.

"How long will it take for Tull's message to reach your world?" Benny asked. The other commander had implied that the Alpha Maraudi leadership would not be thrilled with Vala's decision to allow the humans aboard, despite Benny's insistence that they were there in the name of peace.

"It will take a day for it to reach Calam, my home. Perhaps two," Vala replied. "In Earth terms."

"And, uh . . ." he said. "How do you think they'll react?"

The tentacles on Vala's head swirled around a glowing red ball, spinning it several times. "I am unsure."

"We'll hope for the best, then," Benny said, though he wasn't really sure what "the best" would be in this situation.

Mostly he just prayed that whoever was in charge back on Calam didn't order Vala to shoot them all out of an airlock or something.

Vala turned her attention to the nearby mushroom cap. "This superweapon. What do you know of it?"

Benny sighed. "Honestly? Not much other than the fact that it exists. Dr. Bale—the guy who created it and was working with the Earth forces that took over the Lunar Taj—he's a genius. Pretty crazy and trigger-happy but, still, a genius. Those weapons at the resort? The drones that destroyed the asteroids floating between the Moon and Earth? That was all his stuff. Plasma rays or something like that. So when he says there's some kind of superpowerful doomsday device buried on the dark side of the Moon that's capable of destroying the Alpha Maraudi, I believe him." He shook his head. "It has something to do with electro-magnets, but that's about all I know."

Vala nodded at the electro glove on his hand that he'd used against the Alpha Maraudi. "I assume you know that our bones are made up of metallic minerals."

"Yeah," Benny said. He looked down at the glove himself. "Oh, crap. Should I take this thing off? This isn't, like, a sign that I'm angry or going to attack you or something, just so you know. I kind of forgot about it."

"Do not worry, young human," Vala said. "I think I understand your intentions."

There was a slight shift in the ground. Benny jumped, raising his hands a little and planting his feet.

"The internal thrusters," Vala said. "There's nothing to worry about. We're on our way to Jupiter now." She raised one hand to her chin. "You've searched for this weapon yourselves?"

"We didn't really have time to," Benny said. Then he remembered that wasn't totally true. "Actually, some of the Pit Crew—the older kids—did go out looking for it."

"And they found nothing?"

"They got attacked and shot down while they were on the dark side looking," Benny said.

A harmonic sigh came from Vala's mouth. "I see."

"We do know it's on the dark side of the Moon some-where. Dr. Bale was Elijah's old partner. They, uh . . . had a falling out. Afterward, Bale lived there for years with-out Elijah knowing his whereabouts. Apparently that whole time Bale was preparing for your people to attack, making weapons and gathering allies on Earth. He's a master of stealth technology. If he doesn't want that weapon found, I don't know that it can be." Benny paused for a second, an idea starting to form in the back of his mind. "Actually, we did swipe a few of his stealth drives. Maybe we could learn something from those. I'll ask Jazz."

"Once we have regrouped with the scholars we left behind, they will help you with whatever you need," the commander said. "If this weapon is real—and I believe that it is—it represents a more pressing concern than even our expanding star. Tull obviously feels the same way. In fact"—she paused—"it is possible this weapon is the only reason Elijah West is still alive. Tull realizes that the human is more useful to him as a bargaining chip than a corpse."

"Isn't there anything else we can do to get Elijah back? I met Tull. He didn't seem as . . . *understanding* as you've been." Benny shook his head. "Elijah made a lot of mistakes, but he saved us in the end. Plus, he *is* a genius. And basically the most famous person on Earth. We could really use his brain and his influence."

Vala sat on one of the chunks of black quartz. When she spoke, her eyes were focused on the pool of gold. "The Alpha Maraudi are a peaceful people. We prioritize science and survival. We do not war among ourselves. But that does not mean that we are without such urges. When life is threatened, hands that are normally outstretched can quickly curl into fists. In times like these, with so much at risk, many of our commanders have hardened themselves to the rest of the universe, disregarding the welfare of anything that doesn't help our people. Tull is one of them. I do not believe there is anything you can do save deliver this superweapon to Tull if you want to get Elijah back. He means only to protect our species. It is understandable to you, I hope."

"Yeah," Benny said. And he meant it. In the Drylands, his caravan had made it a point to help anyone in need they came across, but there were plenty of other groups out there that cared only about their own survival. Even people in his caravan family had gotten that way when resources were running low.

"Tull likely also understands that having your friend on board will keep his ship from being attacked," Vala said. "At least by your group."

He's not really a *friend*, Benny thought. But, then, he had no idea what to call Elijah West anymore.

"That makes sense," Benny said. "Ricardo and the Pit Crew aren't going to be happy with that answer, but I guess that's all we've got. We already wanted to find that weapon. Now we have even more reason to." He took a deep breath. "So, let's talk about Earth."

Vala nodded. "Your home planet has nothing to fear for the moment. The only two ships in your solar system are mine and Tull's, and I doubt Tull's craft is in any shape to take on an entire world. Especially now that he's aware of the weaponry the humans have. It was unexpected."

"Uh, it was pretty unexpected for us, too. Top secret," Benny said. "But that's good news. How long will my planet be safe?"

The commander stood, taking a few long strides away from him, her tentacles weaving into a loose bun piled on top of her head, once again spinning the red ball. "You know that we do not hold any ill will toward your species, even though there are many things your people have done that we do not approve of. The state of your planet, for example. You have poisoned much of it. You can imagine that for those of us losing the home that we treasure, this is an unfortunate fact."

"Yeah," Benny said. "I mean, I come from a place that apparently used to be full of people and cities and life. Now it's just a desert. I'm well aware of how badly we've treated the world."

Vala nodded, her back still to Benny. "Our plans were to . . ." She paused momentarily. "We were to clear the planet with what you would call an asteroid storm, then reshape it to suit our needs. Your atmosphere and gravity are already what we require—why Earth is the only planet that will suit us—but there is still much work to be done before it is a comfortable home for the Alpha Maraudi. Tull was to take care of the first step." She turned back to Benny, spreading her arms wide, gesturing to the bounty of alien plants around them. "Whereas my crew was to begin the conversion process. Changing the landscapes. Planting vegetation from our own world. Making it *feel* like home."

Benny began to realize for the first time that the destruction of Calam wouldn't just wipe out the Alpha Maraudi but all the plants and animals—beings he couldn't even imagine—as well. Looking around, he wondered how many species would be lost when the star expanded.

"I get it," Benny murmured. "You were going to try to save everything, along with your terraforming."

Vala's head tilted to one side. "I am afraid I do not know this word."

"I didn't really either until recently. Elijah used it to describe you. He said you could change planets to make them whatever you wanted." He let out a little laugh. "He thought you were going to make some kind of vacation planet out of Earth."

As much of a visionary as Elijah had always been, Benny couldn't believe he'd gotten the aliens so wrong.

"I suppose that is one way of looking at our technology, though it is an oversimplification. It was our hope that the evacuees from Calam would see a world that was in some way familiar once they landed on Earth. To help ease the relocation process."

Benny shook his head, staring at the purple gravel. "That's what would be happening right now if we hadn't stopped Tull. You would be on my planet. Changing it. Everyone else would be . . ." He trailed off, trying to focus on the conversation at hand and not worry about his family back on Earth. He swallowed and looked back up at Vala. "How much time does *your* planet have?"

"According to our scientists, it will be habitable for the

equivalent of perhaps two more Earth months. Even now, the evacuation ships will be preparing."

"They'll head this way," Benny said.

Vala nodded. "And they—*we* will need somewhere to go. We cannot stay on our ships forever."

"A caravan needs a place to park," Benny murmured, more to himself than to Vala. Then he shook his head. "When Tull's ship is fixed, he'll go after Earth again, won't he?"

"Perhaps," the commander said. "We still await orders from home, given everything that happened today. But I warn you: in the end, even if Tull does not attack Earth again, it will not matter. The full Alpha Maraudi fleet will be in your solar system once they evacuate Calam."

A shiver ran down Benny's back. "Unless Bale's superweapon destroys them along with your planet."

Vala was still for a moment. "Yes. But if Calam—if our *people* are destroyed, I know that Tull will not sit idly by. He will take revenge on humanity." Again, her gaze burned into him. "There are other mother ships out there. Even if our planet is destroyed, there will be those to avenge it. And they will still need a new home."

For the briefest moment Benny thought he might have to reach out to one of the nearby rocks for support. It felt as though he were in a Space Runner that was falling out of the sky. He'd been against Dr. Bale's weapon because it meant the destruction of an entire people: he hadn't thought about the ramifications it would have for Earth as well.

"Okay," Benny said. "I guess we both know what we're trying to avoid. It's in the best interest of all of us that that weapon never makes it off the Moon. That's our priority. So, what do we do now?"

"I was about to ask you the same question, Benny Love," the commander said. "I will listen to your suggestions."

Benny thought of Hot Dog and Drue, of Jasmine and Ramona, and of the Pit Crew and the rest of the EW-SCABers now on board the ship. And he thought of his family—always, somewhere in his head, he was thinking of them, no matter how far away they were.

"You've got scientists and scholars on the moons of Jupiter, right?" Benny asked. "Well, we've got an AI and some of the smartest kids from Earth up here. Together, we'll work on a way to find that weapon. Maybe we can even figure out a way to stop your star. Or to make it so you can live on another planet. One that isn't ours. But the weapon comes first, I think."

"You are . . . I do not mean to insult, but you are *children*. You have barely drawn breath."

"We stopped the first attack by ourselves." He paused. "Mostly. Elijah jumped in there at the end."

"Your idealism sounds enticing," Vala said. "But this is no actual plan, only promises that things *might* turn out for the better if our crews work together, with no actual details of how we will do that."

Benny thought about this, silently cursing that they hadn't been able to think of anything more definite. And, speeding farther away from Earth and the Moon, their options were dwindling even further. If only the Earth forces or *New Apollo* or whatever they were calling themselves would be open to other possibilities, like Vala seemed to be, they might be able to avoid this weapon firing altogether.

But of course, the way Dr. Bale and Senator Lincoln had spoken, it sounded like they thought this electromagnetic weapon would solve all their problems and obliterate a hostile alien species. They probably had no idea that doing so would put a death sentence on Earth.

"We can work on figuring out a way to locate the weapon ourselves," Benny finally said. "I'm sure with so many brilliant people up here, that's doable. But you're right. It's not enough. We have to get in contact with the New Apollo forces at the Taj. We have to make them see that this weapon will doom all of us. That's our first step toward peace between our peoples. It may be our best shot."

Vala leaned her head back, a tentacle scratching at the side of her face as she considered this.

"You wish the unreasonable to see reason," she said after

a few moments. "What evidence do you have that they will be able to do so?"

"None," Benny said. "But I also had no idea that you'd listen to me when I boarded your ship."

At that, it looked to Benny like the commander smiled.

"A fair point," Vala said. "What a surprise you young ones can be."

Back on the bridge, Ricardo hadn't moved, and the recording of the call from earlier was playing once again. By this point in the video, Tull had put the mask back over Elijah's face and was now gesturing to someone offscreen. Another alien appeared, grabbing Elijah and pulling him away.

"You'd better be taking care of my cars," Elijah said, attempting—and failing—to plant his feet and hold his ground. "Some of them are American classics! Irreplaceable."

And then the image froze, the call over.

Ricardo stood perfectly still for a few moments before reaching out, his hand hovering over the blinking light that Vala had shown him. But he didn't press it.

"Do we have any idea where they are?" Ricardo asked. "Is there any way we can get him back?" He turned to

Benny. "You told her everything we know, right?"

Benny nodded—he already knew what the answer to this question was.

"Tull's ship has not logged a location since you attacked his asteroid storm," Vala said. "He will not have gone far, though. From what I understand, his ship was badly damaged. It will need to be repaired before it can safely travel out of your solar system."

"So, it's still somewhere close by?" Ricardo asked. "Compared to it being outside our galaxy."

The commander nodded. "But we do not know where."

"We know Elijah's alive now," Benny offered. "That's something."

"Great," Ricardo said. "He's on an *Alpha Maraudi* ship and the best we can say is at least we know he's alive? I already knew that. Somehow, I knew."

"We're going to do everything we can to get him back," Benny said. He turned to Vala. "All of us."

"Of course," the commander said, nodding.

Ricardo looked at Benny. "I know," he said slowly. "It's just . . ." He looked at the hologram once more. "It feels like he's so close."

Griida yelled something from across the bridge.

"He says we're entering a speed that will be easier to launch your Space Runners from," Vala said. "Anyone who wishes to leave." She tapped one of the floating green ribbons of light and the hologram shifted. Elijah was replaced by a star map. "Any farther and your people will have to navigate through the asteroid belt between Mars and Jupiter."

"It's okay to slow down here?" Ricardo asked. "It's safe?"

"We are well out of range of the human ships we encountered on the Moon, but I would prefer not to stay here too long."

Benny nodded. "Then we should see who all wants to go back to Earth."

"Dunzo," a voice said from behind them.

Benny turned to find Hot Dog. Pinky paced the air in front of her as a one-foot-tall hologram.

"Um, should I ask why you're tiny?" Benny said as they approached. "Or . . . Actually, yeah: Why are you tiny?"

"I've sent the rest of my nanoprojectors throughout the ship to give us a working map of the vessel," the AI explained with a satisfied smirk. "I'll copy it to your HoloTek as soon as I'm done compiling data."

"Oh, nice," Benny said.

Hot Dog made her way up to the star map. "Wait, we've passed Mars already?" she asked, her blue eyes wide. "This is like a superfast ship right outta my dreams. We must be going a bajillion miles an hour."

"That's hardly scientific," Pinky chimed in, her voice

coming from the speakers in their space suit collars. She disappeared for a split second before reappearing atop the floating hologram of Mars on the map. "But don't worry. I'm keeping excellent records of the vessel's capabilities as far as I can extrapolate them."

"So, let's focus on evacuating the EW-SCABers who want to leave," Ricardo said. "Does 'dunzo' mean you have an idea of many people we're talking about?"

"While Benny and the commander were having their meeting, we took a survey," Pinky said. "A little over half of the EW-SCABers would like to go home. Fifty-six of them to be exact."

"Basically the same people who went underground instead of flying out to the asteroid storm," Hot Dog added. "Plus a few more."

"Okay," Benny said. "So, if we do three to a Space Runner, that's what, like . . . Some math . . ." He trailed off.

"The McGuyvers have already set aside vehicles they're sure can make the trip," Pinky said. "We'll be in a bit of a short supply once they leave, but we'll still have a few dozen SRs and prototypes left."

"It's a long ride in a Space Runner," Ricardo said, frowning. "We can port Pinky into the guidance systems and autopilot the whole way. But even traveling at top speeds, it'll be over a day back to Earth."

"They *could* stop off at the Taj," Pinky suggested. "Now

that we know the humans have won, they'd be safe there. Senator Lincoln said he intended to ship all of you back to Earth anyway."

Benny bounced on his feet. "I don't know. He may not be too happy that we ran off with the Maraudi."

"Not to mention his son," Hot Dog said. Then she scrunched her nose up. "Actually, from what I've seen and heard, that might not be his biggest concern."

"I can assign a few of my crew to tail your crafts until your people close in on the Moon," Vala said. "In case you'd like extra protection."

Hot Dog pursed her lips and raised an eyebrow. Ricardo glanced at Benny.

"It wouldn't be a bad idea," Benny said, mulling this over. "Especially if they run into any of Tull's fighters who might still be roaming around out there. I'm not sure how our caravan back to Earth would go about explaining everything going on from inside an SR."

He told himself again that they needed to trust each other if this was going to work. And, besides, surely the caravan could handle a few alien ships if something did go bad. Right?

"Okay, then," Ricardo said. "Thank you, commander."

Vala nodded. "It will be done."

Benny sighed. "Right. I guess I should go down to the hangar and let them know what's what. Plus, I need to talk to Jazz and Ramona and Trevone about setting up a satellite or something for us." He waved a hand at the group. "I'll be back in a sec."

He was a few steps away from everyone before he realized he had no idea how to get to the hangar now that the hole to the garden was closed.

"I'm coming!" Hot Dog said, rushing to his side. "I definitely got lost for five minutes trying to find my way back to the bridge earlier, but I can totally get you there."

"Thanks," Benny said, following her lead.

"Plus," she whispered, looking over her shoulder at him, "I want to hear all about that little talk you just had."

She led him through a maze of rock hallways as he updated her on his brief conversation with Vala. Hot Dog listened, nodding occasionally as she peeked into open doorways they passed, investigating the alien rooms. When he was finished, she slowed down her stride, thinking about what he'd told her.

"Okay," she said finally. "So, we've got a lot going on. I can update the rest of the Pit Crew about everything. That's one thing off your plate."

"You sure?" Benny asked.

She flipped her blond curls. "I feel like I was yelling at them a lot back on the Moon, so this'll be a nice change of pace." And then she stopped suddenly and turned to him, so quickly that he almost ran into her. Hot Dog's lips were drawn down in a slight frown, her eyes sharp and boring into him. "Do you trust Vala?"

Benny, surprised by the sudden question, paused for a few seconds. Finally, he took a breath. "After Elijah and Dr. Bale and, I don't know, the entire US government, I'm not sure I really trust anyone anymore. Other than you guys, I mean." He shrugged. "But Vala seems like she's being straightforward. I mean, you met Tull, too. So far the Alpha Maraudi have been pretty good about telling us exactly what they plan to do, even if that includes killing everyone on Earth."

This answer seemed to please Hot Dog. Her expression softened. "Good," she said. Then, she shook her head. "I mean, good that you're keeping your guard up and only mostly trusting them. Not the part about them destroying humanity, obviously."

"What do you think about all this?" he asked.

Hot Dog bit her lip for a second, and then turned away from him, continuing down the hallway. "I think that three weeks ago I was hanging out on the streets of Dallas because I didn't want to have to go home to our cramped apartment and listen to my parents yell at each other. And now I'm on an alien spaceship trying to save the world. I think we're doing the best we can, even though this totally isn't our fault. And I think that if we ever make it back to Earth, we deserve some *serious* rewards."

Benny laughed once. "Like what?"

"A cutting-edge gaming system and a Space Runner of my own. For starters."

"Yeah? What color?"

"I used to imagine cherry blossom pink with baby blue holo-stripes," she said. "But Mustang red is really starting to grow on me. Plus, chrome accents would look way better with that."

"You've thought a lot about this."

Hot Dog let out a long sigh. "A girl's gotta have a dream. Otherwise I'd go crazy trying to keep it together with all these unanswered questions and, you know, *worlds* hanging in the balance." She perked up. "Oh! Speaking of questions, that reminds me: What's with that red ball Vala's always got up in her tentacles? Is it magic or something? A weapon? Or is it just a really hip alien accessory?"

Benny shrugged. "I have no idea. Maybe it has something to do with her control of the ship? Or it's a symbol that she's in charge?"

Hot Dog shook her head. "Priorities, Benny. You should always ask about the hair."

Ahead of them, the hallway opened up into the hangar. Benny could see the wing of one of the purple quartz-like alien ships that they'd faced off against several times in the last week.

"Turns out they keep these entrances to the hangar

open when nothing's taking off or landing and the artificial environment's on," Hot Dog said. "Thankfully. I'm so over having to wear force field helmets."

When they'd boarded the ship, the hangar had been nothing but a vast, cavern-like room, mostly empty but for a handful of Maraudi spacecraft dotting the floor. Now, it was alive with action, people, and noise. The hundred EW-SCABers milled about among the dozens upon dozens of vehicles they'd brought up from the underground city below the Taj—the Space Runners, Moon buggies, and retrofitted muscle cars that the McGuyver siblings had hidden away when trouble started up above. A few Alpha Maraudi stood silent against one wall. Voices bounced off the high ceiling of smooth, greenish stone, creating a wave of sound that Benny and Hot Dog walked into.

It was a little overwhelming.

"Everyone's pretty up to speed thanks to Pinky's note and the Pit Crew," Hot Dog said, leaning against the alien ship beside them.

Jasmine caught sight of the two of them and hurried over. Trevone, the second-oldest member of the Pit Crew, followed her.

"We plotted a route that anyone who wants to leave can travel back to Earth," Jasmine said. "It's kind of the long way around, but it should be safe."

"On that note," Trevone said, "I don't know that we

can send all those kids into space on their own. It's a long way home. Dangerous. Asteroids, other Alpha Maraudi, even the human ships—this isn't the same automated trip you took from Earth a few weeks ago." He shook his head. "Plus, someone's going to have to rally people on Earth and try to explain what we're doing. Especially now that we're out of contact."

"You think someone from the Pit Crew should go, too," Benny said, realizing what Trevone was about to suggest.

Trevone nodded across the hangar where Sahar stood dressed in a yellow space suit, handing out silver pouches of water to several of the new arrivals.

"Sahar is still pretty banged up from being shot down. That girl is fierce, but it wouldn't be a bad idea to get her to an actual hospital, even though Pinky's scans checked her out. Afterward . . . Well, she may be quiet, but she can definitely get things done. And Kai . . ." He paused, his gaze moving to where Kai and Kira stood across the hangar. Kai leaned against his white Space Runner. Kira had a hand on his shoulder and appeared to be talking to him softly. "He's pretty shaken up by all this," Trevone continued. "After watching what happened to Sahar, he's not really looking forward to getting into another battle. I think he'd be more useful back on Earth than here. Both of them."

"You think people will listen to them?" Benny asked.

"Definitely. Especially since people know who they are.

They're part of Elijah West's Pit Crew, and he's still the most famous man in the galaxy. Plus, I think the other kids leaving would feel better with them around."

"Okay," Benny said. Those were two great pilots they were losing, but he understood why, at least. And if he were heading out for a long trek through space, he'd probably want some of the Pit Crew to back him up, too. "That makes sense. If you think it's the right decision, I'm all for it."

"How did things go with the commander?" Jasmine asked.

"Good, I think," Benny said. "Actually, this is great, because you, Trevone, and Ramona . . . Wait, where *is* Ramona?"

"Oh," Hot Dog said, scanning the rows of cars. "She found a case of energy drinks earlier and I'm pretty sure she locked herself in an SR with them so no one else could take any."

Before Benny could respond, Drue was breaking into their circle.

"'Bout time you showed," he said. "I know what you're wondering, and, *yes*, the McGuyvers brought the Star Runners up here with them. Everything is right in the universe." He flashed a big grin.

Hot Dog rolled her eyes. "How is that your main priority?"

"Uh, it's a lot easier to worry about whether or not I'm

going to get to drive a Star Runner again than if the planet's going to be wiped out." Drue raised his arms out at his sides. "How is that weird?"

"In your dreams, kid," a voice came from underneath the nearby Maraudi craft. Ash McGuyver, mechanic extraordinaire, scooted out from under the spaceship. "This place could really use some hover boards," she muttered as she got to her feet, running her fingers through her short, magenta hair. Then she narrowed her eyes at Drue. "We may not be in my garage anymore, but those are still my babies. I'm not lettin' you crash one into the side of whatever moon these ETs are taking us to."

"I've earned a few laps around Jupiter!" Drue said, crossing his arms. "I didn't see you sneaking aboard an alien ship to save humanity."

"And I didn't see you figuring out how to install an artificial environment system into a sports car twice as old as you. Deal with it." Ash wiped her hands on her gray coveralls as she turned to Benny and nodded at the alien ship. "I'll give these squids one thing, their ships are locked up tight. Can't figure out how to get under the hoods. Or where the hoods are, even."

"I don't think we ever thanked you for hiding all those vehicles underground," Benny said. "That saved our butts."

"Don't mention it," Ash said. There was a glint in her eye. "Speaking of muscle cars, I brought up a little surprise."

She pointed across the hangar, where an electric-green Chevelle sat on four shiny black tires. Bo McGuyver leaned against the back of it. His eyes were fixed on the two Alpha Maraudi in the corner of the room, who stood silently observing everything around them.

"The car we rescued Hot Dog in," Benny said.

Hot Dog sighed.

"We didn't rescue her," Drue said. "We just . . . helped her get back faster."

Hot Dog looked a little surprised. "*Thank you*, Drue."

"You're welcome." He smirked. "Of course, you *probably* would have died and turned into a Moon zombie if you'd had to walk all the way back on your own."

"Drue," Benny said.

"Back to the Chevelle," Ash went on. "We towed the beaut up here with a magnetic tractor beam. I couldn't leave her behind. And, seeing as how you apparently aren't bad behind her wheel, I figured she might come in handy."

"Amazing," Benny said. "What about the other kids who want to leave? We have plenty of SRs?"

"Yup. I've got them all moved to one side over there, ready to go. Bo and I've given them the once-over. They're good to fly." Ash paused for a moment. "I'm gonna miss that lug nut."

"What?" Benny asked.

"He, uh," Ash said, "isn't too keen on hanging out with

a bunch of aliens. I told him they probably had all kinds of tech we could look at but, well . . ." She leaned in closer to Benny, nodding toward her mountain of a brother. "He's more sensitive than he looks."

Benny mulled this over. The McGuyver siblings were the best mechanics in the galaxy. Having both of them on board would definitely come in handy if they needed to modify their vehicles in any way. They'd already been a huge help to the Moon Platoon, hiding prototype models from the aliens and Dr. Bale and installing laser mounts on the Space Runners they'd used to stop the asteroid storm. But one of them was better than none, he supposed.

"Plus," Hot Dogs said, "with Bo going, there's someone to do repairs if anything goes wrong."

"But nothing's gonna go wrong, right?" someone asked from a few yards away.

Benny tried to figure out who it might have been, but he was at a loss: a few dozen EW-SCABers nearby all seemed to be waiting for his response.

Hot Dog poked Benny in the ribs. "I think that's your cue."

"Ooo, is it speech time?" Drue asked. And then, before Benny could answer, he had his hands cupped around his mouth. "Hey! Dudes! Listen up! Our fearless Benny Love's got something to say."

"Thanks," Benny said dryly.

Slowly, the noise from the rest of the hangar faded to a murmur. Benny was the focus of everyone's attention. His palms started to sweat inside his gloves.

"How 'bout you get where everyone can see you, kid," Ash said. She pointed to the crystalline wing of the nearby Maraudi ship. With her help, he climbed on top and looked out at the hundreds of human eyes staring at him.

"So," he said. "Hi."

"Louder!" someone shouted from the back of the hangar.

"Hi!" Benny said again. "Uh, so, I just wanted to say that I know this has been a crazy couple of days. None of this was what we expected when we got our acceptance letters to come to the Taj. A lot of you want to head back home, which I understand. I miss Earth and my family, too. As soon as I'm done talking, we'll get everyone who wants to go loaded into Space Runners. If you're going back to Earth, remember you're still one of us. Maybe there's a way you can help out back at home."

He paused, his eyes scanning the crowd. A lot of people looked like they'd been crying. Some were grinning or had wide eyes full of wonder as they looked around the hangar. A few seemed like they were ready to punch the first person—or alien—who glanced at them the wrong way.

Benny swallowed hard and continued. "Look, this has been horrible. I know that. Trust me. You're scared. You're mad. You're confused. You're also completely weirded out by the fact that you're standing on an alien ship. I get it. I'm feeling all those things, too. We didn't ask for any of this to happen, or to be in a spot where we're trying to save our entire planet." He took a deep breath and held his head higher. "But all that fear and anger can't get in the way of the hope that we can figure this out. That we can protect everyone we know and love *and* keep an alien species from being destroyed. We're not just fighting for the future of Earth here. We're fighting to show that humanity deserves to survive. We'll figure out a way to save our planet. Not only from the aliens but from *anyone* who wants to harm it. Elijah brought us all into space because he thought we were the best the planet had to offer. Well, I think we've already proven that to him. Now let's prove it to the rest of the universe."

Below him, Drue raised a thumb into the air. "Come on, Moon Platoon!" he shouted. "What do you say?"

The hangar filled with cheers echoing off the stone walls. Benny watched Kai and Kira Miyamura hug on the other side of the room. Ash gave him a wink. His friends beside him on the ground were all smiles.

In that moment, despite the odds and every way things could go wrong, Benny truly believed that it was possible they could make all this work out in the end.

Following his speech, Benny let the Pit Crew handle
the logistics of loading up the Space Runners that were
leaving and showing those remaining on the mother ship
to their sleeping quarters. He headed back to the bridge
where he and the rest of the core members of the Moon
Platoon watched a holographic projection of the EW-
SCABers making their exits, their Space Runners shooting
toward Earth in a route devised by Pinky and Jasmine. Bo
McGuyver's oversized vehicle led the way, ready to tow any
SR that had problems. His car was flanked by Sahar's yellow Space Runner on the left, and Kai's white one on the
right. Two alien ships followed behind the group. In a few
seconds, they all disappeared from view.

Including the Pit Crew and Ash, there were now scarcely
more than fifty humans left on the Alpha Maraudi ship.

"They'll be fine," Pinky said, coming up beside Benny,

her normal height again. "Space Runners are the safest vehicles ever created. At least by humans."

"I know," Benny said. "It's just . . . kind of weird that they're going back and we're not."

"I wonder how Ash is holding up," Hot Dog said. "I didn't get a chance to talk to her before her brother left. They were doing all sorts of last-minute inspections, so I didn't want to interrupt her. I would ask the same about Kira but . . ." Hot Dog shrugged. "Honestly, she kind of scares me."

"I know I'd be worried about my brothers if they flew out," Benny said, "regardless of how safe it was supposed to be."

Drue came up between Hot Dog and Benny, leaning on their shoulders. "So, guys. What now?"

Benny turned to Jasmine, causing Drue to stumble forward. "We've got a couple of Dr. Bale's stealth drives in the hangar still, right? Is it possible for us to, I don't know, take them apart and see how they work? Reverse engineer them? If he's using that same tech to hide his weapon—"

Something sparked in Jasmine's eyes. "Of course! If we can figure out how they work, we may be able to figure out how to subvert his cloaking." She raised her eyes to the ceiling, deep in thought. "Or we might be able to home in on the frequency that his holograms operate on and use that as a way to track down his weapon. I was also thinking: since it is an electromagnetic weapon of some sort, it's possible that there would be peculiarities in the general magnetic field around it, and if we can use those variances to . . ."

She stopped. Benny blinked a few times. Jasmine nodded.

"I'll get on it," she assured him. "Trevone will be glad to help, I'm sure."

"And I'm at your disposal, of course," Pinky added.

"So, that's what we're staking all our hope on?" Drue asked.

"Our priority is figuring out a way to stop that super-weapon," Benny said. "It's the most immediate threat to both the Maraudi and humanity. Vala's given us even more reasons to convince the New Apollo forces that it would be a bad idea to use it. We need everyone to work together."

Drue raised an eyebrow. "Hold on. You want to talk my dad into getting buddy-buddy with the aliens? Ha. I can't wait to see you try to do that."

"You'll have a front row seat," Benny said, "because you're going to help me."

Drue shoved his hands into his space suit pockets. "Um, maybe you're forgetting that the last few times I tried to tell my dad that I was doing superimportant space hero stuff, he was, uh, less than thrilled."

"Things are different now," Benny said. "I mean, we're on an alien ship. We have an alliance with them." He shrugged. "Plus, you totally saved your dad's life back on the Moon. Turn on that Lincoln charm and remind him that he owes you one. Or that he should listen to us, at least."

Drue didn't look completely convinced by this, but he nodded.

Pinky raised a finger in the air. "Not to bring everyone down, but there's no way I can connect us to the Taj this far away."

"I know," Benny said. "I'm hoping Ramona will help with that."

"Woot," Ramona said, not looking up from her HoloTek. "Major shock."

"You've made satellites for us before," Benny said. "We need you to do it again. A superpowerful one that'll let us contact the Taj." He sighed. "And we need it fast."

"Psh," she said. "No prob. Mega upstreams. I can source parts from the hangar." A mischievous grin overtook her face. "And the mother ship."

"Sure . . . Great." He tried to think of what else they could be doing, but before he could come up with anything, a gigantic yawn forced its way out of his mouth.

This was apparently some sort of trigger for Pinky, who put her hands on her hips and started tapping one foot on the ground.

"What you need now is rest," the AI said. "All of you have been going nonstop for a very long time. You haven't even slept since the invasion of the Taj. I've marked the sleeping quarters on your HoloTeks. You'll be useless tomorrow if you're completely wiped."

"Actually, Pinks is right," Drue said, stretching. "I'm about to pass out standing here."

"We need to get started on these satellites and stuff immediately, though," Benny said. "There's no time to waste."

"I agree," Jasmine said. "But—and don't take this the wrong way—that's up to us, not you. *You* need to be awake to rally everyone tomorrow and, you know, lead."

"Look around you, Benny," Hot Dog said. "The ETs have gone to sleep, too. Or, at least to their rooms? I don't know if they sleep, now that I think about it. Anyway, this thing's on autopilot, and we've still got a while before we're to Jupiter."

"I can't work much longer," Jasmine said. "I'll be right behind you. But I definitely want to take a preliminary look at the stealth drives before I call it a night. I do some of my best brainstorming right before I go to sleep." She looked to Ramona. "Want to come to the hangar with me? I'm sure Ash can tell you what kind of satellite components she might have lying around if she's still up."

Ramona clicked her tongue and made an okay sign with her fingers.

"See?" Hot Dog crossed her arms. "Don't worry. Us

girls can hold down the place."

"As much as I enjoy the idea of an all-female crew," Pinky started, "you should rest, too."

"Oh, I'm going to get my beauty sleep, don't you worry. We'll take shifts." Hot Dog glanced at Ramona, who slugged from a can of soda that seemed to have appeared in her hand out of nowhere. "Even *she* has to sleep sometimes." She paused. "Uh, right?"

Drue headed for the exit, pulling out his HoloTek. "Come on, Benny, my man. Let's see how accurate Pinky's maps are of this place. I'm guessing we're not going to find any Taj-style suites, if you know what I mean, so prepare to rough it."

"Okay, okay," Benny finally said. He turned to Pinky and Hot Dog and shrugged. "I'll see you soon. But if anything weird happens, wake me up, yeah?"

Hot Dog pointed toward the exit. Benny nodded and followed Drue out of the bridge. A few steps into one of the stone hallways he heard Ramona burp behind them. Pinky started lecturing her on the importance of decorum when meeting new cultures, but Benny didn't hear how that decidedly one-sided conversation ended as he and Drue walked through the snaking hallways of the ship.

"Turns out, there's actually another hangar below the one on this level. They parked a few extra SRs down there when space was getting full in the main one," Drue said, holding his HoloTek up. "It explains how the Alpha Maraudi were able to bring so many ships to the Taj. Not that it helped."

"Yeah," Benny said. "The Earth forces really overwhelmed them."

"That's my dad for you," Drue said, a little more subdued. "A Lincoln wins no matter what. Failure is never an option."

Benny was quiet for a few seconds as they continued. His relationship with his father—with his entire family and caravan—seemed to be so different from the way Drue had lived back on Earth. "Are you worried about him?" he finally asked.

"Who, my dad? Nah. He'll be fine. He always is."

Benny nodded. "He, uh . . . Before I left, he told me to make sure you were safe."

Drue slowed down. "Really?"

"Yeah."

"Huh," Drue said. There was a hint of a smile on his face. Then he shook his head, picked up his pace, and gestured to his HoloTek map again. "Anyway, looks like most the rest of the ship is pretty standard when it comes to what you'd imagine a traveling space station to be like. I mean, if you don't count that weirdo garden and some of the rooms Pinky couldn't identify."

Eventually Drue led them to a hallway where the Alpha

Maraudi must have slept when they'd populated the ship. Doorways opened to huge, deep-purple stone chambers that were veined with glowing orange light. The walls were filled with tubes at least five feet in diameter. There had to have been fifty little sleeping holes per room, EW-SCABers dotting the lower rows.

"I shoulda packed my nice pillows," Drue said. He nodded farther down the hall. "C'mon, let's find one with fewer people. I bet some of those guys snore."

As they continued, Trevone stepped out from one of the rooms.

"Hey," he said, seeing them. "Plan on getting some shut-eye?"

"I'm being forced into it," Benny said. "We left the girls on the bridge. We'll trade out when we need to."

"Smart," Trevone said. "That's actually the same idea we had. I'm going to make the rounds. See that everyone's settling in." He pointed a thumb over his shoulder and into the open room behind him. "The rest of the Pit Crew's in here. You should join us."

"Thanks," Benny said.

"I mean, we could probably find a basically empty room if we keep looking," Drue said. "Maybe even with bigger sleep holes? There's got to be, like, an officers' suite, right?"

Benny ignored him. "Tell Hot Dog what room we're in, will you?" he said to Trevone. "For when she needs someone to take her place. And if you're up to it, Jazz was about to head to the hangar. We have a whole project she can update you on."

"Sure thing," Trevone said. He started down the hall before calling back to them. "Oh, and nice work with that speech earlier. You're getting good at those."

Drue elbowed Benny's arm. "I'm rubbing off on you."

Benny groaned. "Please don't say that."

"Hey!" Drue said, his mouth hanging open and eyes narrowed.

Benny tried to keep a straight face, but the exhaustion was wearing on him, and he couldn't stifle a chuckle.

Drue smacked him on the back and went ahead. "You're gonna thank me for everything I've taught you one of these days."

Inside the sleeping cavern, a handful of other kids had already climbed inside the cubby holes carved into the walls and passed out. All he could make of Kira was the soles of her white boots. Ricardo sat on the edge of a tube on the bottom row, his head a foot from the top of the circular frame.

"I call top bunk," Drue whispered. He raced over to the wall, put his feet on the bottom of the first sleeping nook, and then jumped, straining to pull himself up onto the second row. Once there, he craned his neck back, looking at the three rows of tubes above him. "Actually, you know what?" He slapped the side of the rock. "This is fine."

"People are trying to sleep," Ricardo said quietly, glaring at Drue. He looked to Benny. "By the way. Sorry if I was frustrated earlier. This has just been . . . a lot."

"Of course," Benny said. "Don't worry about it. We'll figure out how to find that weapon. Not only is it the way we all survive, it's the best hope we have of getting Elijah back from Tull."

"We will," Ricardo said, climbing inside his bed. "We have to."

Benny crawled into the chamber underneath Drue's, leaving an empty one between him and Ricardo. He'd slept in the little space in the RV that was situated above the front seats on occasion, which sometimes felt unbearably cramped. By contrast, he could sit upright if he wanted to in here, with feet to spare above his head. It was actually kind of cozy, he thought—there was a blanket folded inside, a few round woven bags he assumed were pillows, and a thin mat that was somehow absurdly comfortable.

Drue's head appeared at the foot of his tube, his dark hair wild as he hung upside down.

"Ugh, this thing is totally claustrophobic, right?" he asked. "It's like a cryochamber in a movie. I feel like they're going to freeze us and then we'll wake up and it'll be the year 3085 and they'll be using us as organic batteries or something."

Several people from all around shushed him. Drue rolled his eyes. "Whatever. Good night." And then he disappeared.

The thin veins of glowing amber light threaded through Benny's sleeping cubby, too, giving off just enough glow for him to see his immediate surroundings. On the wall of the tube was an outcropping that held some kind of gold oval—like a little frame that didn't have any glass or picture inside. He pulled it off with his silver-gloved hand and turned it around a few times, inspecting it. Nothing but a hollow ring. But when he placed one of the fingers of his gold glove on it, the device sprang to life. A six-inch hologram appeared. An Alpha Maraudi, unmasked, holding a much smaller alien—perhaps a baby?—came to life in front of him. They both waved.

Benny held his breath, staring back at them wide-eyed. It was only after a few seconds that he realized the image was repeating, not an actual communication. He sighed, trying to calm himself down a bit.

That's when it dawned on him that this tube hadn't always been empty. Someone had called it their own—someone who had probably been shot down over the Taj or had been on the invasion team that went inside the resort. Maybe even an alien he'd faced. Were there holograms, *memories* like this in all these tubes? What was happening to the alien soldiers stranded on the Moon now?

Looking at the waving aliens, he wondered what was going on back at Calam, too. Were the Alpha Maraudi he was looking at now worried? Were they thinking about the alien who had been in this tube the night before? Were they planning their evacuation?

Benny suddenly felt like this hologram wasn't his to see, and placed the little frame back on the wall. Then he put his head down against a pillow and closed his eyes. He let his mind wander back to the Drylands. What were his brothers, Alejandro and Justin, doing? What about his grandmother? Were they okay? Had they realized yet that he wasn't coming home?

His eyes grew heavy, until he could barely keep them open. He half wondered if he'd really used an electromagnetic glove to fly on the back of a Space Runner capable of landing on an alien mother ship just hours before, or if it had all been a dream. Before he could be certain, he'd passed out completely.

Benny woke to something shaking his foot. He jumped, pulling his legs farther into the tube and scrabbling to sit up on his mat.

"*Baka*," Kira Miyamura said, pulling her hand back. "I was just trying to wake you."

"Sorry," Benny said, scrambling to get his wits about him and shake off the remnants of sleep.

"We're almost to Jupiter," Kira said. "They thought you'd want to be on the bridge."

Before Benny could ask more questions, Kira was gone. Benny inched out of his tube, his entire body sore from the events of the previous day. Muscles he didn't even know he had burned as he stood and stretched.

Trevone was doing the same thing a few yards away from him.

"I thought you were on watch," Benny said.

"I was," the Pit Crew member responded, putting his goggles up to the top of his head. "Kira took over for me. We tried to wake you up earlier, but you were *out*." He nodded to the door. "Come on. If we're really that close, I don't want to miss the approach."

In the hallway they found Pinky directing several kids.

"Ah," she said as they approached. "There you two are. The bridge is fairly small, so I'm moving the scholarship winners who are awake to this vessel's version of a mess hall. There's a clear rock wall there they can watch from and plenty of food—though, it will of course be nothing like the feasts I could create back at the resort."

Iyabo, one of the EW-SCABers who'd been instrumental in the attack on the asteroid storm—not to mention in convincing the rest of the kids underneath the Taj that the best course of action they had was to board the alien ship—leaned out of one of the doorways to another sleeping room.

"So, like," she said through a yawn, "where'd we end up putting all our supplies? I know for a fact I made sure to pack a bunch of boxes of that cereal that's mostly marshmallows."

"I believe there are still crates in some of the Space Runner trunks that we haven't unpacked," the AI said. "Though, as you know, I would much prefer you have a balanced breakfast of—"

"Yeah, sure," Iyabo replied, already starting toward the hangar, her silver-threaded braids swinging behind her. "Just point me toward the morning sugar rush, Pinky, and nobody gets hurt."

Pinky sighed, looking back to Benny and Trevone. "If you'll excuse me."

The two boys hurried to the bridge, where they found the core members of the Moon Platoon and what was left of the Pit Crew standing around the hologram that showed their approach to the fifth planet from the sun.

"Hey, sleepyhead," Drue said with a grin as Benny approached.

"You could've woken me up," Benny replied.

His friend just shrugged. "I didn't want to interrupt your desert dreams or whatever. You kept sleep talking about sand."

"I don't believe that," Benny said.

"It was an uneventful few hours," Hot Dog said, sipping

a soda. "You didn't miss a thing."

"We're getting close," Jasmine said. "I wish I could see it better."

Vala turned away from the terminal where she'd been observing Griida. "That's simple enough," she said as she beckoned to Benny and the others. "Come."

The alien walked up the stairs to the egg-shaped throne and stopped in front of a giant stone wall—part of the hull—which must have been at least three stories tall. It was more transparent than the rest of the bridge, but still allowed them to see only the vaguest outlines of whatever was on the other side. The commander raised a hand, and Benny noticed a flash of gold rings across her knuckles. As Benny and the others climbed the steps, the rock in front of them began to change, fading until it was almost imperceptible, giving them a clear view of space.

What Benny saw took his breath away.

They were still thousands of miles from the planet, rushing ever closer toward it. Still, Jupiter loomed larger than he could have possibly imagined, an immensity striped in shades of orange and beige, with occasional wavelike crests of blue. He knew little about the planet other than the fact that it was gaseous and the largest one in the solar system, but seeing it now, with his own eyes, it was hard to even fathom that such a giant was real.

"Holy whoa," he murmured.

"*Max* whoa," Ramona said, hurrying up the stairs to join them, disregarding her HoloTek for once.

"Yeah," Drue said, his voice only a whisper. "Same."

"Over eleven times the size of Earth," Jasmine said. "What we're seeing are mostly cloud belts. Underneath, a liquid surface."

"Kinda makes you feel insignificant, huh?" Hot Dog said.

"It is a sight," Vala agreed. "Though if this lone planet calls significance into question, one wonders how humanity would react to experiencing the true vastness of the universe."

"There," Trevone said. "That dark swirly part. That's the Great Red Spot. It's a storm that's been raging on the surface of the planet for over four hundred years."

"That we know of," Jasmine said, scarcely able to hide the excitement in her voice.

"It used to be at least forty kilometers from end to end." Drue said, "but it's been shrinking over the centuries."

Hot Dog glanced at him.

"What?" he asked. "It's like you guys forget I know stuff, too, and never-ending storms on giant planets are kind of cool to learn about."

"Elijah couldn't race across its surface," Ricardo said. "So I'm not sure he ever saw Jupiter this close."

Kira took a few steps toward the window. "I wonder if

71

we'll ever know what all Elijah's seen."

"We have planets like this in our system as well," Vala said. "Beautiful. Enormous. But completely incapable of habitation. At least for those like us."

"Makes you wonder what *could* be living down there," Hot Dog said.

"Yes," the commander continued. "Though, in our history, we have discovered that often this is an inquiry best left unanswered."

Benny gulped. He kind of felt like he needed to start a running list of all the follow-up questions he had about things that Vala casually mentioned.

"Um," Jasmine said. "Which of the moons are we landing on? I have to admit that I wasn't very familiar with Jupiter's satellites since there are over seventy of them. But according to the info on my HoloTek, a lot of them are very icy and, uh, well, full of volcanoes."

"My people are on the largest of the moons," Vala said.

"Oh, good," Jasmine nodded. "One that I actually know. Ganymede. At least, that's what we call it on Earth."

"So, are we freezing to death or melting?" Benny asked.

"Freezing," she answered. "It's basically a giant ball of ice with rock—and maybe even water—underneath. But Ganymede is one of the places in our solar system that scientists believe could be made to support life one day, though that would take a *lot* of work, planning, and resources. It's also far larger than our moon. The biggest one we know of."

Vala nodded. "We were interested in what lies beneath the moon's icy surface."

There was a subtle jolt on the bridge, the feeling of the room shifting slightly around them.

"Uh, should we buckle up or something?" Benny asked.

"Do not worry," Vala said, taking a seat on her throne behind them. "We are only slowing for the landing. I'll try to make it as smooth as possible."

Seemingly out of nowhere, a new shape filled the mineral window—the polished surface of Ganymede, a steely gray with darker, carbon-colored patches.

"All that's ice?" Benny asked. He was already shivering and they hadn't even landed yet. An entire lifetime spent in the Drylands hadn't prepared him for anything like this.

Trevone nodded. "It's believed to be the smoothest natural surface in the solar system."

"We shoulda brought skates!" Drue exclaimed. "*Rocket skates!*"

"I'm beginning to think we could use some coats, too," Hot Dog said. "These space suits are only so warm. Didn't Elijah have any parkas lying around? The man was *really* into faux fur for a while."

"You'll find that our camp here is comfortable for you. The temperatures our peoples thrive under are very similar."

"Another reason you want Earth," Kira said, glancing at the commander from the corner of her eye.

Vala merely nodded. "Now, if you'll excuse me, I need to concentrate."

As they shot toward the moon Ganymede, Jasmine's nose almost pressed up against the see-through rock wall. "That's odd," she said, pointing at a greenish blip on the surface of the moon.

"It almost looks like it's glowing," Trevone said, stepping up to her side.

It took a moment for Benny to see what they were talking about, but, sure enough, the point they seemed to be flying toward was different from the rest of the landscape. He stared at the location, finally taking a sharp breath once they were close enough for him to recognize exactly what he was seeing.

Alpha Maraudi rock.

"They've dug into the ice," Jasmine said.

"What does that mean?" Ricardo asked.

"That they've made some kind of base here," Trevone said. "They've found a way to live on this moon. At least temporarily."

Jasmine smiled a little. "Underground. They've probably

created an entire livable environment down there."

Griida yelled something from behind them.

"I will take it from here," Vala called back in English.

The commander's hands were clasped together in front of her chest, holding the red ball that was usually spinning around in her hair. Tentacles tipped in gold shot out, touching the sides of the quartz-like throne. Suddenly, the inside of the chair—covered in the same golden metal—began to glow. And then this light spread, until Benny could see webs of it flowing through the floors and walls of the ship like circuitry, little gleaming currents.

"Wow," he whispered as the ship slowed, hovering just above the surface of the moon.

Somewhere far below them, there was a rumbling sound, and then the entire ship shook, just slightly, before going still again.

"It is done," Vala said, her tentacles weaving around her head once again. "We are now one with the rock below." She gestured to the clear wall in front of them. "Welcome to Ganymede. I believe you are likely the first humans to set foot here."

6.

Once the ship landed, everything was in motion very quickly. Commander Vala's harmonic voice rang through some sort of intercom system on the ship, instructing the few members of her people that remained to begin the process of assessing the vessel and its supplies. After a brief discussion, Benny and the Pit Crew decided it would be best for the EW-SCABers to remain on the ship for now, where they had plenty of space and resources. Reluctantly, Ricardo and Kira agreed to stay behind with Pinky to help maintain order. Trevone, the member of the Pit Crew who specialized in science and calculations, joined Benny, Drue, Hot Dog, Ramona, and Jasmine as they followed Vala down several flights of stairs, stopping only once, at the hangar, to pick up a few of Dr. Bale's stealth drives.

Eventually, Benny found himself in the lowest chamber of the alien mother ship, an empty room the size of his suite back at the Lunar Taj, all stone and glowing rivers of energy. Vala stood in front of him.

"This temporary base is home to a dozen of our wisest scholars and science officials," the commander said. "They know you are coming. You have nothing to fear from them. If anything, I believe they will be interested in studying you."

"Cool," Drue said. "As long as we don't end up as lab rats."

"On the contrary," Vala said, nodding to Benny, "they should be able to help you in both creating a way to communicate with the Earth forces and, with any luck, finding a way to track down this superweapon."

"The exterior of the ship fused with the base that was already here?" Trevone asked, looking around. "Interesting. It alleviates the need for any secondary connections or airlocks."

"And creates an instant fortress," Jasmine added.

"Well," Hot Dog said. "I guess now's as good a time as any to check out a secret alien base underneath the surface of one of Jupiter's moons. Just a normal . . ." She paused. "I have no idea what day of the week it is on Earth. So, how do we get in?"

Vala turned to the wall and waved a gold-tipped tentacle, causing the stone in front of them to fall away, revealing a dark staircase leading beneath the surface of Ganymede.

Another flick of the appendage and a webbing of green circuitry began to glow on the walls, illuminating their path.

"Dude, Benny," Drue whispered. "You gotta get better at using that glove of yours."

Vala stepped through the newly opened doorway. "You may follow me."

"This reminds me of that staircase underground at the Taj," Jasmine said as they filed down the steps. "Remember that? Back before we knew about the Alpha Maraudi or that Earth was about to be destroyed?"

"The good old days," Hot Dog muttered.

"I don't know," Jasmine continued. "If it hadn't been for us discovering the underground city, I never would have seen my life flash before my eyes dozens of times. Starting with the way you drove that mine cart."

Hot Dog gasped a little. "We *survived.*"

Drue let out a boisterous laugh. "Jazz! I knew you had a sense of humor in there somewhere."

"I'm only sort of joking," Jasmine said.

"Could've been worse," Benny added. "Could have been Drue driving."

"Hey!" Drue raised a hand to his chest dramatically. "I'm hurt by that, Benny."

"Thin skin," Ramona said. "You'd never last in online forums."

"I have no idea how the five of you ended up as the

driving force behind everything that's happened in the last few days," Trevone said, shaking his head. "Don't get me wrong. I'm glad. But it seems to me like you all should have died several times already."

"There's always tomorrow," Benny joked, not really thinking about what he was saying. He immediately regretted it. The comment hung in the air as they continued their descent in silence.

"How far down does this go?" Jasmine finally asked.

"We needed to dig below the many layers of ice," Vala said. "The moon is at its warmest here, but the surface is still thick."

"And did you find anything interesting?"

Vala nodded toward the dead end they were fast approaching. "You will see."

The commander waved a hand and the wall melted. A rush of cold air shot through the stairwell, but Benny's force field helmet still hadn't deployed—however this base was built, it was running its own artificial environment, just as the ship had. Still, he couldn't help but shiver.

As they stepped out of the narrow corridor, all the humans took deep breaths, eyes wide and trying to take in the sprawling oasis in front of them.

The telltale grayish-green alien rock spread from the doorway and covered almost the entirety of a giant cavern that extended so far up Benny could barely make out the shimmering stalactites above them. Huge glowing boulders dotted the stone floor, providing ample light. Across from where they stood, half a dozen pillars of jet-black rock jutted out of the ground. Several Alpha Maraudi were gathered around them, scanning the outcroppings with instruments and bringing chunks of the mineral to nearby workbenches. Giant alien plants were thriving in one corner, surrounded by more illuminated stones. There were hallways leading farther back into the rock walls, where Benny assumed other rooms must have been located. But the most awe-inspiring thing—what caused the goose bumps to form on his skin—was the farthest side of the cave, where the alien rock gave way to walls of silvery ice and the floor sloped down, leading to a dark pool of water. Melting icicles from the ceiling rippled its surface, each drop echoing through the cavern—an underground lake on Ganymede.

"This is insane," Benny whispered.

"Wha . . . How?" Jasmine stuttered. "Is that . . . ?"

"Those rocks . . ." Trevone said. "Water? But . . ."

"What *is* this place?" Hot Dog asked.

"Our scans found this hollow pocket far below the surface," Vala explained. "We mined down to it, reinforced it with our own elements, and created a temporary environmental system. The lake is full of saltwater that's bubbling up from ever deeper depths. Since we raised the temperature to make us comfortable, the surface of the liquid does not freeze."

Benny shook his head, marveling at the sight. It was strange enough that he was in a cave hundreds of feet below the surface of one of Jupiter's moons and that it was full of aliens—not to mention the fact that they'd turned it into a space where he could stand and breathe normally. But there was something else that leaped out at him, something that weeks ago, sweating in the Drylands, he never could have fathomed. "I've never seen so much water and ice like this before," he said quietly.

"Oh, man, that's right," Drue said. "This must be blowing your mind. I mean, it's blowing my mind and I *didn't* live in the desert my whole life."

"Wait," Benny continued, trying to refocus his thoughts. "If you can turn an ice cave into a livable place, can't you do that to, like, a whole moon or planet?"

Jasmine shook her head. "This is a self-contained environment. Like how the Grand Dome worked. To do something like this for an entire planet would mean creating a synthetic atmosphere. It's theoretically doable, but . . ."

"But you'd need impossible amounts of specific gasses and the perfect balance of gravity," Trevone said.

"They are correct," Vala said. "This is a temporary solution for a small number of my people."

There was the now-familiar sound of the alien language

from somewhere to Benny's left. He turned, expecting to see yet another tall Alpha Maraudi, but the alien running toward them was small compared to every other stretched-out extraterrestrial he'd faced—a whole head shorter than he was, in fact. It wore a silver tunic and no mask over its eyes. Four waist-length tentacles swung behind it, the tips of them an inky black.

"Oh my gosh," Hot Dog whispered. "It's a squid kid!"

The small alien stopped a few feet away from them, all three eyes scanning the group, and then turned to Vala. The two of them spoke back and forth a few times, the child's alien words quicker, more excited than the commander's—or at least, Benny was pretty sure that was what he was hearing. Finally, Vala seemed to smile, and placed the glowing red ball that she usually kept wrapped up in her tentacles into the kid's hand.

"Okay, I still have questions about that thing," Hot Dog said.

"This?" Vala asked, pointing at the ball. "In what way?"

"We thought maybe it was how you controlled the ship or something," Benny said.

Vala stared at him for a beat. "It is merely a child's toy. Something I take with me to remind me of what is waiting for me elsewhere in the universe."

The smaller alien barked something, and then turned to Benny and his friends. When it spoke again, it used English.

"I am *not* a child. I've seen seven star festivals!"

"It talks!" Hot Dog whispered.

Drue leaned in to Benny. "So . . . seven years old?"

The alien let out a snarl. "I was chasing Bazers back on Calam before you'd even crawled out of your newborn nest."

"I have no idea what that means, but point taken," Drue said. "I think."

"This is Zee," Vala said. "He is of my family."

"He's your . . ." Benny started. "Kid?"

"Not exactly. Though I have been entrusted with his care for many cycles."

"You're like a foster parent," Jasmine said. Her lips pursed as she rolled this thought around in her head. "Fascinating."

"I can't believe I'm looking at actual humans," Zee said, his glowing blue eye radiant. The alien's tentacles whipped back and forth as he continued. "I always hoped I'd get to meet one before Earth was depopulated. I have so many questions! Why is your music so simple? How do you *really* see anyone without a third eye? Is it weird to get a haircut? Does it hurt?"

"Zee has been very . . ." Vala started, "*interested* in Earth since he learned that it would be our new home."

"I've been swallowing all the materials I can find about your planet," Zee said.

"You've been . . . eating research?" Benny asked.

Zee's tentacles drooped. "*Swallowing*'s the wrong word? Maybe . . . *chewing*? Is that right?"

"I think you might be looking for *digesting*," Jasmine suggested.

"Or *bingeing*," Hot Dog said. Then she put a hand on her hip. "It's a little creepy to get superobsessed with humanity right before your people come to wipe us out, don't you think?"

"You should take it as a . . ." Zee thought for a moment. "The opposite of an insult?"

"A compliment?" Jasmine asked.

"If you say so," Zee continued. "You have many faults, but I'll admit the Space Runners your people love so much look way colder than most of our ships."

"Cooler," Drue said. "And if you think normal SRs are awesome, you should've seen the Galaxicle I was on yesterday."

"Yeah," Hot Dog said. "Or basically any of the prototypes the McGuyvers brought to the mother ship."

Zee's mouth dropped open, as if it had unhinged for a moment. "You have Earth vehicles?!" he asked. "Here?" His tentacles practically vibrated. "I want to see!"

Benny turned to Vala. They were getting off track, and every minute they stood there talking was time that could have been spent doing something else. "We brought the stealth drives with us," he said to Vala. "And Ramona's our satellite expert. We need to get started soon, before New Apollo has a chance to launch their superweapon."

"Superweapon?!" Zee squealed. "You Earth people are so good at those! What is it?"

Before Benny could answer, Vala spoke to the young alien in their own language.

"I don't care if I'm supposed to have lessons today," Zee replied in English. "Why spend time reading about different cultures when I could actually experience them?"

Vala raised her mask, staring at Zee. Zee grunted and stormed off.

The commander paused for a moment before turning to Benny. "He is older than you all, and yet . . ." She trailed off, shaking her head and returning her mask. "Come. I know there is much to be done."

The commander led them to the work spaces set up near the black rocks. It was only once they were on the move again that Benny realized the rest of the Alpha Maraudi in the cavern had stopped working and were staring at them. He shoved his hands in his space suit pockets, suddenly self-conscious and keenly aware of how quiet it had gotten.

They came to half a dozen different tables that had grown out of the stone floor of the cavern, all pulsing dully with a green light. Each one was piled high with gadgets Benny didn't recognize. One was covered in dark rock samples in meticulously labeled clear vials.

"You're analyzing the minerals down here?" Jasmine asked.

"And the great underground lakes," a nearby alien said as Benny and the others gathered around the work space. "There are secrets beneath every celestial body's surface. We're barely beginning to uncover what this moon might have hidden away."

"This is Pito," Vala said, nodding to the speaker. "He is the top scholar and scientist on my crew. And I would go so far as to say one of the brightest minds across our many ships."

"Commander," Pito said, bowing slightly. "It is unfortunate to hear of what happened at the Lunar Taj."

Something about Pito was different from the other Maraudi Benny had met. A gold mask covered not only the upper part of his face, but much of his head as well, all the way to the back where, symmetrically, there should have been a second tentacle beside the single thick one that was wrapped around Pito's neck like a scarf. There was what looked like scar tissue peeking out from beneath the gold. Obviously, the alien had been through something traumatic, but what? Benny wondered. A battle? A science mishap?

Pito looked at Benny. "The commander told us about this 'superweapon,'" Pito continued. "You have some device you think could be of use in tracking it?"

"That's right," Benny said. "Made by the same person who developed the weapon he says is capable of destroying your species." He nodded to Jasmine. "You can probably explain things a little better."

"Of course," Jasmine said, placing two of the stealth drives on the table. "So, here's what we know."

She caught Pito up on Dr. Bale's use of stealth, the few things they'd learned about his superweapon, and their hopes that by understanding the tech in front of them, they might track down the place where the electromagnetic weapon was hidden on the Moon.

"We've never had a chance to look at much of your technology up close," Pito said. "I admit that I'm interested to see it in action."

"Likewise," Trevone said. "The way your people have learned to control elements is so far beyond anything we have on Earth."

"It seems as though it's not completely new to you," the scientist said. The single tentacle squirmed from around his neck and pointed at Benny's gloved hand.

"Oh," Benny said. "Yeah. I'm, uh, not that great at using it. But if you all could teach me, maybe it could come in handy."

"Fascinating," Pito said. Then he turned his attention to the stealth drives. "Once we've unlocked these secrets, of course." The alien glanced back at them. "Are you all scientists as well?"

"Those three are our geniuses," Hot Dog said, pointing to Jasmine, Ramona, and Trevone.

Drue cleared his throat. "I kind of walk the line between being a brain and being an adventurer. I'm a man of many talents."

Pito looked at Drue for a few seconds before turning to Jasmine and Trevone. "If the future of my people is truly at stake, then I'd like to begin at once."

"Of course," Jasmine said.

Trevone nodded. "I've been itching to take these apart and better understand how they work since I learned about them."

Benny stuck his thumb toward Ramona, who'd been silently eating an energy bar and looking at her HoloTek most the time, occasionally glancing at some of the alien instruments on the tables around them.

"This is our tech wiz," Benny said. "We need to get in contact with the people who are now in charge of Earth's Moon."

Ramona lifted her chin into the air in greeting.

"Oh," Pito said. "Unfortunately, our methods of communication are far more advanced than what you generally use, and the two aren't necessarily compatible." He paused, drumming his four fingers on the table. "Perhaps I could upgrade some of your systems—"

"I'm good," Ramona said.

Benny and the others all turned to look at her. She shrugged, holding up her HoloTek.

"Already mapped out new coding," she said. "What do you think I'm doing all the time? Playing games?" She shook her head. "Newbz."

She reached out and snatched a red metal tool from the workbench and held it up. It had half a dozen prongs sticking out of it—Benny thought it looked like some kind of multitool.

"This'll work," she said. "Ash didn't bring near enough supplies." Then she turned away from them and headed for the stairs, shoving the rest of the energy bar in her mouth.

"That's, uh . . ." Benny started. "Ramona."

He bit his lip, but Hot Dog nudged him. "Don't worry," she said. "I usually have no idea what she's talking about, but she *does* always get stuff done."

"If you'll excuse me," Vala said. "It has been a long flight, and I require time to recuperate. The focus it takes to land my ship can be draining. My crew down here will assist you in any way they can." She nodded to the stairwell. "Or you can return to the ship if you like. Shall we reconvene in two of your Earth hours?"

"Sure," Benny said.

Vala turned away from them, disappearing into one of

the cavern hallways as Jasmine and Trevone began to take apart a stealth drive alongside Pito.

"So what do *we* do?" Hot Dog asked. "I feel kind of out of my league here."

"Well," Drue said, drawing out the word. "We've got some time to kill . . ."

"What are you up to?" Hot Dog asked, narrowing her eyes.

"I just think it'd be a good idea if we take stock of all the cars we brought up from the Taj." He shrugged. "And make sure they're working all right."

Hot Dog's face lit up. "Wow. Okay. I actually agree with you. Plus, you know, we don't want our skills to get rusty."

"Guys," Benny said.

"I'm sure we could teach each other a thing or two," Drue said. "It's for the good of humanity!"

"I am one hundred percent on board with that," Hot Dog said.

"We've got more important stuff to be doing," Benny said.

"Like what?" Drue asked. "Come on, Benny, man. Blow off some steam."

"Think of it as a training exercise," Hot Dog said. She grinned at him. "You're not a bad pilot, but you've still got plenty to learn."

"First one there gets a Star Runner," Drue said. And

before anyone could say anything else, he bolted toward the stairwell.

"There's more than one, you idiot," Hot Dog yelled, chasing after him.

"But . . ." Benny started. He looked around the cavern. The commander was gone. The stealth drives were being inspected. Ramona was working on the satellite comms. He tried to think of what else he could do.

"Go," Jasmine said from behind Benny.

He turned to face her. She shrugged and continued. "Take a break."

"We're fine down here," Trevone said, pulling his goggles down over his eyes as he inspected an Alpha Maraudi tool. "Trust me."

Jasmine's nosed twitched. "Besides, it's making me very nervous that Hot Dog and Drue are getting along. Those two should always have a third wheel."

Benny couldn't argue with that. "Okay," he said. "But I'll be back in a bit. Let us know if you need anything."

"*Go,*" Jasmine said again. Then she turned to Pito and Trevone as she held up a stealth drive that she'd pried the casing off of. "So, I figured out last night that the power source appears to use gel capacitors."

"No good," Trevone said. "We can't track something like that."

"Interesting. And what's the composition of this 'gel'?"

Pito asked. "Perhaps that could be helpful."

Benny took one last look at the three of them as they continued to discuss things he didn't understand at all, and then let out a long breath. Before he could find an excuse to stay, he was at the staircase, starting the long climb back up to the ship.

When Benny finally made it back to the hangar—
sweaty from the many flights of stairs—he was wholly
unprepared for the scene he walked into. On one side of
the room, Ramona sat on the ground beside a gold Star
Runner. Both its doors were open and various electronic
components were on the stone floor around her. It looked
like she had disassembled the entire interior dash. Drue
stood nearby, staring at the craft with a look of horror on
his pale face.

A few rows of cars away, Hot Dog chased after Zee as
the Alpha Maraudi child darted around the hangar. The
alien stopped at every vehicle he passed, opening the door
with a tentacle and shoving his head inside. Hot Dog was
talking quickly, looking exasperated.

"You can't just come in and go through all our stuff,"
she said as Zee slid into the driver's seat of a laser-mounted

Space Runner. "If Ash were in here right now, she'd freak out. Hey, get out of—"

The SR's engine powered on.

"Oh, no, no, no, you don't," Hot Dog said as she basically threw herself into the passenger side of the car, smashing buttons until it turned off.

"Everything okay?" Benny asked, coming around to the front of the Space Runner.

Hot Dog crawled back out and blew a curl out of her face. "What does it look like?"

"Uh, hi, Zee," Benny said.

The alien climbed out and stared at Benny. "You seem to be the leader of the Earthlings up here, right? Great. Remind this human that you're . . ." Zee paused. "Not *hostages*, but . . . there's another word."

"You'd better be looking for *guests*," Hot Dog said.

"Sure. You're our *guests*, which means we're helping you out and you should pay us back by letting me fly one of these things. I've read all about Space Runners. This will be a perfect way for me to find out *why* your planet is so obsessed with them."

"This sounds weirdly familiar," Benny said. He glanced over at Drue, who just kept shaking his head as he stared at Ramona and the Star Runner.

"What have you done to her?" Drue asked. "Do you have any idea how fast this thing could go? It nearly blew

94

the skin off my face. It was *amazing*. And you've stripped it down to component parts."

"Cry somewhere else, flyboy," Ramona said.

"Wait, the gold one is faster?" Zee shoved past Hot Dog, heading toward Drue. "I want to try that one! Put it back together!"

"How did he get up here?" Benny asked as Hot Dog came to his side.

"Must've been while we were all talking to that scientist," she said. "We're just lucky he didn't fire off one of these lasers and accidentally blow up an SR or something."

"How fast does it go?" Zee asked Drue, bouncing on his toes as he inspected the Star Runner's hull.

Drue shook his head. "Faster than anything humans have ever created, I think. I drove one yesterday and it pinned me to the back of my seat. I thought my brain was going to come out of my ears. It was the greatest feeling I've ever experienced."

Zee let out a high-pitched squeal. "That's what I want to do!"

"It's too much engine for you," Drue said.

"Like your"—the alien paused—"your *spleen* could even process the speeds that my people can travel."

"I think you mean *brain*."

Tentacles whipped in the air. "I'm speaking an alien language my mouth can barely stormulate! I don't hear you talking in any intergalactic tongues."

"*Formulate*," Drue said with a smirk.

Zee let out a long, wheezing groan.

"Oy!" Ramona said, pointing the sharp end of the red metal tool she swiped at the two of them. "Mute yourselves! Spam someone else. This is top priority." Then she used another end to open a soda and started tapping on her HoloTek, muttering to herself.

"Well," Drue said, "I guess we do have two more."

Zee scanned the room until he spotted another of the gold vehicles. "Mine!" he shouted, and then he was darting over to the Star Runner.

"No way," Benny said, sprinting and cutting the alien off between rows of cars.

Zee skidded to a stop in front of him. His tentacles braided together and swung through the air back and forth like a pendulum. "I get it. I've read all about your people. You don't trust me because I'm different from you. That's the way you work, right?"

"This has nothing to do with you being an Alpha Maraudi," Benny said. "And humans aren't like that." Despite saying this, he couldn't help but think of all the times that people in cities had looked at him and his family in disgust just because they belonged to a caravan. "Well . . . not all of them, at least. There are a lot of good people on Earth."

"Yeah?" Zee asked. "Prove it." He smiled, eyes looking past Benny and at one of the Star Runners behind him. "No one else even needs to know! What do you want? Alpha Maraudi secrets? I can show you weird stuff on this mother ship you probably didn't even know existed."

"You can't go out in a Star Runner because if something happened to you, I'm guessing Commander Vala would never forgive us," Benny continued. "And that's kind of the opposite of everything we're trying to do here."

"Plus, you *are* part of a group wanting to take our planet," Hot Dog said, catching up to them. "Don't think we forgot that."

Zee let out a frustrated growl. "I've been stuck on this moon with nothing to do but study and help scientists for *so many* sleeps. All I want is—" The alien stopped, staring at Benny's hand. "Wait. Where did you get that glove?"

"Oh," Benny said, crossing his arms and shoving the glove into his armpit. "Uh, I kind of took it from someone on Commander Tull's ship."

Zee's two red-pupiled eyes went wide. "You met *Tull*. And you're still alive?" One of his tentacles rubbed his chin. "Okay. Maybe I am undressed."

"Undressed?" Benny asked.

"*Impressed*," Drue said, coming up behind Zee.

"So," the alien said, ignoring him. "Do you even know how to use that thing?"

"Sort of," Benny said. "I got us on this ship with it."

"It's powerful," Zee continued. "Or at least, it can be in the right hands. *If* you know what you're doing."

There was a bump in Benny's pulse. "Can you teach me?"

"Sure!" Zee said. Then, he grinned, baring rows of gleaming gray teeth. "If you let me take one of the Star Runners out."

"Ha. Nice try. Not happening."

The alien snapped his jaw shut and turned away from them, heading toward the door. "Fine. I'll get Vala to command you to let me do it. I need to train! What if I could learn something about making our own ships better by flying one of yours? It's for science!"

When they were gone, Hot Dog let out a sigh. "Just what we need. An alien Drue."

"I'm going to pretend I didn't hear that," Drue said. "Because the more time we spend fighting, the less time we spend in the drivers' seats of these SRs."

Benny shook his head, taking a few steps away from them and turning his attention to Ramona. "Hey. What's the situation here?"

"Too many users," Ramona said. "Hangar over capacity. Processing speeds radically reduced."

"Right," Benny said. "So, that means . . . ?"

She looked up at him as she used a piece of silver wire

to tie back some of her frizzy strawberry-blond curls. "I did this before back at the Taj, but I def work better in silence, B-Man. Gimme that, and I could have some gonzo uplinks for you in an hour."

Benny looked at the parts lying all around Ramona, and then back at Drue and Hot Dog. "You heard her. This takes priority. And we can't really open a hole in the wall for you to fly out of while she's working here."

Hot Dog snapped her tongue, her shoulders slumping. "You're right."

"Yeah," Drue agreed, but there was a sly grin on his face. "We should take two of the Space Runners parked in the lower hangars instead."

Hot Dog's eyes lit up. "I forgot about those!"

"I'll race you down there!" Drue said, already bolting toward the door.

"Not so fast!" Hot Dog shouted, darting after him.

In a flash they were gone, but Benny stayed behind, looking around the giant room, taking in the sight of so many of Elijah West's creations sitting unmanned on an alien ship. What would Elijah say if he could see them all now? What would his *family* say? He had so many stories to tell his brothers already. He just had to make sure he got the chance to.

"Okay, I should check in with Pinky and Ricardo." He laughed a little. "I wonder how long it'll take Drue and Hot

Dog to realize they need me or one of the Alpha Maraudi to open the hangar for them."

Ramona looked up at him. "*Mute,*" she said.

"Right, sorry," he said.

On the way out, he passed by Ash McGuyver, who flashed him a big smile before popping her gum and heading into the hangar.

Benny only got a few steps down the hall before he heard her scream.

"My baby!" Ash shouted. "What have you done to her?"

On the bridge, he found Pinky standing in front of the central hologram, which now showed the outside of the ship and its surrounding area.

"There are what we would call cameras all over the hull's exterior," the AI said as he approached. "The energies in the minerals record data and transmit it to this terminal."

"Sounds like it would be good for scouting," Benny said as he came to her side. "We could have used it when we were hunting for Hot Dog or Dr. Bale. Shoot a rock toward the dark side of the Moon and see what you can find." He raised his eyebrows. "Hey, maybe we can use that to find the weapon!"

"The range appears to be quite short, so the mother ship would have to be very close by to pick up any transmissions," Pinky said. "From what I can tell."

Benny let out a long breath, but Pinky continued, nudging him, even though her elbow went straight through his. "That's an innovator's mindset. Elijah would be proud." She looked sad for a moment before shaking her head and smiling.

"Are you . . . worried about him?" Benny asked.

The AI shrugged a little. "I learned a long time ago that Elijah West isn't someone you can worry about. It would consume you. Take up all your time."

"Oh. Yeah. I guess that makes sense."

"Or," Pinky continued, "maybe that's just something Elijah implanted into my programming. I couldn't say for certain." Her brow furrowed, and when she spoke again, her voice was much softer as it came through the speakers in Benny's collar. "I'm sure the real Pinky knows. She must still think of him. At least sometimes."

As they stood together in silence staring at the hologram before them, Benny wondered what it must have been like to know that there was another version of you—a flesh-and-blood human—somewhere on Earth. It was hard for him to even fathom. Before he could figure out if it would be okay to ask about or not, he was distracted by two silver vehicles that shot out into space from one side of the holographic ship.

"Are those . . ." Pinky started, stepping around the image to get a better look.

"I guess Hot Dog and Drue got one of the Maraudi to open up the lower hangar for them," Benny said, watching the two Space Runners race each other around the mother ship, weaving back and forth across its surface. "They wanted to take some SRs out."

"Of course they did," Pinky said with a slight smile. "And you didn't join them?"

"I don't think I'd have any fun behind the wheel right now." He paused. "How are the others doing?"

"As well as can be expected. Ricardo and Kira have kept their eyes on everyone, helping to keep them calm."

"That's good," Benny said. "What about you?"

"I've been observing," The AI said. She raised a hand and pointed to a knot of green light slithering in the air. "Every movement—every *thread* of this has meaning. The way the patterns weave, how the ribbons unfold . . . It's a lot to process, especially without any sense of how their vocabulary works."

Benny stared up at the holograms, trying to figure out how someone would even begin to try to figure out what they meant. "My grandmother tried to teach me Spanish for a while, but I wasn't a very good student." He shook his head. "I kind of wish I'd spent more time learning from her instead of out on the sand in a dune buggy."

"Griida was nice enough to explain a few things at first, but he said he had to focus on ship running diagnostics and couldn't be bothered." Pinky's voice got quieter. "I think he was just annoyed, if I'm being honest." She looked back to the hologram. "Oh, dear."

Benny watched as one of the Space Runners flew across the ice surface of Ganymede well away from the ship, its laser on, carving into the surface of the moon. He didn't have to wonder who was driving the craft—after a few passes, the laser turned off, leaving three letters behind, etched into the surface: *DBL*.

"I'm going to kill him," Benny said. "If he doesn't get us killed first."

Pinky smirked a little, pointing to another part of the hologram.

"Careful," she said, "or you'll end up having to get rid of half your platoon."

Benny watched the other silver Space Runner attempt to carve a jagged *H* into the surface of the moon. The connecting line in the middle was too long, a diagonal slash across the other marks. The SR jetted around in circles before finding a new spot and trying again.

"We're doomed," Benny said, though he couldn't help but grin a little.

8.

Benny left the bridge to check in with Ricardo and Kira, who were doing their best to keep the other kids both calm and entertained in the mess hall. The room was, like the hangar, huge and made of stone. One wall was clear, looking out onto the cold expanse of Ganymede—thankfully, not the direction in which Hot Dog and Drue were flying. After spending so much time at the Lunar Taj where every surface was unnecessarily luxurious, Benny was actually starting to appreciate how utilitarian the Alpha Maraudi were. Even the gold-lined throne on the bridge seemed to have had purpose, aiding in the ship's landing.

In the mess hall, he found row after row of tables and benches that had grown out of the floor. They were covered in boxes brought up from the Taj that contained resources like packaged food, water, first aid kits, and spare space suits—basically anything that could be grabbed once the evacuation began. Most of the kids in the room sat in little groups, sharing games on their datapads or munching snacks.

Benny spotted Kira and Ricardo unpacking a stash of fresh fruit at one of the middle tables.

"This'll all go bad soon," Ricardo said to Kira as Benny approached. "We should be eating it first."

"*Hai*," Kira agreed. "I'm already planning on swapping things out as soon as we've taken stock of what we have. We tried to be thorough when we were packing, but we left in a hurry."

Ricardo paused as he saw Benny approach. "Finally," he said, sounding annoyed. "You could have at least sent us an update."

"Sorry," Benny said. "The commander needed some time to rest. Right now we're kind of at a standstill. We're meeting up in a little bit, and you should be there to talk our next steps with us. Jazz and Trevone are doing science stuff. Ramona's in the hangar working on comms. We're doing what we can."

Ricardo handed Benny a banana. "Good."

"We're not used to being out of the loop," Kira said, going back to unpacking the container.

Ricardo nodded to something over Benny's shoulder. "Actually, we're not the only ones who want updates."

Benny turned to see a dozen EW-SCABers all standing

behind him. Even after the last several weeks, there were a few of them that he didn't even recognize, which made him feel like a horrible excuse for a leader, given everything they'd been through together. Before he could say anything or awkwardly try for introductions, however, they began to speak at the same time.

"What's going on down there?"

"Did someone say something about a superweapon?"

"How many ETs are here?"

"How long are we on the ship?"

"Where's Elijah?"

"Did I see a tiny alien running through the hall earlier?"

"Uh," Benny said. "Okay, let's start with what we're trying to get done right now."

He answered as many questions as he could, anxiously glancing at a HoloTek on the nearby table every few minutes to see how much time had passed, not wanting to get too distracted and miss the meeting with Vala. Eventually, Hot Dog and Drue wandered in. They dashed for a few granola bars before joining Benny's side.

"Whoa, whoa," Drue said as he approached. "Let's give the guy some space, huh?"

"Welcome back," Benny muttered. He paused. "Wait, how *did* you get back in?"

"Oh . . ."

"We kinda didn't plan for that," Hot Dog said. "For a

minute I thought I was gonna have to try to shoot through the hull."

Benny's eyes went wide.

"Don't worry," she continued, waving her granola bar through the air. "I just gave the wall a few love taps with the front of my SR and the Maraudi inside got the picture." She sighed. "Thankfully. Anyway, it was a good session. We were both reminded that I'm the better pilot."

Drue grinned. "And that I'm a better shot."

"Yeah, I gotta work on that."

"Wait," Iyabo said. "You guys went *flying*. Hold up, I want to go, too. It's starting to get boring around here."

Several other kids started complaining as well. Drue and Hot Dog looked to Benny for help.

"Nuh-uh," he said, shaking his head as he took a few steps back. "This is all you." He held up the banana he still had in his hand. "I haven't even gotten to eat yet."

Benny hurried over to another table, taking a few deep breaths and relishing the fact that he was out of the spotlight for a moment. After digging around in a box full of drinks, he tried to poke a sharp straw through a silver pouch of water, only to end up spritzing himself in the face. There was a low, breathy giggle behind him, followed by the sound of an aluminum can opening.

He turned to find Ramona. "Oh," he said. "Hey."

"Satellite's installed," she said, taking a swig from her

drink. "In the Star Runner. Max upgrades. Impressed even myself."

"Wait," he said, shaking his head in astonishment. "Really? It's done?"

"Don't ask for repeats, Benzo. You know I'm the master." She took a long swig from her drink. "And Ash helped. Turns out she's super leet. Nice to meet a worthy brain."

"That's amazing!" Benny said. He felt light—*finally* they had something to work with. "Okay. Can you get Pinky from the bridge and look at porting her into the SR? We can get this thing launched ASAP and reestablish comms with the Taj and Earth forces."

Ramona clicked her tongue. "Sure thing, boss," she said, turning away. "I've kinda missed that dumb holo-troll."

As soon as Ramona finished a few last-minute tweaks and Ash cleared them for launch, the satellite Star Runner shot out of the side of the mother ship, auto-piloted on a course set by Pinky. Benny then gathered everyone down in the underground cavern—except Ramona, who decided she would much rather stay in the hangar and try to convince Ash to introduce an entirely new operating system to the SRs. Commander Vala took them to a room in one of the hallways that led deeper into the moon. Inside, egg-like chairs resembling the throne on the bridge sat around an oval table rimmed in gold.

"So," the commander said, "you've launched a communications satellite. What do you do now?"

"Pinky estimates it'll take several hours for the Star Runner to be close enough to contact the Taj," Benny said. "Once in place, we should be able to talk to New Apollo and start trying to convince them not to use the weapon. And, you know, that we can all work together."

"And if they refuse?" Vala asked.

He turned to Jasmine. "How're the stealth drives going?"

Jasmine's face fell. "We're still trying to figure out exactly how they work," she said. "Pito is testing a few of the components right now to see if there's anything the Maraudi have that might be able to track them. If we can detect a stealth field, we can find that weapon."

"Dr. Bale's way of building things is complicated," Trevone added. "It's all very different from Elijah's tech."

"Now that Ramona is done with the satellite, we can use her help as well," Jasmine said.

"What about the other Alpha Maraudi?" Ricardo asked Vala. "Have you been in contact with Tull or your home world?"

The commander leaned back in her chair, the tentacles on her head unraveling and reforming into a tightly coiled bun. "We still await word from Calam. As for Tull . . ." Vala sighed. "I have attempted to communicate with him, but my calls have gone unanswered."

Ricardo clenched his jaw. In the chair beside him, Kira scoffed.

"Perfect," Hot Dog said. "We're being ghosted by an alien."

"Okay, so we keep working," Benny said. "We have some time before we're in touch with the Taj, so let's figure out a game plan for what we're going to say when we do. I'm pretty sure Bale thinks all of you are bloodthirsty world conquerors. If we can get him to see that you're open to coexisting, hopefully that'll change his mind. But we're going to need to be convincing."

"Dr. Bale wasn't too big on talking things out," Hot Dog said. "You may be forgetting that whole threaten-us-with-a-gun thing."

Benny shook his head. "No. But things are different now. And he's not in charge anymore. Plus, I don't think anyone wants to get to the point where we all end up dying because no one will sit down and talk." He glanced at Drue. "Your dad has to be against that."

Drue shrugged.

"As I mentioned to Benny before," Vala said, "if this superweapon is used against our home planet, Calam, that will lead to the full force of the remaining Maraudi ships being directed against Earth." She paused. "If I am being completely honest, I would likely not raise a hand to stop such a retaliation."

Benny frowned, but he wondered, too, what he would do if they failed to stop the Maraudi from taking his planet. Would he have led a charge for revenge?

"I think the term we're talking about is 'mutually assured destruction,'" Jasmine said. "And as a senator, Drue's father will definitely understand the concept. Although he hasn't seemed too excited about listening to a bunch of kids from what I've seen."

"No," Benny said. "But what about listening to an alien commander? And once we've got the weapon out of the way, we can start actual peace talks."

"Convincing the humans to save themselves by not killing us is one thing," Vala said. "But 'peace talks,' as you call them, are another. I must admit that I hold little hope in them succeeding. Or, rather, in any lasting peace being upheld."

The room went silent as everyone turned their attention to the commander. Benny was sure he hadn't heard her right.

"What do you mean?" Ricardo asked. "Because your people would have to coexist with us? Or find another planet?"

"Or do you just not want to work together with the humans?" Kira wondered aloud.

"*Guys,*" Benny whispered.

"Allow me to put it this way," Vala continued. "When

you speak to me—be it earlier on the bridge, or now, sitting here—I think that what you say is true. But we have seen many broadcasts from your planet. The older your people get, the less their words mean."

"Like, people lie more?" Hot Dog asked.

"It's not only that," Vala said. "I listen to you, and I believe that *you* believe what you are saying. You are . . . I think the word is *earnest*. Humanity tends to lose that as they age. Part of the problem is your system of communicating. Your languages have much margin for error."

"What do you mean?" Trevone asked.

"You have so few means of expressing yourself. You say a word like *peace* and it is in a single tone. It's a nebulous idea that could mean any number of things. So easily misunderstood. We say our word for *peace* and, using the multiple tones of our voices, we can say precisely what we mean."

"I get it," Jasmine said. "We say a word and it's a single instrument. You say it and there's an entire orchestra playing a chord. You express so much in a single syllable. You can be exact, down to the smallest nuance."

Vala nodded. "I believe you understand."

"Even in the differences between human languages, there is plenty of room for error," Kira said. "I definitely get that. There are words in Japanese that have no real translation to English. The meanings can be misinterpreted easily."

"So," Benny said. "How *do* we communicate in a way that you trust?"

Vala stood from her chair and slowly raised her mask with a tentacle. The blue third eye on her forehead cast an eerie glow around her head. "It is easier for us to know that you speak the truth and exactly what you mean if we can look at you, in person. There are shifts in energy, in pulse—in many tics we can detect with the eye that you do not have. It is the same for our own people. A way to gauge emotions and intent."

"Then why do you keep your third eye covered?" Jasmine asked.

"Yeah," Hot Dog agreed. "Wouldn't you want to see everyone like that?"

Vala nodded slightly. "To see someone so purely is not without its drawbacks. It is . . . *intimate*. Something we reserve for those closest to us."

"That makes sense," Benny said. "I probably wouldn't want people going around seeing the worst of me."

"Please, I bet you'd have nothing to worry about," Hot Dog said. "Others of us . . ."

"Yeah, I *get* it." Drue groaned. "Go ahead and shoot me the look. I'm ready."

"What?" she replied. "I was talking about *me*."

"You want to meet with the other humans in person?" Ricardo asked. "You do realize you *had* that opportunity already, when you attacked the Taj."

"Would you have lowered your shields for us?" the commander asked. "Would you have let us in without any threat of violence? Would this *Dr. Bale* of yours, the weapon creator, have thrown down his arms to talk of peace?"

Ricardo didn't answer.

"Like I said," Benny said, "things have changed. And now, you've got us. We're . . . I don't know . . . *translators* isn't the right word."

"Peace brokers!" Drue said. Then he hesitated. "I don't know if that's actually a thing, but it sounds cool."

"Peace brokers," Vala repeated.

"Plus, my father is kind of in charge at the Taj now," Drue said, the excitement fading quickly from his voice. "There's no way I could change his mind by myself, but maybe I can at least get him to not hang up immediately." He swallowed. "Probably."

"Listening is a good first step," Jasmine said.

The sound of stomping in the hallway took everyone's attention. In seconds, two figures darted through the open doorway. Pinky stopped at the foot of the table behind an empty chair. Ramona followed after her, wheezing. She half collapsed onto the back of the seat.

"Hologhost . . . ," she managed to get out between breaths, "made me . . . *run.*"

"We might need your coding skills," the AI said. Then

she turned her focus to the rest of them. "There's been an unexpected development. The Star Runner we sent out has already made contact with something. It seems the Taj launched their own deep space probe after we left."

"What does that mean?" Benny asked.

"This new satellite or *whatever* they launched has pinged Ramona's Star Runner. They've been trying to establish open lines for the last few minutes."

"They're *calling* us?" Jasmine said.

Ramona grabbed her side, which must have been aching from her sprinting. "Bingo, J."

Benny stood up. "Then let's answer it."

"Uh, okay, but how do we do that here?" Hot Dog asked. "On a HoloTek?"

"I can do you one better," Ramona said, tapping on her datapad.

"What are you—" Pinky started.

And then the AI disappeared. The swarm of nanoprojectors that formed the hologram instead projected a wobbly blue line that floated over to the middle of the table.

"Oh, you horrible little hacker," Pinky said through the speakers in their collars. "You are not trapping me in your HoloTek again. At *least* prop it up so I can see what's happening."

"Just say when," Ramona said, ignoring the AI. "I'll patch you through."

Benny glanced around at the others They nodded to him. Finally, his eyes landed on Vala. "You want to meet in person?" he asked. "Now's as good a time as any to try to make that happen."

The commander mulled this over for a few moments before speaking. "Then I will leave it to you, Benny Love. Let us see what peace and progress you can facilitate."

Benny swallowed hard, then got to his feet, motioning for Drue to join him by his side. "Okay. Let's do this."

"You got it," Ramona chirped. "I've set the nanocameras to face you two." She let out something that sounded half like a sigh, half like a laugh. "What would you do without me?"

The blue holographic line wobbled a few more times before suddenly changing. There, floating in front of them, was Elijah West's desk in his private quarters. A man sat behind it, his suit perfectly tailored and black hair slicked back. Steely gray eyes stared at them.

Drue slowly raised one hand into the air and tried to smile. "Uh, hi, Dad."

Senator Lincoln stared back in silence, mouth agape,
for two seconds. Then his entire body tensed as his lips
pressed together into a grim straight line.

"Yeah . . ." Drue said, drawing out the word until it dis-
integrated into a breath.

"Where are you?" the senator asked. His eyes were full
of fire, but Benny couldn't tell through the hologram if it
was due to anger, concern, or some kind of relief at the sight
of his son. Maybe it was a mixture of all those things. He
couldn't help but think that this was a great example of
what Vala had been talking about when it came to the dif-
ficulty of interpreting humans. At least where adults were
concerned.

"Well, you see," Drue said, "it's a long story. We—"

"Jupiter," Benny said, before Drue could name the exact
moon they were on, just in case the Earth forces had any

ideas about attacking the Alpha Maraudi there. "Basically. In that neighborhood."

"Jupiter . . ." Drue's father repeated quietly. His eyes wandered around, taking in the stone walls behind the two boys. "How? That's impossible. Where would you even be broadcasting from. Unless . . ." He trailed off, but his entire face seemed to pull back, as if it were being stretched over the front of his skull. "Don't tell me," he whispered.

"Uh," Drue said. "We kind of hitched a ride on the alien mother ship that was at the Taj?" For some reason this came out as more of a question, even though it was exactly what had happened.

Senator Lincoln jumped to his feet and started shouting at people offscreen. "Haven't you tracked this signal yet? Get the New Apollo team prepped. I want a map of every ship and resource we have in space between here and Jupiter and stats on how long it would take for us to reach the planet. Chart a course to the foreign satellite we're connected to."

"The signal you . . . uh, pinged?" Benny asked, looking to Ramona, who nodded. Then he continued. "The signal you pinged isn't coming from the alien ship, but from a Space Runner we launched so we'd be able to communicate with the Taj. Tracking it down won't do you any good."

"Connection to the ship is max encrypted," Ramona said with a grin.

Drue's father looked at Benny with narrowed eyes, then slowly began to sit down again.

"So, you're hostages, then," he said. "What are their demands?"

"Actually, *we* sort of hijacked their ship," Benny said. "But we've formed an alliance with the aliens on board."

"You aren't going to sit there and tell me that the Alpha Maraudi just let you have their ship and took you halfway across our solar system so you can be *friends*. You saw what they did to the Taj. They almost killed all of us. They *would* have killed you had we not shown up."

"They've actually been pretty nice," Drue said. "Though, the beds leave a lot to be desired."

"Nice?" Senator Lincoln repeated, digging into the word. "We are on the verge of intergalactic war and you think the aliens who would annihilate our entire species are being *nice* to you? Have you learned nothing from watching me all these years? You're being used as political prisoners and you don't even realize it."

"Well, when you put it that way, it *sounds* bad, but . . ." Drue trailed off, pulling on the neck of his black space suit a little.

"Benny," Hot Dog whispered from the other side of the table, raising her eyebrows and silently urging him to take over.

"Right," Benny said. "*Nice* probably isn't the right word.

They're being helpful. They're listening to what we have to say."

The senator hunched over Elijah's desk, his hands in fists. "And what *do* you have to say?"

Benny sat up straighter, staring into the hologram. "Things have changed, Senator Lincoln, and if we don't try to work together, both our species are going to destroy each other. None of us will get Earth. None of us will survive. We can find a way to avoid that. We can figure out a way for us to all to be okay. But in order to do that, you have to be willing to give peace between our worlds a chance. And that starts with taking Dr. Bale's superweapon off the table."

He glanced around the room. Vala didn't move. Neither did the members of the Pit Crew, who sat with their lips pressed together tightly, staring at Senator Lincoln from other sides of the hologram. Hot Dog and Jasmine both nodded to him. Ramona yawned.

At Benny's left, Drue leaned in a bit, grinning and talking softly without moving his lips. "That sounded good."

Senator Lincoln simply laughed. "What are you talking about?" he finally asked. "We beat the aliens at the Taj. Humanity has already shown that we can win this battle. The only talks we should be having are the Alpha Maraudi officially abandoning any plans to take our planet and leaving our solar system for good. They should be apologizing to us." He leaned back in Elijah's chair. "Not that we'd trust them to stay away. Not after everything they've done."

Commander Vala made a low, snarling noise as several of her tentacles tapped on the table.

"We have nothing to fear from the aliens anymore," the senator continued. "We may have gotten off to a rocky start, but we've proven we can take them on. If Elijah had let us base soldiers at the Taj to begin with, we wouldn't even be in this mess." He pursed his lips for a moment. "You know that they intend to colonize our planet. You heard it from their own disgusting mouths. So why should we risk letting them live?"

"For one, you're talking about wiping out an entire species," Benny said.

"So are they."

"Sure, but," Drue piped in, "I mean, I get what you're saying, but when you really start thinking about it . . . It's an *entire planet* of people who are in trouble."

Drue's father stared at him for a moment. "And?"

"You would just sit back and watch their planet burn from another galaxy?" Benny asked.

"I would sit in my home country on Earth and continue to exist, along with every other human who rightfully belongs on this planet," Drue's father replied. "I would do it to make sure my *family* was safe." He slammed his fist against Elijah's desk. "I am done wasting my time listening to the fantasies of *children*. You know nothing of what you speak about."

Benny sat in silence for a moment, the senator's words striking something in his core. Of course, he was trying to do all this to keep *his* family safe as well. And if it came down to it, that was the most important thing to him. Despite everything he'd done to try to make peace with the aliens.

But there were other things to consider.

"You don't understand what using that weapon would do," he said firmly.

"This safety you speak of would be nothing more than an illusion," Vala said.

Senator Lincoln looked around, trying to figure out where the words had come from since the cameras were focused on Benny and Drue. "So you've got one of them there with you."

Ramona tapped on her HoloTek, and the swarm of nano-projectors and cameras turned until Drue's father faced the alien.

"I am Vala, commander of this ship and outpost," the alien said. "I have spoken with these humans and have thought long and hard about this 'superweapon,' as your people have taken to calling it. Knowing humanity, I do not doubt its existence for a moment. However, I am also aware of the limited scope of your people's understanding of our shared universe. Of *my* solar system. I am sure that you could send some bomb to my planet. Perhaps faster than we could evacuate. But that would not completely eliminate the Alpha Maraudi. Do you think we have not sent mother ships to the far corners of other galaxies in search of habitable planets? That we do not have outposts across this vast universe? How do you think our commanders would react once they learned of our world's destruction at the hands of a primitive planet in a vulnerable solar system?" The commander's tentacles twisted together, forming two glossy horns that weaved around each other above her head. "It would take only *one* of our mother ships to destroy all life on your planet." She paused. "In fact, that was our original plan. Before the humans around this table involved themselves and saved you."

"Have you not figured out what happens when you threaten us?" the senator asked, banging his fist on the desk. "We will fight you. We'll do whatever it takes to continue to exist."

"This is not a threat," Vala said calmly. "This is simply the logical chain of events that would occur were you to destroy our home world. Despite what you may think, we are at heart a peaceful species. Only the most drastic of situations has led us to the predicament we are in now. But losing so many of our people, I assure you, would bring wrath down upon your planet."

The senator didn't respond, but Benny noticed a bead of sweat fall from his temple. His face, too, looked paler than it had just moments before.

"The commander's right," Jasmine said, the cameras turning to her. "There's no possible way you could destroy every Maraudi mother ship or evacuation ship, no matter how big this superweapon is. We don't even know how many there are out there."

"But I bet this commander does," the senator said. "I bet Vala could tell us exactly how many ships are in the alien fleet."

Benny glanced at the commander, who neither responded nor moved.

"We don't even know where the other mother ship *in our own solar system* is right now," Jasmine continued. "If it gets close to Earth . . . I personally ran the debris projections before our attack against the asteroid storm. I don't know how many of these weaponized Space Runners you have, but is it enough to stop a coordinated assault from two mother ships? A dozen? It would take so few asteroids to wipe all of humanity off the map."

"Uh," Hot Dog whispered, "maybe *don't* tell the ETs how to kill Earth?"

"Trust me," Trevone said. "We've been working with Pito. They know what's possible."

"Uh, Ramona?" Benny asked. The cameras turned

back to him. "Thanks. Senator Lincoln, Commander Vala has agreed to meet with people from Earth to try to talk peace and figure out how we can work together to save both our species."

"*Peace*," the senator half spat. But there was something different about his expression. Ever since Vala had spoken about what would happen if they used the Dr. Bale's weapon, the man had let a hint of concern shadow his face—a slight crease between his eyebrows. Even though Drue's father still sounded like he was laughing off the threat to humanity, Benny could tell he was weighing what they were saying in his head. He was *listening* to them.

"All we want to do is avoid . . . ," Benny started. He glanced at Jasmine. "Mutually assured destruction."

"You don't want the Lincoln name to be connected to the end of humanity," Drue chimed in. "And, you know, I kind of want to go back to Earth and not have to worry about getting exploded."

"Just let us talk," Benny said. "And for the sake of our solar system, don't use that weapon."

Drue's father was quiet for several seconds. "The government—the *planet*—I represent would be . . ." He paused, narrowing his eyes as though he were deep in thought. "We could discuss the remote possibility that there are other options."

"Good," Benny said, his pulse thrumming as he tried

not to make it obvious how relieved he was. "Great! That's all we're asking for right now."

"But, um," Drue added, "it has to be in person."

"We would welcome an envoy of representatives onto the ship," Vala said. "Though, with our current numbers, it would need to be a small delegation. Perhaps—"

"I'm not walking into a trap," Senator Lincoln interrupted. "Dr. Bale has told me of the potential forces your mother ships could hold and of the way you can control certain minerals." He grimaced. "I've been encased in your rock before and that will not happen again. I won't become a hostage."

"That's fine," Benny said. "We have plenty of Space Runners up here. We could, I don't know, meet you somewhere else. Mars, maybe. Just a handful of people from both sides."

"No," the senator said. "I don't want those things coming any closer to Earth or our Moon." He paused, sliding his fingers across the holo-surface of the desk, bringing up several maps.

Ricardo and Kira had stayed quiet throughout the conversation, but Benny heard the leader of the Pit Crew grunt. "That's *Elijah's* desk," he said. "He has no right to sit behind it."

"He has no right to be at the Taj at all," Kira agreed.

But either the senator didn't hear their comments, or he

chose to ignore them. "What about one of Jupiter's moons?" he asked.

"Uh, yeah, maybe," Benny said. Ganymede—with its surface made completely of ice—didn't exactly sound like a great place for a peace talk, and he figured it was better to keep the location of Vala's ship a secret. Still, Jupiter apparently had many, *many* satellites. If only—

"Io," Jasmine said from the other side of the table, tapping on her HoloTek. "It's volcanic, but it's got a rocky surface at least. We'd have no trouble landing there and getting around."

"Uh, we're not going to burst into flames when we get out of the car, right?" Hot Dog asked.

"It also has large ice regions," Trevone added, one side of his mouth curling up in a look of satisfaction. "Well, frozen sulfur dioxide, actually, but similar to ice. That means there are places where the temperature kind of, you know . . . evens out."

"This is true," Vala said. "We mapped several such areas when first observing the moons of Jupiter." She nodded to Benny. "I would approve of this location."

"Io," Senator Lincoln said, staring at a map of the solar system now floating about the desk in Elijah's office. "Yes, we could make that work. Send us the coordinates you suggest and I will have Dr. Bale and our people look over them. If they think this is a suitable location, I'll get back to you."

Benny looked around the table. "Does this sound good to everyone?"

There were no objections.

"Not so fast," the senator said. "Here are our terms: You come alone. No alien vehicles that could trap us in rock. And I don't want to face an entire army of the Alpha Maraudi. The bare minimum. Dr. Bale has ways of detecting the aliens. We'll know if we're being deceived."

"Then you don't bring weapons," Benny said. "We have ways of making sure you don't." He curled up his silver glove on the table.

Senator Lincoln stared at him for a moment before nodding. "Now," he said. "How many of you kids are there?"

"About half the EW-SCABers," Drue said. "Give or take."

"That must mean that the squadron of Space Runners our satellites are tracking . . ."

"Are those who decided to go back to Earth," Benny said.

"We'll make sure they're escorted home, then." The senator pursed his lips. He was quiet, looking down at Elijah's desk for a few seconds before he met his son's eyes. "You'll be at this meeting, Drue?"

"Obviously," Drue said as he crossed his arms. "I'm totally an important part of this." Then, his eyes went wide as he grinned. "Oh, man, are you going to die when I tell you about where I carved our initials."

"What about *my* people?" Vala asked. "The ones you shot from the sky. Those who were at the Taj when you arrived. Where are they now?"

Senator Lincoln raised his eyebrows as the camera shifted to the commander. "You're asking about the invaders we rescued the Lunar Taj from?"

Vala was silent, but her tentacles twitched and writhed as she nodded.

Drue's father stared at the commander for what felt to Benny like a long time before answering. "They're still here," he said. "We've moved them underground." He paused. "Those who survived."

Vala took a deep breath. "It would be a sign of good faith to return those you are keeping prisoner to their home."

The senator let out a single laugh. "I could say the same for you. You've got dozens of underage humans held captive on your ship without permission from any parents or guardians."

"There are no prisoners here," Vala said firmly.

"Prove it, then. Show me those kids are there of their own free will—bring them to the meeting—and you'll get your people back."

There were indecipherable voices from somewhere in Elijah's office, which took the senator's attention away for a moment. He turned back to the camera. "I have to go," he said. "Remember our terms. We'll hold up our end. And, all of you up there"—he focused on Drue—"be safe. I'll be in touch."

And then, the hologram of Drue's father and Elijah's private quarters disappeared, replaced by a wobbly blue line.

Benny let out a long sigh, sinking back into the egg-like chair. "That went . . . good?"

"All things considered," Jasmine said, "I think you're right."

"We will see how well things truly end up," Vala said. "The specifications of this meeting lean heavily in the favor of the Earth forces if we meet their demands."

"Yeah," Hot Dog said. "But Benny's right. If they try anything, we've got the electro gloves to help stop them."

"And you've got your"—Drue's lips twisted—"uh, rock stuff."

"In Space Runners, we'll have the advantage," Ricardo said. "You've got part of the Pit Crew and a few of the other best pilots in the galaxy sitting around this table."

"How long do you think it would take them to get to Io, Jazz?" Benny asked.

The girl shrugged. "Depending on what vehicles they're in, a day? If they really want to push their hyperdrives."

"So we've got some time," Trevone said.

Drue leaned forward onto the table. "At least we don't have to go anywhere far. That's nice. I guess it's a good thing they're scared the Alpha Maraudi would try to attack again if we went back to the Moon."

"Right." Jasmine frowned. "Or they just don't want us anywhere near Dr. Bale's superweapon."

And with that, the room went quiet.

Once again, all they could do was wait. There was a churning in Benny's stomach as a familiar feeling from the past few weeks began to creep through his body.

Helplessness.

But Benny was determined not to let that get the better of him. Or any of his friends for that matter.

Jasmine, Trevone, and Ramona went back to work with Pito. Pinky—in her holographic form now that the call was over—returned to the bridge to continue monitoring the Alpha Maraudi tech, trying to learn as much as they could about it, hoping to find something useful. In the meantime, she assisted Griida in determining suitable coordinates for the meeting to send off to New Apollo.

Hot Dog and Drue were more than happy to join Ash McGuyver and help her prep the remaining Space

Runners since if all went as planned they'd be moving out again soon—though, Benny was pretty sure part of their exuberance was because helping out would give them the chance to claim which vehicles they wanted to drive. That left Ricardo and Kira, who Benny spoke with in the great underground cavern once they'd left the meeting room.

"This is dangerous," Ricardo said. "Dr. Bale and Senator Lincoln plotted to take over the Taj—for who knows how many years, by the way. While Elijah was still there, running the place. All behind his back. I don't trust them any more than I really trust the Alpha Maraudi. Maybe even less."

"*We* could be the ones walking into a trap," Kira added.

"I know, I know," Benny said, glancing around to make sure none of the aliens filtering through the cavern were listening. "But it's our best bet right now. Something we *can* try." He shrugged. "Plus, I don't think they're going to attack the aliens when a bunch of kids are around. It'll basically just be us and Vala and maybe a few of their guards."

"They could try to make us come back," Ricardo said.

"You're the best drivers around besides Elijah. You said it yourself. How are they going to make you do anything you don't want to?"

Ricardo didn't look convinced, but he nodded. "We need to be prepared for anything."

"Right," Kira said. "What would Elijah do?"

"What can *we* do?" Ricardo asked. "SR prep? Strategizing?"

Benny shifted his weight on his feet. "I need you to keep looking after the rest of the EW-SCABers."

Kira said something in Japanese that Benny could only imagine was a curse. Ricardo glared at him.

"We're the Pit Crew," he said. "We're not babysitters. And you do realize that *you're* an EW-SCABer, too."

"I know," Benny said. "But I—"

"Look, I appreciate everything you've done so far. But you can't keep sidelining us like this."

"It's not because I want to keep you out of the action," Benny said. "It's because they look up to you."

Ricardo scoffed. "I could say the same about you."

Benny shook his head. "It's different. You're both older, one. And two, they knew who you were before any of them flew to the Moon. We *all* did. You said you're the Pit Crew? That's the reason you have to keep being there for them. I can make speeches, sure. And, honestly, I'm not even sure how I've managed to do those. But one-on-one with them? I freak out. I mean, I'm getting better, but not *that* good. And the last thing they need to see is the guy who's supposed to be their leader totally losing his cool."

Ricardo grunted, but he didn't disagree. "I *hate* this," he said.

"I know," Benny said. "I'm sorry."

"What are you going to do, then?"

Benny glanced down at the golden glove on his hand. "I'm going to make sure *I'm* prepared, too. I'm going to get some answers." He looked back up at them. "This thing has helped us out so much and I don't even know how it works. Imagine what it could do if I actually had a clue what it was."

Ricardo nodded in agreement. "Not a bad idea," he said. Then he turned to the stairs leading up to the mother ship. "It's a long climb, Kira. You'd think these aliens would have come up with elevators."

"I wonder if Pinky can get in touch with the caravan that left," Kira said, following him. "I just want to make sure Kai's okay. And Sahar, too."

Finally alone, Benny let out a sigh, trying to collect himself a little before making his next move.

Ricardo paused halfway to the staircase and called back to him.

"One more thing," he said, turning his head slightly, to where he was almost looking over his shoulder. "Don't think for a second we've forgotten about Elijah."

"Not at all," Kira agreed.

And then they were off.

Benny took a deep breath, mentally going over a checklist of where everyone was and what they were doing, making sure that he wasn't missing anything. At least somewhat sure that everything was in order, he looked for Vala, who'd begun to make the rounds, updating her crew. He eventually spotted her on the far side of the cavern, standing among the alien plants that were thriving among huge, glowing boulders. When he got closer, he realized the commander wasn't alone.

"Oh, you," Zee said, spotting Benny. He crossed his tentacles and turned back to Vala. "That human wouldn't let me take any of their ships out earlier."

"Good," Vala said. "Your experience with solo flight is practically nonexistent. You would have hurt yourself. Or others."

"Whose fault is that?" the alien kid countered. "The closest anyone ever lets me get to flying is . . ." Zee paused for a moment, then said something in the Maraudi tongue.

"I'm sure there are words for that in Earth's languages. You should ask our guests about them."

Zee gritted his teeth, and then spoke again in English. "All I get to do is drive the videos with the fake ships. You know what I mean."

Flight simulators, Benny thought. The Alpha Maraudi must have had their own version of flight training.

Vala let one of her tentacles alight on Zee's shoulder. "Even a Bazer must learn to walk before it leaves the ground behind. Do not get ahead of yourself. You have many, many cycles to live through."

Zee groaned in a tone that sounded like metal wrenching against metal to Benny and turned away. Then he snatched something yellow and doughnut shaped off a nearby vine and bit into it viciously.

Benny blinked. "Um, is this a bad time?"

"I was checking in on Zee's lessons," Vala said. "He has been . . . *distracted* since your arrival."

"You're the one who told me I could learn from these humans," Zee said through a wad of half-eaten food. From what Benny could tell, the fruit or vegetable had caused the inside of his mouth to glow purple. "Even if a lot of it is about what not to do."

"Actually, speaking of lessons," Benny said, holding up the gold glove, "I was wondering if there was anything you could teach me about this. You saw me back in the garden. I'm not very good with it."

Zee's four tentacles weaved over the back of his head in a crisscross pattern. "And why does he get to have that? He's a . . . a *newborn* basically. Earlier than me! And I'm not supposed to get one of them for how many more cycles?"

"If you listen closely, perhaps this will be informative for both of you," Vala said. She held a hand out toward the dark lake at the other side of the cavern. "Come. Let us

137

move to a more suitable location."

The commander started walking. Zee made a gargling noise in the back of his throat, buried the scraps of his food under some soil, and followed, with Benny bringing up the rear. The farther they got from the front of the chamber, the colder the air was, and Benny couldn't help but shiver in his space suit. He was beginning to realize he was definitely not cut out for lower temperatures.

"What *do* you know of the glove?" Vala asked.

"Not much," Benny admitted. "It's made up of elements we don't have on Earth. And somehow it can control alien rock. I mean, that glowing rock that you guys use." He motioned to the walls. "It seems like everything you have that's gold can . . . make the minerals grow or move? Whether the gold is on your tentacles or a glove or even inside your chair on the bridge of your ship."

Vala nodded. "You are observant."

"It's pretty obvious," Zee grunted.

"What I don't get is how it works," Benny said. "I've used it a few times, but I have no idea how, really." He shrugged. "Mostly I've just punched rocks away."

"Humans," Zee said. "Maybe I *do* know everything I need to about your kind."

Benny flexed his fingers. "I've used it to melt rock, too. When I got covered in it back on the Moon. And to open a hole in the hull so we could get into the hangar of the mother ship."

"It is strange, as I mentioned, that you can use it at all," Vala said. "These gold items, as you call them, are what we refer to as . . ." She was silent for a few beats. "I think they might translate into something like *keys* in your language. They're usually tuned to a single Alpha Maraudi because one must be so *precise* in their intent when using them. So sure of what they are to do." A tentacle scratched beneath the commander's chin. "Perhaps it is because you are so young that you can tap into its power. So earnest, as I said before. Or perhaps it is because you *believe* it will work."

"Or maybe it's a mistake," Zee said. Then he grinned. "Let me try it on and see."

Benny looked at Vala, but the commander shook her head, continuing her stride.

"Benny Love of Earth has earned the right to wear this glove," Vala said, in a tone that gave no room for disagreement.

Zee rolled his two red-pupiled eyes and didn't say anything else about the subject.

The farther they walked into the cavern, the harder it got to see. In fact, it seemed like Vala was leading them toward the darkest section of the chamber. Benny was just beginning to have to squint to make sure he was still walking on solid ground and not about to trudge into the inky lake when the commander stopped abruptly. Benny half tripped over himself to keep from running into her.

"Careful, two eyes," Zee said with a snort.

Benny assumed that nickname wasn't a compliment.

"Can you see?" Vala asked. "I'm unsure how much light your kind needs."

"Uh, not really," Benny said. Even with his eyes adjusting to the dimness, he could barely make out the two aliens in front of him. Sweat started to prickle his brow as a nervous flutter erupted in his chest—why had they brought him this way?

"Good," Vala continued. "I've seen you manipulate rock, even if you weren't able to close the hole you created in the wall of the bridge. But can you tap into the light inside it?"

"You mean that circuitry-looking stuff that glows?" he asked. "And the veins that light the sleeping tubes?"

"That's right."

Benny shrugged in the darkness. "I wouldn't know what to do."

"Crouch down," the commander said. "Touch your glove to the floor. Close your eyes. Imagine the light inside you flowing through the key and into the stone."

"That's all it takes?" Benny asked.

"Try it," Vala insisted. "We will see."

Benny looked at the gold glove—which seemed to shine softly, even in the darkness—and took a long breath. Then he got down on one knee, placing the palm of the glove on the rock floor. He closed his eyes, unsure what Vala meant by "light." After all, it wasn't like he had a glowing third eye or anything like that. Maybe there was something he was losing in translation. And so he tried to focus on happy things, figuring that was close to whatever Vala was talking about. He thought about racing over sand dunes in his dirt buggy back home in the Drylands, his brothers, Alejandro and Justin, shouting from the backseat, begging him to go faster. He remembered the taste of the cinnamon cookies his grandmother always seemed to be able to make on special occasions, no matter how limited their supplies and resources were. The way his dad used to laugh for no reason every time he'd tear open the RV door at the end of the day before collapsing onto their threadbare couch. And moments from more recent days filled his mind, too. The thrill of seeing a satellite shoot by the window during his very first ride in a Space Runner. The electric feeling that came from stopping Tull's asteroid storm. The relief of knowing that his friends had his back. That he wasn't in this alone.

He pictured all of this pouring out of him, through his palm and into the glove. He imagined the ground bursting with rivers of light so bright that others around him would have to shield their eyes. The key was warm, vibrating at the same frequency as the buzzing in the back of his chest. He was doing it, he was sure.

Benny smiled as he opened his eyes.

If anything, it seemed even darker than before.

"Was that it?" Zee asked.

Benny stood slowly, nodding his head. "Yeah. I tried."

"Maybe it is not meant to be," Vala said. "Or maybe the time has simply yet to come."

The commander waved a tentacle. There was a flash of gold, and then suddenly veins of light shot through the ground below them, up into the wall a few yards away, illuminating the entire area and reflecting off the edge of the dark lake nearby.

"As I said," she continued, "the keys are meant to work in harmony with individual Alpha Maraudi. Who knows what you can and cannot do with them as a human. Light may be beyond your control, unlike the rock itself."

Benny stared down at the glove, now reflecting the glowing webs in the ground. He knew he shouldn't think of himself as a failure for not being able to light the stone up— that this was something no human had ever done before. Still, he felt like he should have been able to do more.

One of Zee's thick tendrils brushed a stray piece of food from the shoulder of his tunic. "No wonder the humans never got as far into exploring the universe as we did."

For a moment, Benny thought about smashing his finger down on the side of his *other* glove, and holding Zee in the air just to watch him squirm. But the flash of annoyance passed.

"What about moving rock?" he asked. "Can you tell me how to get better at that?"

"You said it earlier," Vala said. "It worked for you when you were acting on instinct. You must trust yourself." The commander stepped forward, raising the gold mask from her eyes. "On our planet, we show our faces not only to see another's true self," she said, "but to allow another to see that we are speaking truth as well." Vala glanced at Zee to make sure he was listening, and then looked back to Benny. "You faced a most fearsome enemy and lived to tell of it when you were taken aboard Tull's ship. You earned this golden prize, Benny Love. It would do you well to remember that. The actions you are taking for your people are . . . admirable."

All three of them were quiet for a moment. It felt to Benny as if the blue, glowing eye in Vala's forehead was boring into him, and despite the fearsome mouth and inhuman proportions of the alien's features, he almost felt like she was looking at him with respect.

It felt good.

The silence was broken by an alien call from the other side of the cavern. Vala stiffened up.

"I must go," they said. "My people need me."

"Yeah," Benny said. "I should check in with my friends."

Zee put his hands on his hips. "Good idea. I'll help you out. Make sure the lasers are still working."

"Your lessons, Zee," the commander said.

"But—"

A tentacle whipped through the air, snapping in front of Zee's face so quickly that were it not for the *crack* that echoed off the walls, Benny might not have noticed it at all.

Zee didn't say anything, just groaned deeply and plodded away.

Benny bowed slightly to Vala. "Thanks for the info. I'll try to keep it in mind."

"Perhaps we will have a moment to test how well you can control rock in the future. To hone that," Vala nodded to Benny's glove. "Take care of the key. May it serve you well."

"All of us," Benny said. "Not just me."

As Vala walked away, catching up to Zee in a few long strides, a tendril—maybe the same one that had whipped the air moments before—snaked down from her head and rubbed the kid's back. One of the young alien's four tentacles wrapped around Vala's arm, squeezing it just for a moment.

Benny suddenly felt such an ache of longing for home, so far away from this cold cavern, this freezing lake. And

he felt something else, like he had when he'd seen the hologram of the Alpha Maraudi back in his sleeping tube. The
sinking reminder that the aliens had real lives and feelings.
They had families and friends. They had people they cared
about and wanted to protect.

Standing alone among the glowing stone, he felt as
though two worlds were on his shoulders.

11.

On the long climb back up to the mother ship, worry again settled in Benny's stomach: it felt as though everything now rested on a single meeting between the humans and the Alpha Maraudi. He decided to bring these concerns to Pinky, and found her on the bridge with Hot Dog, who was halfway through what looked like a big hunk of jerky.

"You should try this stuff," she said, one of her cheeks bulging as she chewed. "I've had a lot of jerky in my day, and this is pretty good. Even if it is fake meat, I think."

"I'll get some later," he said, stopping in front of the two of them. "How're things in the hangar?"

"They're going. I needed a breather. And some food. Protein's important, Benny. Keeps your energy up."

"You've been hanging out with Pinky too much. Next you'll be reminding me to brush my teeth."

She shrugged. "I'm not going to apologize for looking out for my friends."

"Nor should you," Pinky said, raising a single eyebrow while staring at Benny.

"Anyway," Hot Dog said, "what about you? How are things downstairs?"

Benny took a long breath. "I'm kind of nervous about this meeting," he admitted. "I mean, I'm glad we got it set up, but now that that part's done . . . how's it going to go?"

"You're right to be anxious," Pinky said. "In all likelihood, a gathering of this magnitude has never taken place before in our solar system."

Benny frowned. "I know. But I wish you didn't agree with me."

Pinky shrugged. "It's not technically against my programming to lie to you, but I don't think it would be to anyone's advantage if I did."

"Thanks." He sighed.

"Then let's talk it out," Hot Dog said. "That helps sometimes, right?"

"Sure," Benny said.

"Okay, so, what are you worried about? Just things going smoothly?"

"Or what our next step will be if everything falls apart and they start fighting?" Pinky asked.

"Oh!" Hot Dog exclaimed. "You're probably thinking

about your family back on Earth, right?"

Benny just stared at them for a few seconds before nodding. "Uh, yeah," he said. "All of that stuff."

Hot Dog sucked in a breath through clenched teeth. "We're . . . probably not helping."

"Perhaps you're thinking about things the wrong way," the AI said.

"What do you mean?" Benny asked.

Pinky adjusted her glasses and looked at the ceiling far above them. "Maybe you should ask yourself if you've gone through every possible outcome in your head and what sorts of probabilities each outcome has of occurring, cross-referenced against what you hope to gain from the meeting."

Benny blinked, trying to process what she was suggesting. "Yeah," he said slowly. "I guess I could do that."

"Hold on," Hot Dog said, wrapping up the jerky and shoving it into her pocket. "I've got an easier way of looking at this maybe. Before I was super into flight sims, I was into fighting games."

"Right," Benny said. "I think you mentioned that when you were explaining how good you were at kicking alien butt." He glanced over his shoulder at Griida, who sat at the controls. "Uh, no offense," he murmured, but the Alpha Maraudi didn't appear to care.

"Well, before that, I was super into role-playing games,"

148

Hot Dog continued. "And I'm not talking about fluffy 'oh, look at that cute little fairy' ones. I mean, 'take a wrong turn and you're instantly dead and lose three hours of work and all your coin' kinds of RPGs. I'm talking skeleton dragons breathing acid fire."

"I'm afraid I don't see the correlation," Pinky said.

Hot Dog let out an exasperated breath. "I'm *getting* there. So, I'd be walking around as a totally powerful elf warrior or whatever, but I'd never know if the cave I was going into was going to have a bunch of free treasure in it or, like, a demon that would kill me with one shot. Or if the dwarf I was supposed to get an enchanted sword from was a friend or a foe who was going to sneak attack me. So, what did I do?"

Pinky and Benny both stared at her.

Hot Dog grinned. "Before I'd do anything, I'd ask myself 'What's the worst possible thing that could happen' or 'How could the thing inside that cave be trying to ruin everything I've worked for.' Then I'd make sure I had the magic or potions or whatever to handle that."

"So," Benny said, furrowing his brow, "what you're saying is we should make sure we have a bunch of healing potions in case someone gets hurt?"

"I'm saying that if we think about what the worst-case scenarios are, we can be equipped to deal with them before we get into trouble. Even if we don't have magic potions."

She nodded to the far side of the bridge and led Benny and Pinky to the see-through wall looking out onto the icy surface of Ganymede—far out of earshot of Griida, who remained at the controls.

Hot Dog's voice was quiet when she spoke again. "Let's look at this from both sides. First, what's the worst thing the Alpha Maraudi could do?"

"Well, Vala and the others have all been pretty good to us so far." Benny said.

Hot Dog shook her head. "Not what I asked."

Benny stared out at the frozen moon. "I mean, they could try to kill all of us, but that's not going to get them anywhere. It's not like it would make a difference in the grand scheme of things."

"You're forgetting something important, though," Pinky said. "What could the Alpha Maraudi gain from attacking the human forces?"

"Aside from getting their people back?" Hot Dog asked. "If Drue's dad even brings them, that is."

"Info," Benny said, his ears pricking up. "About the superweapon!"

"Ahh!" Hot Dog half shouted. Then she covered her mouth and spoke through her fingers. "You're right. We should think about what they're afraid of! They could capture Drue's dad or Dr. Bale and find out all about that electromagnetic bomb or whatever. They probably have all sorts of weird third-eye ways of interrogating humans."

Benny's lips twisted as he weighed this idea. "But if that were true, wouldn't they have tried to do it to us?"

"Maybe they did," Hot Dog said. "Maybe we just didn't realize it."

"You look doubtful, Benny," Pinky said.

"It's just . . ." He paused, thinking of the interaction he'd had with Vala downstairs in the cavern. How it had made him feel. But he knew he couldn't let himself be swayed by that. So instead, he tried to look at things logically. "Vala doesn't have the manpower—or *alien power* to pull something like that off right now, does she? Especially not if we're all there in Space Runners and not Maraudi ships. There's, like, only a dozen aliens here."

"Yeah, but don't forget that a dozen aliens could do some *serious* damage, even with our electro gloves," Hot Dog said. "I know Vala's taken a liking to you and all, but maybe don't fall too much for the überchill alien commander. We don't know her. Not really."

Benny nodded.

"On the *other* hand," Hot Dog continued, "I know what you mean. And this whole info thing can go both ways. Did you catch Drue's dad talking about how Vala probably knew where all the mother ships were?"

"Oh, man. You're right." Benny shook his head. "If the

New Apollo forces captured the commander, they could try to pump her for all sorts of info."

"Strategically, the Alpha Maraudi are at a disadvantage given the terms," Pinky said.

Benny bit his lip. For a second, he thought maybe they should call Jazz up to help talk things out. But of course, she and Trevone were working on *another* element of this interstellar problem. A backup if things did go poorly. Drue could have been there, too, offering up outlandish ideas on what to do. But, then, they were talking about his father. And the Pit Crew likely would only be concerned about how any of this would help them get Elijah back.

Everything suddenly felt very, very complicated.

"Okay, so we need to be prepared," Benny said. "Whatever we can do. We could plant scout ships beforehand, so we have an idea of what to expect before we get there? Or send more of those rocks that relay info and video back?" He pointed to the hologram that showed the outside hull of the ship.

Pinky nodded. "I'll discuss this with Griida and come up with a full report of capabilities."

Benny glanced over at the alien manning the controls. "Is he being helpful?" he asked quietly, trying to get any sort of sense of how cooperative the rest of the alien crew had been so far.

"In his own way. I'm not sure if the grouchy tone is because he's annoyed or just because he has to speak in another language. But, I'm learning." She shouted a few alien words. Griida barked back.

"Whoa," Hot Dog said. "That sounded just like them. What does it mean?"

Pinky shrugged. "I believe it's how Griida refers to me, so I can only assume something like 'friend.'"

"Yeeeaah," Hot Dog said, drawing out the word. "I'm sure you're right."

Benny began to pace in little circles. "I feel like there's something we're missing." He paused, turning to Pinky. "Let's imagine the Earth forces tried to kidnap Vala. If you were you, but under Dr. Bale's control again, how would you do it?" He set his jaw. "What would evil Pinky do?"

"I don't particularly enjoy this line of thinking," Pinky said. But then she smirked a little. "Let's see. I'd suggest they bring weapons that didn't have any metal elements so that your electromagnetic gloves would be useless, but on such short notice, they likely won't have time to manufacture anything."

"Well," Benny said, "that's good at least."

"Score one for Elijah's gloves!" Hot Dog said.

"Mmhmm," the AI agreed. "But that's likely the only good news. I would also suggest some sort of cloaked surprise attack—perhaps using Dr. Bale's stealth shields."

Benny nodded. "Another reason to figure out how they work."

"Right. But most important, I'd figure out a way to take control of every Space Runner at that meeting. That would ensure that they retrieved not only the alien commander but the remaining EW-SCABers as well. They'd want you all back on Earth." Pinky sighed.

"Crap," Benny said. "We need to be ready for that."

"Maybe Ash can help rewire them so it's impossible for that to happen?" Hot Dog asked. "Is that a thing?"

"We can look into it," Pinky said. "And we can have Ramona serve as a firewall. But I imagine that's what they'll try. And as ingenious as Ramona is, we don't know what kind of tech gurus they may have with them in addition to Dr. Bale."

"What about if Vala attempted something?" Hot Dog asked. "Like, taking out everyone in the hopes that it somehow keeps the superweapon from being launched?"

"We've got our gloves *and* the numbers," Benny said. "If the aliens tried anything, we could stop them. I think Drue's dad is who we need to keep an eye on. And Dr. Bale."

"Ugggghhh," Hot Dog groaned. "I really don't want to put my money on the aliens being the good guys in this scenario, but . . ."

Pinky adjusted her glasses. "From what I've assessed and witnessed of the Alpha Maraudi and humanity—in particular Vala compared to Senator Lincoln and Dr. Bale—I think you're on the right track."

"This is so frustrating." Benny groaned, shaking his head. "If something happens to Commander Vala at a meeting for *peace* talks that we set up, all our hope of getting the aliens to work with us goes out the airlock. There's no way they'll trust us again." His heart was starting to thrum in his chest as he took a deep breath.

"Hey, hey, calm down, Benny Love," the AI said. "I know you're stressed out, but we can take this one step at a time." She reached out and put an intangible hand on his shoulder. "If I had a body, I'd hug you right now."

"Thanks," he murmured. It was so easy for him to forget sometimes that Pinky was nothing more than an artificial intelligence. They relied on her so much, and even though she could walk through walls or appear out of nowhere—at least, at the Taj—she felt like a real person. In fact, if Benny had walked onto the bridge without knowing any better, he would have sworn that she was actually alive.

And that's when a spark went off in his brain.

"Uh, oh," Pinky said. "I recognize that look. Elijah used to get it right before he proposed something he knew I would think was ridiculous."

"What is it?" Hot Dog asked.

"Just thinking of a way we might be able to stay one step ahead of the Earth forces," Benny said. He turned to Pinky, then held his arms out at his sides and shrugged, giving her an apologetic smile. "Um . . . how mad would you be if we needed to take away your body again?"

12.

Senator Lincoln got back to them early the next
morning. Slightly more familiar by then with the Alpha
Maraudi technology, Pinky was able to use the big hologram on the bridge to take the call once everyone had raced
there from their sleeping tubes. The senator was in a Space
Runner, already closing in on the asteroid belt that lay
between Mars and Jupiter. He was on the line for less than a
minute, allowing them no chance to negotiate or ask questions: he and the envoy from Earth would be arriving on Io
within a few hours.

"Not exactly giving us a lot of time to get ready," Hot
Dog said as she pulled her fingers through her hair, trying
to work out a few tangles.

"Good thing we did all the heavy work yesterday," Drue
said.

"Heavy work? You spent most of your time buffing the

exterior of the Star Runner you claimed."

"*And* a Space Runner," Drue said with a grin. "Don't you forget that the shiniest ones are mine."

Benny, his friends, and the Pit Crew had all gathered on the bridge. Vala was there, too, along with Zee, who had been trailing the commander when the call came in. Now, all of them were abuzz. The meeting was happening. They just had to make sure everything went off without a hitch.

"We've got to wake everyone up and get them to the hangar," Benny said. The other kids had already been briefed on what was going on. Though many of them—especially Iyabo—were less than thrilled when they heard it was possible the human forces might try to take them back to Earth, they seemed to understand that their presence was necessary. Plus, it meant they got to get out of the mother ship and fly around in open space, which everyone seemed excited about.

"We should get to Io before the Earth forces show up," Trevone said. "It'll give us time to assess the terrain ourselves."

"Good idea," Benny said. "But we don't need the EW-SCABers landing on the surface. We can keep them in Space Runners floating above the moon. That way it'll be easier for them to get out of there if they need to."

"I want to be on the ground," Ricardo said.

"I have some thoughts about formation strategy,"

Jasmine said, pulling out her HoloTek. "Just something I've been thinking about while we worked downstairs."

"Your brain is so freaky, Jazz," Drue said. "I'm actually jealous."

After presenting her ideas and a brief discussion, they agreed that it would be best to have as few people on Io's surface as possible in the event that something went wrong. Vala, Benny, Drue, and Ricardo would talk with the senator and whoever else was with him. Hot Dog and Kira would pilot Star Runners, ready to swoop in and rescue the ground team if necessary. Meanwhile, Jasmine, Ramona, and Trevone would stay in the sky with the rest of the refugees from the Taj, combatting any technical interference and keeping an eye on radars and maps along with Pinky. Everyone had a role to play, and in that sense, at least, it felt like they had many of their bases covered.

Once they'd agreed on how to proceed, they split up, running toward either the hangar or the sleeping capsules, anxious to take care of any last-minute preparations before powering up their hyperdrives.

"Make sure everyone on the ground has their electromagnetic gloves!" Pinky called after them, heading to the hangar herself.

Benny stayed behind on the bridge, wanting a moment to talk to Vala.

"You'll bring some kind of keys with you to the meeting,

right?" Benny asked. "They'd be easy to hide in your tentacles."

"You wish to talk me out of doing so because the humans say they will not bring weapons?" Vala asked.

"No," Benny said. "I'm making sure you do because they may try to harm you. Even if Senator Lincoln says he won't . . . I'm guessing he'll bring Dr. Bale with him, and that guy isn't very trustworthy when it comes to your kind. This could be dangerous for all of us, but especially you. They might try to kidnap you and get you to tell them everything you know. That's why we're trying to take so many precautions."

"I am aware of all of this," Vala said. "But, as I believe you would say, this is bigger than both of us. Make sure you are looking out for yourselves as well."

Benny nodded. "Thank you."

"Wait," Zee said, running over to the two of them from a spot where he'd obviously been eavesdropping. "These people are going to try to hurt you?" His tentacles were practically vibrating. "No way. They're just humans. They don't have the—the . . ."

"Firepower?" Benny asked. "Guts? Planning? Because I can tell you right now, they have all those things."

Zee bared his teeth, groaning in frustration. Then, he said something in the alien tongue.

"You might translate it into 'the right,' I think," Vala said.

Benny laughed once. "If you think not having the right to do something will stop them, you really do have a lot left to learn about humans."

"This is crazy!" Zee said. "We should bring fighter ships with us. Someone needs to protect you!" He planted his feet and raised his chin. "Give me a key. I can look out for you."

"Absolutely not," Vala said. "I want you down in the cavern until I return."

"But—"

The commander let out a single alien tone so loud that Benny actually jumped.

Zee stared at Vala for a second before turning on his heel and darting off the bridge.

The commander sighed. "I have thought long and hard about what this talk will mean for the future of our peoples. I am sure the burden is on your shoulders as well."

"Yeah," Benny said. "I mean, it's weird. We're not even going there because we have a solution to all these problems. We're just there to try to get everyone to agree there may *be* another solution. It seems like such a small thing. But . . ."

"But it is everything."

"Yeah." Benny nodded. "At least it feels like it. But our main priority is still to keep them from using that weapon and dooming us all. We should start with that, I think."

Vala nodded. "I agree. It would be best if they would hand the weapon over to us so that we did not have to take them at their word. But we shall see how trustworthy these men are."

There was a flash of blue behind Vala's mask as she walked to the egg-like throne, waving a gold-tipped tentacle. A compartment rose from the ground, and she removed a shiny red mask. Benny recognized it as the same kind that the Taj invaders had worn.

"It lets you breathe when there's no air?" Benny asked.

Vala nodded. "We could attempt to adjust the devices so that you could use them as well. Though we are not experts on your anatomy."

Benny knocked on the side of his space suit collar. "I'll stick with a force field helmet for now. But thanks. I'd offer you one, but . . . you know. Tentacles."

The commander let out what Benny thought was a little laugh as she stared down at the red mask in her hands. "I heard from Calam in the night," she said. "They are sanctioning this talk. But I am told that Commander Tull is against it completely. If things go poorly, they will likely give him clearance to retry his assault on Earth."

Benny took a deep breath. "Okay," he said. "Then things

go perfectly. No big deal."

"More of your humor," the commander said. "I hope that it is a relief to you. Come. Let us join the others. We begin."

They found the hangar to be a mess of people, with the Pit Crew ushering the EW-SCABers into their assigned Space Runners and prototype models—the same ones they'd flown up from the underground shelter. Most of them were in pairs, making it so they'd have to take fewer cars and allowing the better pilots among them to fly those without as much experience.

Iyabo came up to Benny when she spotted him.

"Hey," she said with a grin. "Just so you know, I'm keeping my finger on the laser button. Anything starts to look fishy, and I've got your back."

"Thanks," Benny said. And he believed her: Iyabo had been a great fighter against the asteroid storm and had rallied the EW-SCABers when he and the rest of the core Moon Platoon members hadn't been around. "But hopefully it won't come to that. And if it does, I'd rather everyone just get out of there. Jasmine will be calling the shots. Listen to her."

"Yeah, yeah," Iyabo said. She turned away from him and sighed as she made her way to a Space Runner with Mustang-red stripes across the side. "I just wish we could figure out a way to do all this without having to rely on a bunch of old dudes. That never works out well for us."

On one side of the hangar, Hot Dog gave him a thumbs-up before sliding into a Star Runner. Beside her, Drue was wiping off the windshield of one of the laser-mounted SRs. Ramona and Jasmine walked up to Benny, Pinky in tow.

"This is it," Jasmine said. "Are you ready?"

"I better be," Benny said.

"Time for holo-jail," Ramona said to Pinky, smirking the whole time.

The AI sighed. "I look forward to one day being powered by more than just a datapad or SR system. I miss my old self."

Then Pinky disappeared, and the swarm of nanoprojectors and cameras that had been creating her image flew back to the silver band on Benny's wrist—a holographic bracelet that Elijah West had given him as a reward for leading the Mustangs to victory in a video game battle against robots back at the Taj, which now seemed like ages ago.

Benny raised the band to Vala and nodded to her.

"Here," Ramona said, holding a collar out to the commander similar to the one that produced Benny's force field helmet. "Audio perfection."

"She means you can use it to connect to our radios," Jasmine said.

Vala took the collar, looking at it for a few second before fastening it around her neck.

"Bad news," Ash McGuyver said, jogging up to Benny. "Pinky told me about your worries that the Earth guys may try to hack your vehicles, but I haven't had a chance to figure out a way to completely reconfigure the operating systems of all the cars in here." She shook her head. "Sorry, but the SRs are still vulnerable."

"That's okay," Benny said, though his brain was filled with images of him and his friends trying to get hijacked Space Runners back under their control. "It was a long shot anyway. Thanks for trying."

The mechanic shook her head. "That's the problem with the new models. The interface is incredibly advanced, but I don't think Elijah ever imagined he'd be facing something like this when he was designing it. Security was always something that came second, after performance. I think he figured no one would ever be able to understand his designs enough to break them. Let's hope Ramona and the others can fight off whatever they throw at us."

Two words repeated in Benny's head. *New models.*

His eyes darted across the landing area to the electric-green hood of a car in the back corner.

"You seem . . . *excited*," Vala said. "Is this a positive thing?"

"Jasmine," Benny yelled, "do we have any of those stealth drives that are still put together that we can use?"

"Just one," she said. "It's in the Comet Catcher."

"One is all I need." He turned to Ash. "Feel like making a quick run to another moon with us?"

"Sure thing," she said, snapping her gum. "What's the job?"

"I think I may have a backup plan in case they try to take down our Space Runners," Benny said. "At least something that would let us get Vala out of there if things go bad."

"And what plan would that be?" the commander asked.

Benny grinned at her. "Have you ever heard of the term 'American Classic'?"

Soon, they were shooting through space, a small caravan of kids from all over Earth and the commander of an alien mother ship. Ash McGuyver brought up the rear, her oversized tank of a Space Runner towing the Chevelle that had been retrofitted to serve as a moon buggy behind it.

Benny rode in the car that took point, Ricardo driving. Vala sat in the backseat, the gleaming red mask covering her mouth. Zee's shiny ball sat atop her pile of tentacles.

"The insides of your vehicles are more comfortable than our own," Vala said, her long fingers pressing into the supple fake leather of the backseat. "Our goal in creating ships has always been efficiency, using only what is needed. We give little thought to aspects that are not completely necessary."

"Yeah," Benny said. "I kind of noticed that over the last

few days." He shook his head. "Say what you will about humanity's progress, but I guess we really are advanced when it comes to luxury. At least in places like the Taj."

"Yes," Vala continued. "Of course. But not all of humanity. The class system on your planet is so extreme. Tell me, is your place on Earth one of riches or squalor?"

Ricardo scoffed. "Everyone in this group came from nothing."

"Yeah," Benny said, thinking it best not to get into the fact that Drue had originally paid to get an invite to the Taj. "I come from the Drylands. That's what we call the western part of the United States."

"Ah," the commander said. "The great desert. That's right. There are very few colonies there, as I recall."

"It's mostly caravans," Benny said, staring out the passenger window, checking on the ships behind him in the side mirror. "A bunch of rusted trailers and RVs traveling the sand, looking for water and a permanent place to settle down for good. Mine is a hundred people, give or take. *Great* people."

"I see," Vala said. A few beats of silence passed. "And have you found a permanent home?"

Benny shook his head. "No. I was going to make sure we did when I got back from the Taj, but now . . ." He trailed off.

Ricardo glanced in the rearview mirror. "Now we're just

trying to make sure we have a planet to go back to."

Vala nodded, leaning back into her seat. "Your planet is so far away from ours, your civilizations so much younger. Perhaps we forget sometimes that you have the same basic needs and desires as we do, despite your short cycles."

"I told Commander Tull when I met him that I understood why you were after Earth," Benny said. "That I knew what it was like to just want a place to live. I don't think he believed me."

"Maybe he did not," Vala said. "Or maybe he deemed that his ultimate task would be easier if he chose not to."

Benny thought about this for a moment. "What makes Tull so different from you? I mean, I know we met under different circumstances, but I pretty much can't imagine Tull sitting in the backseat and not trying to kill me. That dude is intense."

Vala lowered the red ball into her hands, turning it over a few times before answering. "Commander Tull was not always as 'intense,' as you describe him. As you have been told, colonizing Earth is a last resort for my people. We have tried many other ways to ensure the survival of our planet. None of them were successful. And some of them resulted in great casualties. Commander Tull's life mate was a scientist named Jarm. You should have seen her—bigger than Tull, as intelligent as she was strong."

"Sounds terrifying," Ricardo murmured.

"Jarm had a theory that a contained explosion in the heart of our middle sun could keep it from expanding," the commander continued. "Or at least ensure us more time. It was a dangerous idea to pull off, but for the good of our people, Jarm led an expedition. It . . . did not go well. Many lives were extinguished, including hers. Many who returned were injured. Pito, for example." Vala stared down at the red ball. "We lost many of our best on that day."

Benny let out a long breath, considering all of this. "And so Tull led the fight to take Earth."

"To make sure that our people *did* survive," Vala said, pulling the ball back up into her tentacles. "So that our sacrifices were not in vain."

And then they were quiet for a while.

Eventually, Io was before them, a sphere of lava, ice, and sickly yellow-green plains dotted with rocky cliffs. Looming in the background was the hulking mass of Jupiter itself, its surface roiling with storms and swirling gasses.

"Those mountains on the moon below?" Jasmine's voice came over the comms. "Some of Io's active volcanoes. There are over four hundred of them."

"Super comforting, Jazz," Drue said. "Glad you picked the sketchiest possible place for us to meet."

"Someone sounds scared," Hot Dog said, and Benny could picture the exact way she must have been smirking in her Star Runner.

Jasmine sighed. "We'll be fine as long as we stay at our coordinates. So far, there are no signs of Earth ships on the radar."

"What are the chances they're all equipped with stealth devices?" Ricardo asked.

"No way of knowing," Jasmine said.

"I'm pinpointing the coordinates of the meeting location now," Pinky said, her voice piping through the SR's speakers.

A blinking light appeared on their windshield, directing them where to go. When they were closer to the moon, Jasmine spoke again.

"We can hold up here while the ground team continues," she said. "Sound like a plan?"

"Let's do it," Benny said.

"I'm following you," Drue said as Ricardo's Space Runner broke away from the group.

Hot Dog chimed in. "I'm taking a flanking position near one of these cliffs in case I need to swoop down fast. It'll be easier if I don't have to worry about the rest of the group getting in the way."

"Same," Kira said.

"Good luck down there," Trevone added.

Benny sat up in his seat. "Thanks. Pinky, keep the comm channels quiet except for the core units. Only what we need to hear."

They soared down, past a few rocky mountains coursing with thin streams of lava, until finally they landed in a
huge, shallow crater.

"Temperature readings are adequate," Pinky said.
"Quite comfortable, even."

"Great," Benny murmured as he watched Drue land a
few yards away from them.

Ash's voice crackled over the comms. Her SR and the
Chevelle were floating above them. "Where do you want
her, kid?" she asked.

"Give me a second," Benny said. He turned to Ricardo,
tapping on his neck and manually deploying his force field
helmet. "I'm going to scope things out. Will you stay with
the commander?"

Ricardo nodded, turning on his own helmet as the cabin
depressurized and Benny stepped out onto the yellow surface of Io.

The gravity wasn't too different from what it had been
on the Moon, so at least in that sense Benny had a good idea
of how to maneuver himself. The crater they were in had
walls that sloped at low inclines, meaning it would be easy
to drive out in any direction—one lucky break, at least.

He spotted a small boulder not too far away, the top of
which was more orange than the rest of the landscape.

"There," he said, pointing to it. "You see that? Can you
put it beside the rock?"

"You got it, boss," Ash said.

She sat the Chevelle down with such care that it barely bounced on its shiny, heavily treaded tires, the hood almost touching the orange boulder. And then Ash shot off into the space, ready to wait in the wings in case someone needed to be towed.

"I'm going to get the escape car ready," Benny said. "You guys okay here?"

"Duh," Drue scoffed.

"Make it fast," Ricardo said.

Benny jogged to the Chevelle as quickly as he could. The keys were in the ignition, meaning that at least he wouldn't have to hot wire it—unlike the last time he'd been behind the wheel. A simple twist, and the retrofitted muscle car powered on, the specialized engine barely even humming as it idled. The dashboard lit up.

"And here we go," Benny murmured.

He reached forward and pressed the blinking red button of the stealth drive he'd swiped from the Comet Catcher. The hood and rest of the exterior of the car disappeared.

"Nice," Drue said. "You're totally invisible." He paused. "Uh, just remember where you parked it."

"Right," Benny said, glancing again at the boulder in front of them. "If the SRs are hacked and frozen, this'll get Vala out. I'll make sure of it."

"You can drive it?" the commander asked through the comms.

Benny grinned to himself. "Oh, yeah. Yeah, I can."

"Guys," Jasmine said, "I've got two dozen SRs approaching. *Fast.*"

"This is it, people," Ricardo said.

Benny got out of the Chevelle and did his best to make a mark on the ground outside the driver's door with his boot, ensuring he'd be able to find it again. Then he hurried over toward the other two Space Runners.

The Earth forces paused far above the surface, sending only four vehicles to the ground itself. Benny spotted plasma cannons on the sides of each of them, the kind that had shot down so many of the Alpha Maraudi back at the Taj.

In a way, there was a symmetry between the two sides with lines of SRs in the sky, and only a few cars on the ground.

Almost as if they were preparing for battle.

"Where are my people?" Vala's voice came through the comm on Benny's collar.

"Jazz?" Benny asked.

"Um . . . That's weird," Jasmine said.

"What?"

"Well, I'm using Dr. Bale's scanner that Ramona

modified," she said. "But I'm not picking up any Alpha Maraudi with them."

"Okay. Okay." Benny stood in front of Ricardo's Space Runner, his eyes on the vehicles still far above them. "Maybe they're shielded from the radar? Or coming later?" He wanted to at least pretend that he was giving the senator the benefit of the doubt. "Maybe they're even out of range? We didn't get to test the lengths of that radar very well."

"Maybe. But that's not what's weird. I'm picking up *two* on our side. The commander and . . . one in your trunk, Drue?"

"Huh?" Drue asked, his voice cracking.

A spike of panic and confusion shot through Benny, and before he even knew what he was doing, he was bounding toward Drue's car.

"Pop the trunk!" he shouted.

"I'm on it," Drue said, as Benny made his way around to the back of the car.

The trunk flew open, and there, staring up at him was a small Alpha Maraudi kid with four short tentacles. A red mask covered his face.

"Zee?" Benny asked.

The alien raised a hand as if in greeting.

Vala's voice roared over the comms, a flood of minor tones.

"Take him back to my ship," she said afterward. "Now."

"We can't just leave," Drue said "Not when there's so much—"

"It's happening," Trevone shouted over the comms. "They're trying to hijack the SRs."

Benny looked through the back window of Drue's car. Inside, there were red lights all over the dashboard. Drue tapped on several buttons, but it was obvious he was getting no response.

"Already?" he asked. "Ramona? Pinky?"

"Right now everyone is stalled," Pinky said. "We're working on regaining control."

"Ramona, get us back online!" Benny said.

"Trying B-Man," Ramona said. "Unknown virus. Smart hackers. Give me a second."

And then, across the yellow landscape, the doors to the New Apollo Space Runners from Earth opened.

13.

Benny looked from the figures stepping out of the weaponized Space Runners to Ricardo's car and then back at Zee.

Things were already not going as planned.

"Stay here," he shouted, glaring at the alien.

Benny couldn't tell if the Zee understood him since he didn't have a radio connection, but before the alien could react, Benny slammed the trunk shut. The last thing they needed was an Alpha Maraudi kid running around and possibly causing huge problems for them.

Drue and Ricardo both jumped out of their Space Runners. Vala stayed in the backseat, as they'd discussed before leaving the mother ship. If nothing else, this would give the three human boys a chance to address the forces from Earth first and provide an extra layer of safety for the alien commander. Space Runners weren't built to withstand heavy attacks, but they did at least offer some protection thanks to the force fields that served as environmental shielding. Plus, Vala could still use her third eye to analyze the humans as she saw fit.

Benny, Drue, and Ricardo gathered in front of the Space Runners and then walked toward the four figures making their way across the expanse between either side of vehicles. Benny recognized all of them. Senator Lincoln took the lead, several medals glinting on his sleek space suit. On his left side, Dr. Bale marched with his chin raised in the air, a HoloTek in his hand. His two assistants, Todd and Mae, followed him closely, tapping on their own datapads, no doubt behind whatever was happening to the Space Runners.

"Jazz, Ramona, keep us posted on the status of the SRs," Benny said. "I want to know as soon as we have control again. Pinky, connect our comms."

"You've got it," the AI said. "Communications established in three, two . . ."

His collar speaker beeped just as the four new arrivals came to a stop ten yards away from them.

Drue stepped forward. "Hello, sir," he said.

"Son," his father replied. "You look well."

"I could use a few fresh space suits, to be honest."

"Senator Lincoln," Benny said. "Dr. Bale. Thanks for coming."

The senator looked around. "Where are the Maraudi?

Did they send you as their ambassadors? I should be insulted, but this will make things easier I suppose."

"You're unarmed?" Ricardo asked. "Like we agreed?"

The senator held his hands out to his sides. "See for yourself."

"But you *are* trying to hijack our ships," Benny said.

Dr. Bale smirked. "Correction. We *have* hijacked your ships."

"They're fighting it," Mae said, not looking up from her HoloTek.

Dr. Bale's mustache twitched as his lips curved down into a deep frown. "Let them try."

"It's a precautionary measure," the senator said. "We're simply making sure that you don't try to pull some sort of attack on us. We're all very exposed out here."

"So much for trust," Ricardo muttered. "We're not the ones with plasma guns on our Space Runners."

"No. Just lasers."

Benny was sure there was more to it than that—that the Earth representatives wouldn't hesitate to force all of them to return to the Moon or their home planet. But he was getting ahead of himself.

"We're making progress," Pinky said through Benny's collar speakers. "We can beat this. We just need more time."

"This little rebellion against your own kind has gone on for long enough, don't you think?" the senator continued.

178

"I don't blame you. I was a child once as well, and in those days I might have thought there was some way for all of us to live side by side in constant sunshine. But that's not how the world—the *universe* works. This is real life. Sacrifices must be made."

"Are you forgetting what the commander said?" Benny asked. "If you attack the alien home world, Earth is still doomed. There's literally no way for us to win if we don't try to find another solution. Think about it logically."

The senator was quiet for a moment before glancing overhead. "You brought the rest of Elijah's scholarship winners, yes?"

"And you were supposed to bring the Alpha Maraudi," Ricardo said. "So where are they?"

"In these ships of course," Drue's father said, motioning to the Space Runners in the sky behind him.

"Not true," Jasmine whispered, the communication only going through to those on their side. "We'd be able to pick them up. I'm sure of it. And I'm still not seeing anyone but Commander Vala and Zee."

"It would be wise not to begin these discussions concerning the future of our peoples by lying to each other, Senator," Vala's voice came through the comms.

Drue's father grimaced.

Benny clasped his hands behind his back as he looked over his shoulder to see the rear door of Ricardo's Space

Runner open. Commander Vala stepped out, rising slowly to her full height, her gemlike body armor shining and her third eye blazing blue. She walked slowly, deliberately forward, until she was standing a few feet away from Benny and the others.

"Now," Vala said, "shall we begin with where my crew really is?"

Drue's father raised his head a little, until he was looking at the commander over the bridge of his nose. "I deemed it necessary to keep them at the Lunar Taj. We have much to learn from them, especially considering your thinly veiled threat the last time we spoke. And, if these children are not hostages as you claim, then what is the advantage of us turning your soldiers back over to you?"

"Do they yet live?" Vala asked.

The senator paused. "Most of them."

A low growl filtered through the collar speakers and made the hair on the back of Benny's neck stand on end. He moved the thumb of his left hand over the trigger of his electromagnetic glove, hating that this was his first instinct, but at the same time ready to stop Vala if she decided to attack.

"I'm sure you understand," the senator continued. "You are willing to do whatever it takes to ensure your people's survival. So are we."

"That's why we're here," Benny said. "To make sure we *all* survive."

"And do you have any sort of plan?" Drue's father asked.

"Of course not. This is an adolescent fantasy. The Alpha Maraudi would destroy all of us to take our planet."

"And you would destroy us without a second thought," Vala countered. "Even if it didn't save your people in the end. That's not strategy. That is spite."

"Hey," Benny said. "Maybe stop arguing about how we're all going to die and start talking about how we might not?"

"Then tell us," the senator said. "How do we all hold hands and keep on living in the same universe?"

Benny's thoughts shifted to all the things he'd witnessed since coming aboard Vala's ship. "We start by understanding that we're probably more alike than we are different. That the Alpha Maraudi have families and friends and dreams just like we do." He shook his head. "They're not whatever bloodthirsty invaders you think they are."

"Give them the superweapon," Ricardo said. "Or dismantle it. Or just tell us where it is and let us guard it. Let that be a first step. Then we can work together to figure out how we can share the universe."

"And what is the benefit of that?" Dr. Bale asked. "It would be safer for us to exterminate them."

Vala growled.

"The benefit is humanity surviving," Benny said, exasperated. "How is that so hard to understand?"

Drue took a step forward.

"Guys, I've been living with a bunch of aliens for the past few days, and it's pretty obvious that they've got crazy tech that we never even dreamed of," he said. "*But*, there's plenty of stuff they could really use. I mean, they sleep in rock tubes and, from what I can tell, there's not a comfortable place in their entire mother ship to sit. And don't get me started on the lack of video games and stuff. It's like living in the most boring supercool flying asteroid ever."

"What does your boredom have anything to do with this, son?" his father asked.

Drue raised a hand, dismissing his father. "I'm *getting* to a point. As much as the Alpha Maraudi know about space travel and making rocks move and stuff, they still have a lot to learn." He turned to Vala. "Like, I know you don't know much about electromagnetic fields. So I bet you guys don't have nuclear bombs or anything like that, either."

Vala's forehead creased. "We do not deal in such destructive sciences."

"Right," Drue said. "I bet you haven't done too much research into plasma weapons and stuff like that, either. Even if that tech isn't used for 'destructive sciences' or whatever, it can *still* be superuseful."

"He's right," Benny said, stepping up beside him. "They're very advanced, but there's still stuff they don't know."

Drue winked at him. "Thanks."

"And with our help—with all of us working together—who knows what we could accomplish?"

"So you want us to give the aliens our own knowledge?" Dr. Bale asked. "That's your solution? For us to abandon our weapons—to render ourselves defenseless—and hand over brand-new ways to obliterate us should their own methods fail?"

"If we share what our civilizations know, maybe we can find *another* solution to this," Benny said. "The commander was just telling us that they tried to cause an explosion in their expanding star that might stop it. That failed, but what if *we* could make it work? And that's just one possibility."

"Why bother?" Dr. Bale asked. "We can stop whatever forces the Alpha Maraudi send against us once their home world is dealt with. *You* stopped them once. With mining lasers. I'm sure they wouldn't be a problem for those of us who actually know what we're doing."

"Sure," Drue said. "Just like you were positive the Grand Dome wouldn't collapse."

Dr. Bale snarled as Drue's father turned to him.

"Could something like an explosion actually stop a star?" the senator asked.

"You aren't actually thinking about working with them," Dr. Bale scoffed. "I thought we were in agreement about this."

"I'm asking you a simple question," the senator said. "You'll answer it."

Dr. Bale looked away, shrugging slightly. "The likelihood of that scenario being effective is incredibly slim. I don't even know that I could calculate it."

"Well, not without data from the Alpha Maraudi, duh," Drue said.

"But it's possible?" Ricardo asked.

"It's science, boy," Dr. Bale said. "*Anything* is possible."

"And there's plenty of stuff we can learn from the aliens," Benny said.

"He speaks the truth," Commander Vala said. "Have you considered what illnesses we have overcome? What science we have perfected?" The commander's tentacles twisted into a long braid down her back. "The world you have is one that we would change to suit our needs, true. We could change it, too, to suit yours. It is not too late to heal the wounds you have opened up on your planet."

Benny inhaled sharply. With everything that had been going on, he hadn't even dared hope that somehow the Alpha Maraudi technology might be able to save the Drylands, or at least turn it into a place where people could live comfortably again. He'd been too busy just making sure there were Drylands to go back to.

"These are pretty thoughts," Senator Lincoln said. "What makes you think we could be successful in helping you, though?"

"I was . . . skeptical. But you have bright minds on Earth," Vala said. "We have always known this, despite the admittedly low regard we hold for many of your people. In the last few sleep cycles, however, I have seen these minds at work myself. I have observed the intentions of the young humans being housed on my ship. They have shown me a resilience and hopefulness that I thought your people did not have." She clasped her hands in front of her chest. "I do not wish to see these children—or those like them who are still on your planet—harmed. I have faith that if we did work together, we could find a new solution. Your scientists and ours. You have followed paths we did not."

"And even if we don't," Benny said, "at least we tried to find another way."

Vala looked at him and nodded. "Together."

Senator Lincoln stared at the alien for a moment that felt to Benny like a lifetime as he waited for the man to speak again. Eventually, Drue's father let out a long breath.

"All right, then," he said. "You can consider this a temporary armistice. We will not attack you for the time being as we look into other possible solutions. *If* they exist."

"You can't be serious," Dr. Bale said.

"Doctor, you will work with these aliens and their scientists or I will find someone else who knows how to follow orders and replace you. I already blame you for half our problems on the Moon. Do not give me another excuse to remove you from Project New Apollo completely."

Dr. Bale glared at Commander Vala.

Senator Lincoln took a few steps forward, holding out a hand. "Are we in agreement, then?"

Vala hesitated, glancing at Benny.

"Uh, guys," Jasmine said through the comms. "I've got something strange on the radar."

"What?" Benny asked.

Across from him, Mae and Todd hurried to Dr. Bale. He glanced at their datapads, and then grabbed Senator Lincoln's shoulder, showing him the screen.

"What's going on?" Ricardo demanded.

"I'm not sure," Jasmine continued. "There's activity on Jupiter. It's coming in blips and static. We can't get a read on what it is, but it looks like something big is coming from the planet."

"No, no, no," Benny murmured. "We were finally getting somewhere."

"Maybe it's just another storm?" Drue asked.

"There!" Trevone shouted. "In the great red spot! That's where it's coming from."

Benny looked up at the massive planet above them, his

eyes darting directly to the rust-colored whorl near its center. He squinted, but saw nothing.

"You sure?" Drue asked. "All I see is a bunch of gas."

And then there it was. Just a pinprick at first, but growing larger with every second as it shot toward Io. A spherical chunk of alien rock, like a giant asteroid—though as it got closer, Benny could tell that it was missing a big piece out of one side.

He recognized it, of course: Commander Tull's mother ship.

"That fool," Vala seethed.

"Oh, no," Benny whispered. He turned to Ricardo and Drue, the three of them all looking at each other with bulging eyes, unsure of what to do.

Suddenly everyone was shouting at once, each voice fighting to be heard.

The senator whipped his head around to Benny and the others. "We agreed on no ships."

"That's not ours!" Benny said. "It's another one. The one we stopped with the asteroid storm."

Above them a steady stream of shard-like crafts began to pour out of Tull's ship, shooting straight for the surface of Io.

"You have to get out of here," Vala said. "Now! You're all in danger."

"I knew this was a trap," Dr. Bale said, stepping forward.

"What are you doing?" Senator Lincoln shouted.

Benny was so distracted by what was happening in the sky that he saw the small weapon in the man's hand too late. Benny smashed his finger against the side of his silver glove, activating an electromagnetic burst. The doctor's gun flew out of his hand, flying far across the surface of the moon.

But only after a golden bolt of energy shot straight through the center of Commander Vala's chest.

Chaos erupted in the crater.

Commander Vala stared at her chest. She made a noise that sounded like a curse in the alien tongue and then spoke a single, furious word: "*Tull.*"

And then she disappeared.

"Where did she . . . ?" Dr. Bale started.

"You idiot," Senator Lincoln yelled as he pushed Dr. Bale backward, the man's assistants catching him. "This may have been a setup, but we could still use the commander alive."

"It wasn't a setup!" Drue said. "I promise! Dad!"

But his father ignored him and started barking orders. Overhead, the weaponized Space Runners flew into action, darting toward the oncoming swarm of Maraudi ships.

"We're stuck up here," Jasmine yelled.

"You've got to let our SRs free," Benny yelled at the

senator. "They're sitting ducks. You'll get them all killed."

Senator Lincoln pointed to Todd and Mae.

"It will take a few minutes," Todd said.

Mae nodded. "They've been fighting us, and now the programs are all tangled up."

"We don't *have* a few minutes," Benny said, making a break for Ricardo's Space Runner. "Come on, guys!"

Above them, Earth's forces began to clash with Tull's soldiers, filling the space over Io with flashes of energy blasts as a full-blown battle broke out. Silver bolts of energy rained down on the surface of the moon as a wave of purple alien ships shot over the crater they were standing in. Io shook as the ground around Benny erupted in plumes of dust and scorched rock.

Senator Lincoln's Space Runner must have been caught in the line of fire, because when Benny looked over his shoulder, it was flying through the smog of debris, headed straight for him like missile.

And then it stopped suddenly a few yards away from him, floating several feet off the ground.

"Gahhhh," Ricardo shouted as he waved his right fist, using the electromagnetic glove to move the vehicle out of the way, placing it on the surface nearby. "Go," he yelled. "Get Vala out of here."

"I'm trying to," Benny said as he rounded the side of Ricardo's car.

Already the back door was open, and Commander Vala—the *real* Commander Vala—leaped out. Benny glanced at his wrist. The nanoprojectors that had constructed the hologram of the alien leader had returned to the silver bracelet Elijah had given him.

Their precautions had paid off. If Vala had actually been standing there, she'd have a hole burned through her chest now and the entire meeting would have been even more of a disaster than it was turning out to be.

At least Pinky could never say that he'd borrowed her body for nothing.

"Can't you tell Tull you're down here, too?" Benny shouted.

"Don't you think he knows that?" Vala asked. Her eyes were wide, frantic. "Where's Zee?"

"Oh, crap," Benny said. "I forgot about him."

"Incoming!" Jasmine shouted. "Benny, watch out."

Benny looked up just in time to see a huge comet of silver energy shoot straight for him and the commander, growing larger every second.

Vala reached out and pulled him close with her tentacles, his face smashing against one of the pieces of armor on her forearm.

"Hold on," she said quickly.

There was a flash of gold, and then suddenly, a small chunk of alien rock began to grow at an impossible speed, encasing the two of them in darkness before Benny could so much as begin to formulate a question.

The commander had shielded them in a sort of stone cocoon right before the blast hit.

To Benny, it felt as though the entire universe was shaking. It was impossible for him to tell exactly what was going on while they were encased in rock, but he had the distinct feeling that they were flying through space. With every passing second his heart beat faster as panic set in.

Something squeezed his arm. Vala was still gripping his bicep.

And then they were crashing. Vala's side of the rock seemed to take most of the force of the collision. Cracks of light appeared around them. At first he thought this was because the commander was making the stone glow, but the impact of their landing had actually fractured parts of their shield.

They skidded to a stop, and the rock began to melt away.

Benny gasped, taking in deep breaths once his chest was free to expand again, and crawled a few inches, trying to get his bearings and see what was happening.

They'd been blown clear past his invisible escape car, toward the far end of the crater. Above him, alien and New Apollo ships were both being shot down or careening wildly into the cold expanse of space. Another purple craft dropped bombs of silver energy across the meeting place, obscuring Benny's vision. He couldn't even make out Drue or Ricardo because there was so much dust. All he could see of the Space Runner they'd been standing beside moments before was a smoking shell of metal.

"Not good, not good," Benny murmured. "Hello? Anyone?" he called into the comms, desperate to hear from his friends.

"There you are!" Ricardo yelled. "Are you two okay?"

In his daze, Benny hadn't thought to check on the commander. Vala was on one knee, swaying a bit, a hand on the side of her face. A trickle of purple blood seeped from one of her temples.

"Vala?" Benny asked.

"I . . ." she said groggily. "Zee."

"Get out of here," Ricardo yelled through the comms. "We already got the little one. We'll take care of him."

"I'll pick you up in the Chevelle," Benny said.

"Please, we've got our own ride," Drue said.

"The SRs are free?"

"Almost," Jasmine said through the comms. "Ramona needs one more minute."

"Then how . . . ?" Benny asked.

"We're taking my dad's car," Drue said.

Benny could make out two figures in space suits darting

toward the weaponized Space Runner Ricardo had saved with his silver glove, a short Alpha Maraudi trailing behind them.

Vala was trying to stand, and Benny reached out, helping her to her feet.

"We have to move!" he shouted.

"But, Zee . . ."

He looked into the commander's eyes as best he could, considering he only had two. "We're taking care of him," he said. "I promise."

A beat passed and Vala's blue eye flashed before she nodded, clearly still dazed from the crash. And then they were off, Benny half dragging the commander across the yellow plains toward the orange boulder.

"My arm," Vala murmured, and it was only then that Benny noticed that the commander's other hand was hanging useless at her side.

"It must be broken," Benny said. "Are you—"

"I'll be fine."

He almost knocked the breath out of himself as he crashed into the invisible car, groping for the passenger door handle. Finally, he found it and pushed Vala in as carefully as he could, slamming the door behind him before racing to the other side of the Chevelle, his hand on the hood as a guide.

He buckled his seat belt once he was inside. The engine

purred as he revved it, the steering wheel vibrating ever so slightly.

"Hold on!" he shouted.

Vala's tentacles wrapped around the roll bar above her head. Benny's foot was already slamming down on the gas pedal, sending them rocketing in reverse. He spun the steering wheel, straightening them out, and then they shot away from the scene. Apart from faint trails of dust, they sped invisibly across the pocked landscape.

"Okay, okay, okay," Benny said, glancing in the rearview mirrors to make sure they weren't being followed. "Where am I going? What are we doing?" He paused. "Jazz, updates?"

"Ricardo, Drue, and Zee are in one of the Earth cars, fleeing the . . . well, the battlefield," she said.

Vala sighed in relief in the passenger seat.

"We've just regained control of the SRs," Jasmine continued. "I'm sending everyone back to the mother ship." She paused. "I don't think anyone will chase us? They seem to be pretty engaged above Io."

Benny clenched the wheel as they hopped the side of a new crater. The Chevelle flew through space in a low arc, finally touching back down on the ground, bouncing and jolting both passengers.

"Guess Ash got around to putting those titanium axels in after we messed this baby up the first time," Benny said quietly. He eyed their surroundings. They'd left the immediate danger behind, but now he had no idea where they were heading.

"Talk to me, Jazz," he said. "Can Ash pick me up? Where's a safe rendezvous point?"

"Of course I can," Ash said over the comms. "But I'm gonna need to see you to do so. That stealth is a beast."

"Oh, right," Benny said. He leaned forward, figuring that since he'd gotten the commander out of there, they were safe, and tapped on Dr. Bale's drive. The electric green of the hood appeared through the windshield. "You spot me?"

"Ten four," Ash said. "You're on my radar. Give me a minute to get to you."

"Wait . . ." Jasmine said. "I see you, too. And according to Dr. Bale's alien radar . . ." She gasped a little. "Benny, look out! Three Alpha Maraudi on your tail!"

"Huh?" Benny asked.

He could just make out a few swaths of deep purple in his rearview mirror.

"Ooooh, this is bad," he said, kicking the Chevelle up another gear. He turned the stealth back on, but it was no use—the Alpha Maraudi ships opened fire, shots of energy landing all around them. A thin coating of dust now covered the car, rendering Dr. Bale's stealth drive useless.

Beside him, the commander cursed in her alien tongue.

"They're going to kill us," Benny said. "Can't you tell them you're in here with me somehow?"

"I think that would only make matters worse," Vala said.

"What are you talking about?"

"Think, Benny Love," the commander continued. "If word got back home that I was killed during what should have been peace talks with the humans, all hope for your planet would be lost. There would be no more conversation. No shared science. Simply destruction. Tull is making sure of that."

"You're telling me Tull would kill you just to get permission to eliminate all of humanity."

Vala nodded. "I believe he would."

Dead ahead of them, more energy bolts rained down, and Benny wrenched the steering wheel to the left just in time for them to avoid the blasts. The Chevelle wobbled, and for the briefest second he lost control of the machine. But then the wheel was responding again and he exhaled loudly as they continued forward.

He scanned the landscape, desperate to get out of harm's way. To one side was a series of tall mountains. To the other, a deep crater. Ahead of them, nothing but flat surface for as far as his eyes could see.

"We need cover," Benny said. He bit his lip for a second. "I'm going to try something."

"What?" Vala asked.

Benny shook his head. "It's either really stupid or really smart. I guess we'll figure out which."

"Well, if that's the case," Hot Dog's voice crackled over the comms. "I'm in."

Benny glanced in the rearview mirror and saw the shining gold of Hot Dog's Star Runner weaving through the alien crafts. It wasn't weaponized, but it was definitely faster than the Alpha Maraudi ships. As she looped around them, the alien pilots seemed confused, unsure where to fire.

"Hey, Ace," Benny said. "I was wondering where you were."

"Just waiting to save your butt," she said. "So what's the plan?"

Benny jerked on the steering wheel. The Chevelle skidded across the surface of Io, drifting sideways. Vala shouted in surprise as the car straightened out.

"Wait, don't tell me . . ." Benny wasn't sure if Hot Dog's voice was full of excitement or horror.

"Yup," Benny said, pressing the gas.

They shot forward toward a space between two tall mountains just wide enough for three cars to drive through side by side.

"As a commander, I must say this seems like a poor choice," Vala said.

"Only if this thing dead-ends or something," Benny said.

"Ugh. Why would you even say that?" Hot Dog groaned. "This *is* a bad idea." She paused. "I'm right behind you."

"You don't have to be," Benny said. "It's a narrow canyon. Not a lot of room to fly."

"Psh. Have some faith in my skills, cap'n."

Benny glanced at Vala. "Um . . . this might get bumpy."

The commander nodded as her tentacles tightened around the car's roll bar.

They sped into the pass between the mountains. Hot Dog followed high above them, the three Alpha Maraudi ships swooping in after her. They fired, but she rolled and maneuvered the superfast Star Runner as though it were second nature to her, avoiding outcroppings and rock bridges that had formed across the canyon.

Benny was pretty sure he heard her giggle, but he couldn't be certain.

The aliens didn't seem to be quite as adept as Hot Dog. One of them clipped the side of the canyon wall, causing the ship to spin and crash against the *other* mountain, eventually falling to the ground behind them.

"Well, that's one down," Hot Dog said.

No sooner had she spoken than the two remaining aliens opened fire again. This time they didn't seem to be trying to hit Hot Dog or Benny's car—instead, they were aiming at the walls of the pass itself, causing parts of it to collapse around the Star Runner and Chevelle.

"Watch out!" Hot Dog said. Her Star Runner shot straight up, narrowly avoiding impact.

On the ground, Benny kept his eyes bouncing between the rocks falling from above and the path ahead of them which, fortunately, seemed to be opening up a little not too far ahead.

"Come on, come on, come on," he muttered as he slowed down and swerved to avoid one falling boulder, then sped up to avoid another.

Above them, Hot Dog's craft flew in a loop, cutting off one of the alien crafts and causing it to jerk to the right—straight into a falling chunk of rock dislodged by its own shots.

"Two down!" she shouted. "I thought this game was gonna be in hard mode."

"Benny!" Vala shouted, pointing a tentacle forward.

That's when he saw it. Ahead of them, the path was indeed opening up into a wider space, some sort of cavern. Unfortunately, it looked as though there was a gorge ahead, a gap in the makeshift road—a space they'd have to jump if they were going to keep going.

"I can clear that," Benny said. "I just have to—"

A geyser of molten rock shot out of the gorge, fifty feet up at least. It wasn't just a break in the ground—they were going to have to jump a river of lava.

"Benny?" Hot Dog asked. "I'm guessing you saw that

since a pillar of fire is kinda hard to miss?"

"We can make it," he said, gripping the wheel, his palms sweaty beneath his gloves.

"As long as you don't get toasted!"

"You get out of here. Who knows how high those geysers can go?"

"Are you kidding?" Hot Dog asked. "I've beaten this level plenty of times before."

Benny glanced at Vala. "We don't have a choice," he said. "Even if I put the car in reverse, half the pass is collapsed back there. This is our only way out."

Vala looked at him in silence before nodding.

He glued his eyes to the terrain ahead of them, spotting the edge that looked like it had the biggest incline and would give them the highest arc through the air. He said a silent prayer, sending it through the expanse of the galaxy and into the Drylands, to the RV where his family was: an apology for not being able to save them in case this failed.

Benny changed gears and smashed the gas pedal so hard that for a second he thought his boot might go straight through the floorboard. And then they hit the incline, the bottom of the Chevelle sparking against the rock as they took to the air in a long arc.

He allowed himself only the briefest glance out the driver's side window, where there was nothing but roiling lava as far as he could see. He reflexively pulled back on the wheel as though it were a flight yoke—as if he could will the car to climb even higher as they began their descent toward the other end of the fiery gorge.

Both he and Vala screamed, their voices forming a horrible drone of sound that filled the car.

The Chevelle landed with a jolt, the back tires just barely catching the edge of the rock on the other side of the gap. And then they were shooting forward once more.

Benny screamed again, this time out of pure relief as he glanced into the mirror and saw Hot Dog shoot over the lava as well.

The third alien ship wasn't so lucky. A geyser erupted just as it was halfway across the river, striking one of its crystalline wings. The craft careened to one side, out of sight. It was the last Benny saw of it.

"We're alive!" Hot Dog yelled.

Benny took a few huge breaths, trying to calm down. As he did, he realized that they weren't going as fast as they should be. It felt like the car was dragging.

"I think my tires are melting," he said.

"Don't let off the gas!" Hot Dog said. "I see the end of the pass ahead!"

And sure enough, in a few moments they were out of the mountains and back onto the flat plains. Benny let the car slow once they were there, searching the sky for any signs of ships.

"That was an insane thing to do," Jasmine said over the comms.

"Yeah," Benny said. "I'm aware."

"We were tracking you. But it didn't seem like a good time for distractions. Stay put. We're seconds away."

Benny parked the Chevelle and leaned back in the seat, looking over at Vala, who was inspecting her broken arm.

"You are an exceptional pilot," the commander said.

Benny shook his head. "I'm not a pilot. I'm just good with wheels."

Hot Dog landed her Star Runner beside them, and, seconds later, Trevone's car parked on the other side. Ash's oversized SR hovered over them.

Benny got out of the car and assessed the damage. There were several dents from the falling rock and debris all over the vehicle's exteriors, and the tires were caked in dirt mixed with melted rubber.

"You poor baby," Ash said through the comms as she engaged the towing tractor beam. "Don't worry. Momma will fix you right up."

"Sorry," Benny murmured.

Hot Dog opened her door and jumped out. She looked like her entire body was coursing with electricity.

"That was such a rush," she said.

Benny turned to Trevone's car. "Jazz, what's going on?"

"I have good news and bad news," Jazz said as she got

out, Trevone following her. "Good news is, most everyone is well away from here, on their way back to Ganymede."

"Most?" Benny asked.

"That's the bad news. Tull is still fighting the Earth forces. And since his ship is so close . . ." She trailed off.

It took a second for Benny to understand what she was getting at. And then his heart seized. "No."

"I tried to talk Ricardo out of it," Trevone said. "But he knows Elijah's there." He shook his head. "To be honest, if it weren't for us needing Jasmine out here, I'd have flown my car up there, too."

"Don't tell me they're going to try to break into Tull's ship." Benny shook his head. "How would they even get in? They don't have a key or anything."

"No," Jasmine said. "But they're driving one of the Earth Space Runners equipped with Dr. Bale's plasma cannons. They can likely shoot their way inside."

"Zee!" Vala said, stumbling out of the Chevelle. "Where is he?"

"Oh, no," Benny murmured. "With Ricardo and Drue."

"Then we must go after them," Vala said.

Benny turned to the commander. "You're injured. Plus, someone's got to man your ship. What if the Earth forces go after you? What if *Tull* does?"

"The child is my responsibility," the commander said.

"Yeah. I get that. And in some ways, all those kids on

their way back to your ship are mine." He paused. "We'll go after Zee and the others."

"I would actually feel kind of bad if Drue ended up in Tull's human zoo," Hot Dog said. She raised her silver electromagnetic glove in the air. "And this time, we're prepared at least."

"We need you on your ship," Benny said to Vala. "Someone's got to send word to your homeland about what happened here. The truth."

Vala was silent for a moment. "Bring him back to me."

Benny nodded. "I promise."

"Uh, we should probably hurry if we're doing this?" Hot Dog said.

"I'll help us stay out of trouble as best I can," Jasmine said, holding up Dr. Bale's alien radar.

The back door of Trevone's car popped open, and Ramona stumbled out, her complexion green.

"Hate . . . flying . . . " she muttered.

Ash landed her SR on the ground. "Anybody who's comin' to the mother ship, hop on in," she said. "This Chevelle's ready to go."

Ramona started for Ash's car. "Barf . . . bag . . . " she croaked.

"There's room for one more in here," Hot Dog said, starting for her Star Runner.

Benny turned to Vala. "We'll be right back," he said.

Vala took a long look at him and then nodded.

Jasmine and Trevone got into their Space Runner. Benny bounded over to Hot Dog's shiny gold vehicle and slid into the passenger seat.

"Buckle up," she said with a grin, and she pressed holographic buttons on the dash.

In seconds, they were shooting through space, straight toward Commander Tull's giant ship.

15.

Tull's ship floated between the immensity of Jupiter and its fire-and-ice moon, Io. Above the orbiting satellite's surface, Earth forces continued to fight against the commander's troops. It was impossible for Benny to tell who was winning as Hot Dog's Star Runner closed in on the asteroid-like mother ship.

"Nice driving back there," Hot Dog said.

"Nice *flying* back there," Benny countered.

"I gotta admit, I was kinda nervous about that whole lava thing."

Benny sat back in his seat and let out a long breath. "You and me both."

"I've been in touch with Ricardo," Trevone said over the comms. "He's landed in the hangar. Kira, Drue, and Zee are with him. It took some convincing, but he's agreed to wait for us to get there before he goes any farther. As long as we arrive in the next few minutes."

"Not a problem," Hot Dog said, pushing a few buttons on the dashboard and speeding them up.

"Jazz," Benny said. "What's that alien radar telling you?"

"Quite a few Alpha Maraudi on board," she said. "Dozens. It looks like they learned from us sneaking on to Vala's ship and didn't send *all* their soldiers out at once. Still, I think they probably lost a lot of people the first time we faced them."

"Right. We have to be on our guard." Benny glanced at Hot Dog. "I can't believe we're going back to this ship voluntarily."

"Meh." She smirked. "You know, it's probably not the weirdest thing we've done."

As they got closer to Tull's ship, the damage wreaked by Elijah West's exploding hyperdrive became more apparent. A chunk of one side was missing, the stone scorched and blackened. Near the center of the blast zone was a hole that looked like it opened up into some sort of chamber.

"That must be where Ricardo shot through," Benny said.

Hot Dog nodded. "Follow me, Trevone. We're going in."

They slowed only slightly as they approached, then squeezed through the gap barely big enough for their car.

Inside, they found themselves in a hangar, though it looked smaller than the one they'd been sucked into by a tractor beam last time.

"Must be the lower deck," Hot Dog said.

"Yeah," Benny agreed. "But it still feels a little too familiar."

They parked beside Kira's Star Runner, Trevone following suit. Ricardo and Kira stood off to one side, looking at the back wall of the room. Drue inspected the New Apollo crest on the front of his father's stolen Space Runner. Meanwhile, Zee paced back and forth on the other end of the hangar, tentacles flitting about around his head, the red mask still covering most of his face.

"Thanks for waiting," Benny said as he got out of the Star Runner and approached the others.

Ricardo pointed to Benny's gold glove. "It seemed smarter for you to get us in than for us to try to shoot our way through this entire ship with the senator's car."

"Did you see what happened to him down there?" Drue asked. "There was so much dust. . ." He trailed off.

Benny shook his head. "No. Sorry."

"I'm sure he's fine," Hot Dog suggested. "He seems like a survivor."

Drue nodded. "Totally. No way he'd let an alien ambush get the best of him." He shrugged slowly. "He's probably on his way back to the Taj now." And then he grinned, but the space between his eyebrows remained wrinkled with concern.

Zee stepped forward, gesticulating wildly with both his hands and his tentacles. Benny had forgotten that without a collar, there was no way for the alien to talk to them in the depressurized hangar.

"We need to find him a comm or get the environmental systems going," Jasmine said.

Benny walked over to the hangar wall, trying to clear his mind and think of everything Vala had told him about how the keys worked. On instinct. With determination and decisiveness. He'd done this exact thing before—he just had to do it again.

And so, he didn't think too hard about it. He walked up to the hole, certain of what he had to do, and placed his glove against the stone wall. He envisioned the gap closing, and slid his palm across the rock in one smooth, defiant motion.

The hole closed up.

Whoa.

"Nice one," Drue said. "You've been practicing."

Benny held the glove up, staring at it. "Not really . . ."

The environmental systems must have kicked in, because one by one, their force field helmets began to disappear.

Zee pulled off his mask, letting it hang around his neck, and then breathed an accordion sigh. "Finally. This thing is annoying. And nobody could hear me talk."

"We're taking you back," Benny said. "If you got hurt, Vala would never forgive us."

"I'll be fine," Zee said. "This is the first adventure I've ever gotten to go on! Vala always makes me stay behind. Plus, I know where the prisoner cells are probably locomotioned!"

"You mean located," Drue said.

Hot Dog shook her head and groaned.

Benny stared at Zee for a second. "Vala thinks they might have been trying to kill her. That means they probably wouldn't think twice about doing the same to you."

"Or taking you as a hostage," Jasmine suggested. "That would make more sense if Tull is aware that Vala cares for you."

"I know," Zee said, a little more quietly than he usually spoke. "I heard everything while I was in the car." There was a flash of concern on his face, and then, just as quickly as it appeared, it was gone. "Which is why I'm going to help you guys out. I think you call it payback? It's also why I should get a weapon." Zee's lips spread all the way to the back of his head in a smile. "Come on. You're humans! Don't you guys have laser pistols or something like that?"

Benny sighed and pulled the electromagnetic glove off his left hand. He held it out to the alien. "Here. It won't fit your fingers right, but you should still be able to manage if you just hold it like this. There's a button on the side—"

"I've got it," the alien said, snatching the glove. "The overconfident one showed me earlier."

Benny looked at Drue, who shrugged.

"What?" he asked. "We had time to kill waiting for you."

"You gonna be okay without that?" Ricardo asked.

"As long as you guys have my back," Benny said.

Ricardo nodded.

"I'm getting rough scans of the ship's interior," Jasmine said, tapping on her alien radar. "But I have no idea where Elijah might be."

Zee came up beside her. "Here," he said, pointing with one of his tentacles. "Our ships don't normally have places to put prisoners, but we do have rooms where we lock away prescient cargo."

"*Precious*," Drue whispered to himself, smirking, his eyes on the ceiling.

"So," Jasmine said, "you're telling me Elijah's probably in this room a floor down that looks like it's being guarded by six Alpha Maraudi."

The alien kid shrugged. "What else would they be guarding?"

Drue's eyes went wide.

"What?" Benny asked. "You think it might be interstellar treasure instead?"

"No," Drue said with a grin. "I'm just realizing how much Elijah's going to owe us for busting him out of alien jail."

"We're wasting time," Kira said. "Let's get on with it."

"Ummm," Jasmine said, looking back and forth between the rear of the hangar and the radar. "Let me see where the hallway would be."

Zee jogged up to one of the walls and leaned against it. "It's right here."

"How do you know?" Hot Dog asked.

"Can't you see the difference in the stone? It's a little darker."

Benny squinted, but it all looked the same to him.

Zee just shook his head. "How do you people get around with only two eyes?"

"Benny," Ricardo said, pointing to the stone. "You're up again."

In a few seconds, Benny had created a hole big enough for them to squeeze through. It wasn't pretty by any means, but he *was* getting better at using the key at least. And since they were about to go exploring an alien ship full of enemies, that was more than Benny could have hoped for.

"See," Zee said once they were all in a hallway made up of smooth, pale blue walls, "aren't you glad I'm here?"

"Shhh," Ricardo whispered.

"Oh. Right. We have to be sneakers."

Benny and Hot Dog both looked at Drue, but he just shrugged.

"That one kinda works," he said.

"This floor is clear," Jasmine said. "They must be too focused on the fight outside to realize we snuck aboard."

"This is probably a storage level," Zee whispered as they continued. "So there wouldn't be any soldiers here anyway."

"Good." Jasmine tapped on the radar and stepped to the front of the group. "Follow my lead."

They did, as quietly as they could, all of them constantly checking their backs, peeking through open doorways, and looking cautiously around hallway corners. But Jasmine was right—they didn't see a single Alpha Maraudi.

Eventually, she stopped them in front of a thick slab of glossy red stone that looked like some sort of doorway.

"There's a huge chamber here," Jasmine said. "If we cut through, we can save ourselves some time getting to the stairwell."

"Right," Benny said, raising his hand to the wall.

Zee grabbed his wrist before he could touch it. "Don't." His voice was grave.

"Why not?" Kira asked, stepping closer to him and holding her head high, accentuating the solid foot she had on him.

There was a rumbling sound on the other side of the stone, followed by some sort of low bellow that Benny swore he could feel through the soles of his boots.

"Did Vala tell you that our ship was going to bring some of our plants from home to Earth?" Zee asked. "Well, Tull's was bringing animals. All sorts of them."

"Space pets!" Hot Dog whispered excitedly, standing on her toes.

"Maybe somewhere on board," Zee continued. "But a red door means whatever's back here is something we don't want to face."

Hot Dog's heels hit the floor again. "Oh."

"Let's go the long way," Trevone said.

"Agreed," Benny said, lowering his hand.

So they continued. Eventually, they came to a stairwell lined with a glowing banister, which they descended two by two.

"You aliens really love stairs, don't you?" Drue asked.

"I forget how lazy you humans are," Zee said.

"Elevators aren't lazy. They're efficient."

"Is that why your dad's car had massaging seats that got hot when you turned them on?" the alien asked. "Because they're efficient?"

"You know," Drue snapped, "you could really stand to learn a thing or two about luxury. You need a week at the Taj."

"You mean the building with all the holes in it now?"

"*Guys*," Ricardo snarled.

"This is the right floor," Jasmine whispered as they came to the bottom of the stairs. She motioned for them to be quiet and tiptoed to a spot where another hallway connected to the one they stood in. "Just around the corner are six Alpha Maraudi."

"Well," Ricardo said, "we've got seven gloves between us."

"Be careful," Hot Dog said. "Maybe it was just because it was the first time I'd seen an alien, but I remember Tull's guards and crew being a lot faster and more hard-core than Vala's."

"Yeah," Benny said. "Same."

"We should come up with a plan," Trevone said.

"I've got an idea," Zee said.

And before anyone could stop him, Zee grabbed Jasmine's arm and dragged her out into the hallway. Jasmine yelped, staring back at the others before she was pulled out of sight.

Benny jumped forward, stopping just short of exposing himself to the guards. Then he peeked around the wall and watched, silently cursing the little alien.

Zee kept pulling Jasmine into a big room that appeared

to be empty apart from six masked guards. When they spotted the unlikely pair, their tentacles flexed, bowing out at their sides. Two of them stepped forward, the muscles in their bodies tense. Zee called out to them in the alien language. One of them barked a response. They went back and forth like this for a few seconds before Zee finally groaned.

"Well, that didn't work," he said in English.

"What did you say?" Jasmine asked.

"I told them you were a prisoner."

"And did they believe you?"

Benny watched as two of the guards crouched, their tentacles flashing with bladed tips, ready to pounce.

"No." Zee said. "They did not."

"Go!" Benny shouted.

He darted around the corner, the others in tow, all charging into the room. Jasmine and Zee caught the two front aliens with their electromagnetic gloves, but the rest immediately sprang into action. The air was filled with the whiplike sounds of flailing tentacles.

"So much for a plan," Hot Dog muttered.

"We're pretty good at winging it," Drue said.

"Sure," Benny agreed, raising his fist into the air as one of the Alpha Maraudi soldiers darted straight for him.

It was only then that he remembered he'd given Zee his glove.

"Oh, crap," he murmured.

The alien guard leaped, two thick tentacles bulging from either side of his head, like lances tipped in shining silver. In seconds, they'd be slicing into Benny.

The guard suddenly shot backward, slamming against the rear wall. Benny looked over and saw Kira Miyamura glaring at the alien. She nodded to Benny, and then picked the guard up off the floor with her glove, holding him in the air.

"Thanks," Benny said.

In a matter of seconds, all six guards were floating off the floor. After so many horrible encounters with the Alpha Maraudi back at the Taj and before on Tull's ship, it was almost unthinkable to Benny that this had been so easy.

"What do we do with them?" Jasmine asked. Her face was a mixture of wonder and concern, and her arm began to shake slightly as the guard in her grasp tried to squirm, thin tendrils lashing about around his head.

"Uh," Benny said. "Good question."

"Do we . . ." Drue asked. "Are we supposed to . . ."

"We're not *killing* them if that's what you're asking."

"No, no," Drue said. "Of course not. Good."

Zee pointed to a spot on the wall with one of his tentacles. "There. Benny. Open that up."

Benny carefully made his way to the wall, making sure to avoid any thrashing blades along the way. Once there, he melted the rock as quickly as possible, opening up a doorway to another room.

"Perfect," Zee said. "They'll be fine inside."

"Can't they get out with a key?" Benny asked.

"They're just guards. They don't have them yet."

And so, as quickly and carefully as possible, they placed the guards inside. Benny had a split second to close up the wall before they lunged out once the electromagnetic gloves were turned off, but he managed it. Afterward, everyone was quiet for a few seconds, the sound of their heavy breathing the only thing filling the chamber.

"Where's Elijah?" Kira asked.

"Well, if he wasn't in *there* . . ." Zee said, eyeing the wall Benny had just closed.

Ricardo took a few heavy steps forward. "You said he'd be down here. You were sure—"

"Relax," Zee said, interrupting him. "If he wasn't in that sealed-off room, he's probably in there." He pointed to another wall. "Or in there." He pointed to another. "Or, somewhere else entirely," he whispered quietly.

Benny rushed over to the nearest spot Zee had pointed to. He was starting to feel like they'd been on Tull's ship entirely too long, like at any moment the walls around them might close in and trap them there, regardless of what key he had on his hand. As the stone in front of him fell away, he imagined them trying to leave, only to find that their Space Runners had been destroyed or that an army was waiting for them in the hangar or that Tull had—

The hole was opened, and slumped against the floor across from him was Elijah West, unmoving, a gold mask covering his face, his head leaning against the wall.

Ricardo pushed past Benny, the rest of the Pit Crew on his heels.

"Elijah," Ricardo said, softer than Benny had ever heard him speak before.

Elijah seemed to be roused from sleep, looking around blindly. That's when Benny realized that his hands were sealed together, encased in alien rock.

Ricardo got down on one knee in front of him and carefully pulled the mask off Elijah's face. The man blinked a few times against the light, and Benny couldn't help but notice the dark circles around his eyes. When Elijah finally focused his gaze on the leader of the Pit Crew, his mouth dropped open, a dry rasp escaping it.

"Am I dreaming?" he asked.

"That's usually what gets you into trouble," Ricardo said. "But not right now."

A moment passed. Then Elijah smirked, and the charming, world-renowned explorer and inventor they'd all known him to be once upon a time reappeared. "Please tell me you brought coffee, at least."

And in a flash, the three members of the Pit Crew were

huddled around the most important person in the universe to them, tangled in an embrace that neither Benny, nor anyone else in the room seemed to want to break up, no matter how much danger they were still in.

The Pit Crew helped Elijah to his feet as a tangle of half-formed sentences spilled out of his mouth.

"Just concentrate on moving," Ricardo said, looping one arm through Elijah's.

"We'll explain everything later," Trevone added. "Right now we need to get you out of here. You must be exhausted. Probably dehydrated, too."

"Also," Kira said, "evil aliens."

Benny stepped into the cell, the rest of his friends following. "Let me see your hands."

A bewildered Elijah West obeyed. Benny smashed his gold palm down against the alien rock and it crumbled, revealing a pair of black, studded driving gloves.

"What . . ." Elijah asked, his bloodshot eyes narrowed in confusion as he wiggled and stretched his fingers. He looked to Benny and then to the golden glove. "But where did you . . ."

"It's good to see you, Elijah," Drue said with a grin. "I'm Drue Bob Lincoln the third, just in case you forgot."

"We didn't get a chance to thank you for knocking us out of that tractor beam back during the attack on the asteroid storm," Hot Dog said. Then, quietly, she added, "Even after everything that happened at the Taj before that."

"We could really use your brain," Jasmine added. "Things have gotten . . . difficult."

"I've read a lot about you," Zee said, tentacles arching out from his head and resting on his shoulders. "It's great to meet you. I always figured you'd be dead before I got the chance to."

Elijah noticed the alien for the first time and flinched, taking a step back and hitting the wall behind him.

"The squid kid is with us," Hot Dog said. "Mostly."

"*Squid kid?*" Zee asked, opening his massive mouth in shock. "Listen . . . female . . . child . . ."

"That's not an insult."

Elijah turned to Ricardo. "I have so many questions."

"Trevone's right," Ricardo said. "We'll get you out of here and then—"

"We've got company!" Jasmine shouted. Her focus had been on Elijah and the relief of finding him, but now her eyes were back on the radar. Her head snapped up, and Benny followed her gaze.

There was movement at the other end of the hallway as an Alpha Maraudi guard walked by. It stopped in the middle of the corridor and looked directly at Benny and the others. For a beat, everyone froze. And then the alien's half dozen tentacles all shot out at once as it darted from view, charging in the opposite direction of the stairwell they'd come down.

"We have to stop them before they—" Zee started.

Red and purple lights flashed in the ceiling as a wailing siren blared through speakers hidden somewhere in the walls. Benny recognized what was going on—the same thing had happened when he and Hot Dog had been on the ship before.

It was an alarm.

Zee exhaled loudly. "Now *that* is not good."

"Run," Ricardo said.

"Now!" Benny shouted.

They darted through the hole Benny had made, all scrambling back into the main chamber where they'd fought the guards, the Pit Crew helping Elijah along.

"Wait, wait," the man said as they were almost into the hallway.

He looked around, his eyes finally landing on what looked like a stone cube in one corner. He hurried over to it, kicking it with his gold-capped boot—and then cursed in pain when he failed to break it open.

"What's the matter?" Kira asked.

"I need what's in this box," Elijah said. Then, there was a glint in his eye. "Hold on. Benny. That glove of yours. Do you think . . ."

Benny sprinted over and slammed his palm down against the top of the cube. It crumbled inward.

"Ah, wonderful," Elijah said. "That glove seems quite useful."

He reached in and pulled out a dark coat with a fur collar, quilted with maroon thread that pulsed with a light of its own. After shaking some stone and dust off, he put it on. It was the same thing he'd been wearing the first time Benny had ever seen him in person, when he'd stepped out of a custom car in front of the Lunar Taj right after the EW-SCABers had landed on the Moon.

"We had to stop for your *coat*?" Hot Dog asked, shaking her head. "Seriously? Even I would leave that behind."

"Trust me, Ms. Wilkinson, it's worth it," Elijah said. "These pockets are full of important things. The keys to my favorite car *and* my safe at the Taj are in one of them." He flipped the collar up. "Plus, it's custom."

"You're in for a rude awakening about the Taj and your cars," Jasmine murmured as they once again started for the stairwell.

It seemed as though Elijah was fully awake now, or at least up to the task of matching the pace of Benny and the rest of his rescuers as they climbed the stone steps to the hallway that would lead to their exit. They passed the big red door, sprinting ever closer to the lower hangar and the vehicles waiting for them. Ricardo stayed at the back of the group, constantly glancing over his shoulder.

"I've got skeletons ahead!" Jasmine shouted through short breaths as she looked at the radar. "Lots of them."

"Skeletons?" Elijah asked.

"We'll have to power through," Ricardo said, clenching a fist.

"Almost there," Benny said, leading them toward the hole in the wall ahead. "We just have to—"

A thick black vine of tentacles swung around a corner and caught Benny in the stomach, sending him sliding backward, crashing into his friends. Hot Dog and Drue hit the ground alongside him.

Commander Tull stomped in front of them, the alien's sheer enormity causing everyone to recoil. Even Zee seemed to be in awe—and horror—of his size. Tull's muscled arms and legs were covered in polished red plates, his chest protected by a thick layer of gold. Countless slick-looking tentacles curled up into two thick masses and formed looped horns on either side of the commander's head. The roar that emanated from his belly was so loud that Benny almost had to put his hands over his ears.

"Children," Elijah said, stepping over Benny as he balled up his fists. "You have to get out of here. Now. I'll try to stall him. Just find another way to escape."

"No offense," Drue said, getting up to one knee and aiming his glove at Tull. "But we're kind of way more prepared than you are."

"Is that . . . ?" Elijah started, but he never got to finish his question.

Drue fired off a blast from his electromagnetic glove, sending Tull flying back into a wall. The commander hit it with a crash, then slid down to the stone floor. As Benny and Hot Dog picked themselves back up, the Pit Crew stepped forward and pressed their thumbs onto their trigger buttons as well. The giant alien was tossed back and forth through the air, slamming into the hallway walls.

"You think you'll stop me this way?" Tull shouted. "I will make you watch your planet burn before I deal with you."

"By the rings of Saturn . . ." Elijah whispered in astonishment, watching as his protégés got the upper hand on an alien commander.

"There are more coming down the hallway!" Jasmine said.

"Hey, Ricardo," Trevone said. "You ever go bowling in Brazil?"

"No," Ricardo said with a smirk. "But I know how to score a goal when I need to."

"Less talk," Kira said. "More throw."

Benny got to Ricardo's side just in time to watch the three members of the Pit Crew use the combined force of their electromagnetic blasts to send the alien commander rocketing down the hallway. His body rammed into the group of Alpha Maraudi guards sprinting toward Benny and the others, knocking them over.

But Tull was down for only a split second, and then he was on his feet again, barreling back toward Benny.

Zee shook his tentacles. "You're just making him *angrier*."

"Run!" Trevone said.

And they did. They were almost at the hole Benny had made into the hangar when suddenly it snapped shut—Tull was already behind them again, and must have closed it, intent on trapping them.

"Benny!" Ricardo yelled.

"On it," he replied, pushing through the group and banging his fist against the wall. There was no time for concentration or precision. They needed out of there—fast.

And it worked. The rock exploded into the hangar, opening up a space big enough for them to get through one by one.

"Go, go, get inside," he shouted.

They shoved Jasmine in first, followed by Drue and Elijah. Ricardo and the others shot blasts at the commander and the guards running toward them, but Tull weaved and ducked, as though he could spot the invisible electromagnetic beams and outmaneuver them. With a flick of his tentacles, sections of the walls jutted out, blocking their attacks.

"I got this," Hot Dog said, stepping toward the oncoming commander, aiming dead center at his chest.

But in the split second before she pressed the trigger, Tull reached back with a tentacle and grabbed one of his soldiers, tossing the Alpha Maraudi forward. That's who Hot Dog's blast caught in the air; and before she realized what was happening, Tull batted the floating alien out of the way and lunged at her.

It was Zee who finally managed to land a shot. He held his silver glove with two of his tentacles and caught Tull in midair, sending the commander rocketing backward once again, crashing into more of his soldiers.

"That's for trying to kill Vala," the young alien said.

Tull's growl was ferocious, filling the hallway.

"Inside," Ricardo shouted. "Now. Now!"

When they were all finally back in the hangar, they darted toward their cars.

"A *Star* Runner?" Elijah asked, astonished.

"Long story!" Hot Dog shouted.

"Come on!" Ricardo said, pulling on Elijah's coat sleeve. "You're with me."

In seconds they'd all piled into their vehicles and were floating in the small hangar, just as Tull and the rest of his guards were rushing through the break in the wall.

"We're not going to get out of here using my glove," Benny said. "You're gonna have to make us an exit."

"I know," Ricardo said. "It's taking a second for the guns to warm up."

Benny could hear Elijah speak from the backseat. "Who the devil designed this car?"

Benny looked out the window at Tull, who was now on one knee, a few gold-tipped tentacles against the floor.

"This does not look good," he murmured to himself.

The entire hangar began to shake as, suddenly, sections of the floor and ceiling began to close in on them.

"Definitely not good!" Benny shouted.

"We're almost ready!" Ricardo said. The weapons mounted on the front of Senator Lincoln's Space Runner began to glow.

"Uh, if we blast a hole in the hangar," Hot Dog asked, "what happens to them?" She nodded toward the Alpha Maraudi outside their car.

"Sudden depressurization," Jasmine said. "They'll be sucked out into space."

The ceiling continued to press down on them.

"Firing in five seconds," Ricardo said.

For a moment, Benny wondered if they should warn the Alpha Maraudi what was about to happen. After all, part of the reason they'd gone through everything they had in the last few days was so they could stop anyone from dying unnecessarily. But then, another part of him wondered if this would solve several of their problems. Commander Tull seemed so intent on destroying humanity—why not let this be his end? Wasn't he their enemy?

Thankfully, Benny didn't have to come up with an answer. It appeared that Tull realized what was about to happen, and after unleashing another roar, he barked at his soldiers. In seconds, they were back in the hallway. But Tull stayed, closing the wall of the hangar after the last of his guards was through. He stood, snarling at the humans. Benny noticed stone rising out of the floor and wrapping around his legs.

"Fire!" Ricardo shouted.

Gold bolts of plasma energy shot from the weaponized Space Runner Ricardo was piloting. The hull in front of them exploded out into space, the depressurization sucking all the debris into the vacuum.

Ricardo raced through, the others following. Benny and Hot Dog were the last ones out, the ceiling threatening to slam into their craft in the second before they escaped. Benny glanced back—he could see Tull for just a blink before the rock closed back up, sealing him inside.

As soon as they were clear of the ship, all their eyes were on the battle that continued to rage above Io. Benny could spot plenty of downed ships—human and alien alike—dotting the rocky surface of the moon.

"Do we help them?" Hot Dog asked.

"I don't know that we can," Benny said.

"It would be smart to use this battle as cover," Jasmine said over the comms. "To make sure no one follows us back to Vala's."

"She's right," Ricardo said. "We should get away from this ship as fast as we can, before Tull has a chance to send anyone after us." He paused. "We *just* got Elijah back."

A wobbly blue line suddenly appeared in the top right corner of the Star Runner windshield followed by a video feed. Benny immediately recognized the background as the bridge from Vala's mother ship. The commander stood beside Ramona.

"Heyo, newbz," Ramona said. "I've been tinkering with the ET comms."

"Zee!" Vala shouted.

"I'm *fine*," he replied.

"We're moving servers," Ramona said, tapping on her HoloTek. "Too much malware around. No longer docked at Ganymede. Coordinates incoming."

A new route appeared on their screens.

"Elijah!" Pinky said over the comms.

"Pinky!" The man's voice was filled with astonishment. "I never thought I'd be so happy to hear you."

"You're always happy to hear me," she said. "Even if you pretend otherwise."

"That's probably true," Elijah replied. "Now, who wants to tell me what in the name of Orion's belt is going on?"

17.

The coordinates directed them to Vala's mother ship, which was moving away from Jupiter and its moons at a rapid pace—though slow enough that the four cars could catch up to it. Jasmine kept her eyes on the alien scanner, but as far as she could tell, no one was following them.

As they flew across the dark expanse of space, the largest planet in the galaxy slowly growing smaller behind them, they did their best to catch Elijah West up to speed. Benny, Drue, and Hot Dog said little, letting the Pit Crew do most of the talking, which seemed right to Benny. Zee initially inundated Elijah with questions, but a few stern words from Ricardo shut him up.

For the most part, Elijah was quiet, and when he did speak, he asked short, softly spoken questions. By the time Ricardo finally got to the meeting on Io and the battle that eventually allowed them to break into Tull's asteroid and rescue the most famous man on Earth, they were approaching Vala's ship. It floated in the distance like a cliff that had been lopped off the side of a mountain and shot into the far reaches of the Milky Way galaxy.

"And . . . here we are," Ricardo said.

"You're back," Kira said. "Safe. I have to get word to Kai and Sahar."

"We'll figure out what to do next once we're on the mother ship," Trevone added.

"Hey," Drue said. "We can check 'saving Elijah' off our giant list of things to do! Next up, save a couple of worlds."

The comms went silent after that, and Benny listened closely, waiting to hear what Elijah would inquire about next. Would he ask about the current state of the Taj? How quickly they could take the resort back? How badly it had been damaged? What cars and prototypes were safe?

But instead, he said only two words.

"Thank you."

There was another brief silence before Ricardo spoke. "Of course. We were always going to come rescue you. Even before we knew where you were. We never doubted you were alive."

"Not for that," Elijah said. "Don't get me wrong, I'm eternally grateful. I owe all of you a debt I will never be able to repay, though I intend on trying. What I'm thanking you for is . . . well, everything, I suppose. For continuing to fight." The man laughed a little. "Despite my own influences."

There was something different in Elijah's voice, Benny thought. The man still had the assuredness and quick wit that they'd all grown accustomed to in their brief days with him at the Taj. But his words were tinged with a heaviness Benny couldn't quite put his finger on. It reminded him of how his grandmother's way of speaking had changed after his father's death. She had sounded mostly the same, but there was one almost imperceptible difference—a weight that those who didn't know her as well as Benny and his brothers might not have picked up on.

"Elijah," Ricardo said, a hesitancy to his voice. "What happened to you on that ship? Were you in that room the whole time?"

Several seconds passed before he answered.

"Not always," Elijah said. "They had . . . many questions. But I think mostly I was in that cell. Unable to really move. Blinded by that blasted mask." He laughed again, just once. "Plenty of time to think about everything I've ever done wrong in my life." He took a deep breath through his nose; and when he spoke again, he was upbeat, almost jovial. "*And* to worry about you all. I can't tell you what a relief it is to find out you're okay. Not only alive and well but, from what I can tell, thriving, even in such bleak times. Every last one of you. That includes the scholarship winners. If it weren't for you, we wouldn't even be here."

Right, Benny thought, we'd still be back at the Taj and Earth would belong to aliens. But he kept his mouth shut. He was pretty sure Elijah had meant this to be a *good* thing.

There was quiet on the comms again as they drew closer to Vala's ship. Eventually, Benny leaned forward in his seat. "Uh, maybe this isn't the best time to tell you, but I just jumped your Chevelle over a river of molten rock on Io and ended up melting its tires." He paused. "Hot Dog almost got hit by a lava geyser in this Star Runner, but it's fine. Obviously."

"It was never even close to me!" she said, smacking his arm.

"Wait, wait, wait, you guys did *what* without me?!" Drue shouted over the comms. "I was risking my butt trying to make sure some alien kid didn't get exploded, and you were off having fun?"

"I took care of myself!" Zee said. "You saw me back there. I stopped Commander Tull! And I'm *not* a kid. You're the one who's barely out of a . . ." There was a harmonic grunt. "What do they call those things babies go in? It's right on the tip of my brain!"

The two of them started squabbling while Ricardo tried to get them to knock it off. In the background, though, Benny could hear Elijah West laughing. Not at what has happening, Benny figured, but at the absurdity of everything. The laughter spread, contagious, until it caught all of them—the relief that they'd made it this far together. That they were alive. In that brief moment, at least, it was nice to pretend that was all that mattered.

Vala and Ramona were waiting for them on the bridge beside the hologram that displayed their new trajectory.

"Maybe it's just the company," Elijah said, as he walked into the room, "but this definitely feels cozier than Tull's ship did."

Vala hurried over to Zee, pulling him close in a web of tentacles. The kid struggled for a few seconds before relenting, wrapping one tentacle around the commander's waist as well. The arm Vala had broken back in the crater on Io was now encased in a clear, gemlike cast.

Then, Vala noticed the silver glove Zee carried.

"Where did you get that?" Vala asked.

"From Benny." The alien grinned. "I blasted Tull just for you."

The commander turned to Benny sharply, her lips drawn tight across her face.

"Uh, are you okay?" he asked, pointing to Vala's arm, hoping to deflect any anger.

"I'll return to normal conditions in a few days," Vala said. She looked back at Zee, and then turned her attention to the newest arrival. "Elijah West. I am Commander Vala.

I have heard much about you, even before these children made homes on my ship. It is an honor to have you aboard. If only it were under different circumstances."

Elijah bowed a little, though he didn't take his eyes off the Maraudi leader. "Commander. Thank you for all you've done for my friends. I'm sorry to hear how badly the meeting went."

"We were so close," Benny said.

"Yeah," Drue said. "My dad agreed to a temporary truce even."

"He meant it, too, I believe," Vala said.

"And then Tull . . ." Ricardo muttered.

"It's unfortunate that at such a crucial moment, one of your people showed up and ensured that any conversation about peace fell apart," Elijah said, staring at Vala.

Vala was quiet for a few seconds as she raised her gold mask, exposing all three of her eyes. "Tull acted on his own accord. I have already sent word to our home world, explaining the situation. As you were Tull's captive, I assume you understand that he can be . . . impulsive. Just as your Dr. Bale did not hesitate to shoot what he thought was my actual body."

"Yo," Ramona called from a few yards away. "Pinky's killing me. Keeps un-muting herself. Wants to be made of light and polygons again."

"Oh," Benny said. "Right."

He tapped on his metal bracelet as Ramona fiddled with her HoloTek. The nanoprojectors took to the air, and in seconds the AI was standing before them, face lit up even brighter than usual.

She clasped her hands together in front of her chest. "Elijah!"

"There you are," the man said with a grin. "Look at you, on an alien ship a million miles from home." He shook his head. "I bet you'd never thought you'd be somewhere like this."

"Are you kidding? As your assistant, I'm surprised I haven't seen other galaxies, to be quite honest." She sighed, giving him a warm smile. "Welcome back, Mr. West." Then her face darkened a bit as her eyes narrowed. "You overrode my programing and forced me to let you get yourself sucked into an alien ship. Not to mention you kept my real personality locked away for years." She took a few long strides toward him, until her face was inches from his, and then poked an intangible finger through his chest. "Don't you think for a second I forgot about any of that. When all this is said and done, we're going to have to have a long, long chat about my autonomy."

"Where are we headed?" Trevone asked, walking to the hologram map in the center of the bridge. "Back toward Earth?"

"That direction," Vala said. "But given the perceived hostilities between us and both the Earth forces *and* Commander Tull's soldiers, I thought it best to stay as hidden as possible until we decided upon our next course of action."

Jasmine peered at the blinking spot of the hologram that marked their destination. "Is that . . . the asteroid belt between Mars and Jupiter?"

"It is," Vala said.

From the other side of the room, Griida let out a groan.

Vala nodded. "It took Griida some time, but he found a suitable space for us to fall in line with the asteroids."

"Clever," Trevone said. "Hide a ship that looks like a giant hunk of rock among a bunch of actual hunks of rock."

Kira shook her head. "Always asteroids."

"At least these don't explode," Hot Dog said. Then she paused. "Right?"

"Have you been in contact with the Earth forces?" Drue asked. "Any word from my dad? Do we know what happened to them?"

"Negative." Ramona said. "Dead air."

Pinky raised both palms. "That doesn't mean anything, though," she said. "Their communications could have been knocked out. Our satellite might be getting too far away from their ships, or . . . Well, there could be any number of reasons."

"Sure," Drue said. "No big."

"What about Pito and the stealth drives we were working on?" Jasmine asked.

"We packed up everything when we evacuated Ganymede," Vala said. "All your materials are downstairs."

"And the other kids?" Ricardo asked. "Pinky said they made it back okay. Was anyone hurt?"

"Only in the sense that Ash had to practically pry some of them out of their Space Runners," Pinky said. "They wanted to fly around Ganymede or alongside the mother ship as we left."

Hot Dog gasped and turned to Drue. "Our initials! Please tell me you took a pic with your HoloTek while we were out there."

"I thought you would!" Drue cried. "We have to go back!"

As all this was happening, Elijah's head practically never stopped moving. Either he was taking in the many wonders of the bridge or staring at the people talking as if he'd never heard them speak before. He must have noticed Benny looking at him, because he glanced at the boy and shook his head a little.

"You kids . . ." he murmured, one side of his mouth curling up in a grin.

"We need to focus," Ricardo said. "We don't know if this armistice is still in place, or if Senator Lincoln thinks the whole meeting was a trap."

"Ugh," Hot Dog groaned. "If he thinks it was a trap, then he definitely didn't see how hard a bunch of ETs were trying to kill Benny and Vala." She flipped her hair over her shoulder. "I wish we had an instant replay of that whole run."

Benny couldn't hide a dejected frown. "I think we failed. Even with everything we told them . . . I wouldn't be surprised if the Earth forces launched their weapon."

"Earth forces," Elijah said. "You mean Project New Apollo."

Benny snapped his head toward the man. "What *is* that? I keep hearing it."

"I recognized the insignia on my dad's Space Runner," Drue said. "He used to have files marked with it sometimes. Stuff that no one else was ever supposed to see."

Elijah nodded. "New Apollo is an initiative the United States government tried for many years to get me involved with as a contractor. They wanted weapons. Space Runner tanks. Deep space probes. The ability to build an entire force of space marines." He shook his head. "It appears that when I turned them down for the umpteenth time, Austin—*Dr. Bale* picked up the slack." He paused, frowning. "Using my designs."

"But why?" Hot Dog asked. "What did they want all that stuff for?"

Elijah glanced at Commander Vala. "Partially to be able to defend Earth from any outside invaders. At least someone in the government must have believed Bale when he brought word of the Alpha Maraudi to them."

"And the other part?" Jasmine asked.

"Colonization," Elijah said. "Seeking out new worlds. Assessing threats. Possibly leaving Earth behind one day. Their reasoning changed with every meeting." He laughed a little. "Not only does the name of the initiative recall the beginning of our obsession with space exploration but the ancient Greek deity as well. Apollo was symbolized by bows and arrows. The patron god of colonists. I'm sure someone thought that was very clever at some point."

"If these peace talks are a failure, then we have to stop New Apollo from launching that weapon," Trevone said. "I just hope we're not too late."

"What should we do?" Ricardo asked, turning to Elijah.

He looked almost taken aback by the question. "You're asking me?"

"Well, yeah."

Elijah looked around at all of them. "Seems to me like you're the ones who have this under control. I'm still trying to wrap my head around everything that's happening. Just point me to where you think I'll be the most help and I'll do what I can."

Everyone looked at each other, unsure of how to continue.

Benny didn't realize how independent they'd become since they'd last seen Elijah West in person. All of this they'd done by themselves—with a little help here and there.

Trevone spoke up first. "We could use your eyes on Dr. Bale's stealth drives. The programming is . . . well, it's not like anything we've worked with."

Elijah nodded. "I remember that man's designs. They worked, generally, but they were needlessly complicated. Impenetrable, even. You should have seen his plans for the Grand Dome." He sighed. "You know, I always meant to get around to reinforcing that one day, but I guess I got distracted."

"Right," Pinky said. "A lot of those distractions are sitting in the hangar right now."

"I saw. Which reminds me, I need to quadruple Ash's salary." He paused. "Assuming that salaries are still a thing a month from now."

"All right then," Ricardo said. "So . . . let's get back to it."

Elijah hesitated. "If you don't mind," he said, "I've been wearing this space suit since I blew up a hyperdrive in Tull's hangar. I don't suppose . . ."

Pinky smirked. "There it is. I'm still well aware of how demanding you can be. I had them put a spare change of clothes in a private room for you."

"Not demanding," Elijah said with a pout. "Just very, very smelly."

"Oh, right," Ricardo said, looking a little flustered. "You probably want to rest, too. Sorry."

"I just need a few minutes," Elijah said. "This room . . . ?"

"I'll show you," Pinky said, starting toward the hallway. "Follow me."

Elijah paused a moment to take in everything around him one more time. He looked as if he was going to say something, but in the end he simply smiled and followed the AI.

"Ramona," Trevone said. "You mentioned you were tooling with . . . the Alpha Maraudi communications?"

"You heard right, goggles," she said, motioning to a terminal near Griida where it looked like a Taj HoloTek had been spliced into the alien tech. "I like that ET," she continued. "He's quiet."

"Hmmm," Trevone continued. "Can you show me? And do you have the specs on that satellite you put together?"

"Roger, roger," Ramona said. "Watch and learn."

Hot Dog sidled up next to Benny. "Hey," she whispered. "Elijah's different, right? A little more . . . chill?"

"Yeah," Benny said. "Definitely."

She shrugged. "I guess a couple days alone in space prison will do that to you."

Almost everyone began to disperse from the bridge. Vala beckoned for Benny to follow her up the steps to the throne that looked out onto the expanse of outer space. The commander stood with her hands clasped behind her back, staring out at stars located light-years away. Benny stopped beside her.

Slowly, she pulled something from the mess of tendrils on her head and handed it out to Benny—his silver electro glove.

"Oh," he said. "Thanks. But we have a couple more stashed away. Zee can keep it if he wants."

Vala let out a wheeze Benny hoped might have been a laugh. "I fear what he would do with such a device. He is behind in studying the cultures that once lived on Pluto. I can imagine him using it against his tutor on an especially long day of lectures."

Benny's mouth dropped open. "Cultures on Pluto?"

"Oh." The commander sounded a bit surprised, then smiled a little. "Of course. They were extinct long before your kind ever walked the Earth. You might find their lives and eventual demise interesting. We can discuss them in the future if you like. Fascinating creatures. A pity about the Brood Wars."

"I . . ." Benny started, once again reeling at the vastness of things he didn't know about, even in his own solar system. "Sure," he finally managed, taking the glove back. "But if he ever needs this again . . . or if *you* do . . . If Tull attacks . . ." He trailed off.

"Thank you," Vala said. "For bringing him back."

"Yeah, well, it wasn't exactly the safest rescue mission. Things got a little hairy there at the end."

The commander nodded. "So I understand."

"Yeah . . ." Benny said. "So, uh . . . speaking of Tull . . ."

"You're wondering what this means for this ship and your people."

"Yeah, I guess. I mean, they tried pretty hard to blow us all up."

Vala nodded, still staring out into space. "You know, we never thought of humanity as our enemies. I am not sure if that is a compliment or an insult to your kind. You were always simply a different civilization. But now . . ." Her tentacles constricted slightly. "Now I am not sure what we are. The same can be said of Commander Tull. The Alpha Maraudi have not warred among ourselves in many, many generations. Argued, of course, but always acquiesced and moved on. We *value* peace. But we also put the preservation of our species above all else. These two things go hand in hand. So when there is a conflict between our want for peace among our people and our will for them to survive . . ." Vala shook her head. "I am not sure what Tull is now. An enemy? A vigilante? A shepherd for our kind? Someone who will bring about a new age for the Alpha Maraudi? And by that line of thinking, what am I? A *peace broker*, as you all called yourselves? Or something else. A traitor." She turned to

Benny, looking down at him. "We try to be a people who believe in absolutes, but in this universe, that is sometimes difficult. Absolutes are constructs that we have invented. They don't occur naturally. After all, fire and ice can exist on the same moon, but so do places in between where the two balance out. Nebulous, gray areas. Tell me, young one. How do you traverse this terrain?"

Benny stared up at the commander, trying to parse exactly what she was asking, his mind very thoroughly confused. Eventually, he shrugged, and tried to answer as best he could. "I don't know. I guess I just try to do what feels right and to face the world . . . well, the *universe* head-on."

Vala thought about this for a moment before nodding. "Perhaps that is a wise way of looking at life."

"I think so," Benny said. "It's something the best person I ever knew taught me."

After speaking with the commander, Benny realized
how hungry he was and headed down to the mess hall to
grab a bite to eat. The room was so abuzz with EW-SCAB-
ers recounting the details of the space battle they'd just
witnessed and Kira Miyamura catching them up on Elijah's
return and their flight to the asteroid belt that he managed
to sneak in, grab an apple and some of the faux-meat jerky
Hot Dog had told him about, and pop back out with only
a few people noticing him. In the hallway, he let out a long
sigh and began to do what was fast becoming second nature
to him: go over a mental checklist of where everyone was,
what they were doing, and how they were actively trying to
save Earth.

He was so lost in his thoughts that he didn't realize Pinky
was in the hallway until he was walking right through her.

"Ahem," the AI said.

Benny paused, part of his arm inside hers.

"Ah!" he yelped, jumping back and spitting flecks of fruit everywhere. "Whoa, sorry, I was just . . ."

"Think nothing of it. I was actually coming to find you."

His eyes widened, chest thumping. "What's wrong?"

She waved one hand a few times. "Nothing. At least, I don't think so. Elijah wants to have a chat with you."

"Oh," Benny said, allowing himself to breathe again. "Yeah. Of course. Uh, can you show me the way to wherever he is?"

He followed her past the sleeping quarters he and the rest of the EW-SCABers had been using and to a different hallway, where he found Elijah and Ricardo in a more private room—albeit one much smaller than Elijah's quarters at the Taj had been. The ceiling glowed with stubby stalactites, but for the most part, the place was bare. Ricardo sat on a stone bench that had grown out of the floor. Elijah wore a new blue space suit and inspected one of two large sleeping tubes in the wall.

"Those things are actually pretty comfortable," Benny said.

Elijah turned to see him, a grin on his face. "Benny Love," he said. "The dirt buggy king of the Drylands. A hologram connoisseur. The leader of the Moon Platoon, I believe you called yourself and your friends." He raised both his eyebrows toward Pinky. "I see you've been putting that bracelet I gave you to good use."

"I'll leave you boys to it," Pinky said. "If I'm not mistaken, I think I might be able to plot a course that will shave minutes off our travel time to the asteroid belt." She smirked. "Griida is going to hate me."

"It's come in handy," Benny said. "I think Commander Tull was actually scared when I made a giant holographic spider appear on his bridge. It's the only way Hot Dog and I managed to get out."

"I don't believe that," Ricardo said. "I've seen her fight a few times—and been on the receiving end of her anger. And you've managed to slip by more than one gang of Alpha Maraudi soldiers. My guess is the two of you would have found another way to escape."

Benny bounced his head back and forth. "Well, she *did* headbutt an alien while we were trying to get back to our Space Runners."

"That girl's got moxie," Elijah said.

"You should see her fly," Ricardo added. "Speaking of which, I want to hear about this lava river you apparently jumped."

"There's not much else to say," Benny said. He looked to Elijah. "But no one's gonna be driving the Chevelle for a while."

"If you're concerned that that's why I wanted to talk to you, there's no need to worry," Elijah said, crossing his arms. "Ricardo here has been filling me in on the finer details of everything that happened in my absence. You and your friends have taken a lot of risks."

"Yeah," Benny said. "I guess. We just tried to figure out how to fix things." He exhaled a long breath. "And somehow managed to mess everything up even more."

"No. Things were already a mess. You just got thrown into the middle of it all." Elijah looked to Ricardo. "Both of you. I'm happy to hear that the two of you and your teams managed to find common ground. I regret that I left things in a place where that couldn't happen immediately."

"You sacrificed yourself for us," Ricardo said. "You did more than enough."

Elijah's eyes went to the floor. "It never should have come to that." He was quiet for a few moments before looking back at them. "The kids here—and those who flew back to Earth—look up to you both. This is not new information. But, if you'll indulge someone who has recently been forced to come to terms with the fact that maybe he is more flawed than he ever realized, I have some advice to share."

Benny looked at Ricardo. They nodded to each other.

Elijah continued, pacing around the room as he spoke. "You both exemplify what it means to be a leader. You've proven that already. I guess what I want to say is that no matter how high your status or large your following, never think that you are above them or that you know better.

Because you aren't, and you don't. At the end of the day, we're nothing but a cluster of cells and atoms. We're all human. If we don't look out for each other, then what are we here to do?" He sighed. "I realize how hypocritical that sounds, given the way I behaved at the Taj."

In the words Elijah spoke was a glimmer of something Benny's father had once told him about the importance of the caravan looking out for one another, and it made goose bumps form on Benny's arms.

"Well," Elijah said, "I guess not *all* of us are human." He shrugged, poking a straw through a silver pouch of water he picked up from the sleeping tube. He seemed to relax a little. "That Zee seems like quite a handful."

"I appreciate the advice," Ricardo said, getting to his feet. "But I don't think you have to worry. At least not about one part of what you said." He looked at Benny and smiled just a little. "From what I've seen, we've been doing a pretty good job of watching each other's backs."

Benny smirked. "Yeah. Once you stopped acting like you were going to punch me every time I did something you didn't like."

"Hey," Ricardo said, stepping forward. "I was just trying to make sure—"

"Kidding," Benny said, raising his hands.

Elijah flashed a grin that was all gleaming white teeth. "I knew I was right to put you in the same team back at the

Taj." And then the smile faded. "I can't imagine what the resort looks like right now. I feel like one of the great loves of my life has been taken from me, and there's nothing I can do to get her back."

"The resort can be rebuilt," Benny said. "I mean, yeah, it looked pretty bad, but I think the New Apollo troops are still using it." He paused. "Not that that probably makes you feel better."

"The Taj is an incredible place," Ricardo said. "But it's not all the tech and fancy stuff inside that makes it wonderful. It's the spirit. And the people."

Benny didn't look at him, but he knew Ricardo was referring to a conversation they'd had on the dark side of the Moon when they'd been waiting for Drue to come back to them with information about what would turn out to be Vala's fleet.

"Yes," Elijah said. "Of course." His eyes went wide. "Ah, that reminds me." After taking a big swig of water, he pulled his coat out of the sleeping tube and fished around in one of its inside pockets. "Before I flew from the Taj the last time, Ash told me you had something I'd be very interested in seeing for myself, Benny. So you can imagine my surprise when I found *this* aboard an alien ship."

He held out a small silver object: the abstract figure of a human that looked as though it was flying through space, its arms stretching back like wings. One side of it was blackened, and the bottom still had stray bits of Benny's Space Runner hood stuck to it—the car he'd been forced to leave behind when he'd escaped from Tull's ship the first time.

Benny felt as though a piston had slipped in his chest.

"The hood ornament from a 2025 limited edition Rolls-Royce," Elijah continued. "Fewer than ten produced in the world. A true collector's item." He sighed dramatically. "I would've loved to have driven one of those. I thought they were all gone. Pity about this scorching, but that's easy enough to clean up."

"My father gave it to me," Benny said, not even trying to hide the wonder from his voice. "He found it in an abandoned garage out in the Drylands. In what used to be California." He couldn't stop shaking his head. "I didn't think I'd ever see it again."

Elijah held it out to him. "Stranger things have happened."

"Where . . ." Benny said. "How?"

Elijah half smiled and shrugged. "One of the first things I was ordered to do on Tull's ship, after a . . . *long* interrogation, was to clean up the mess I'd made. This was mixed in with the scraps of my Space Runner and what I assume was yours."

Benny practically leaped forward, grabbing the little metal statue and cradling it in his hands. It felt so familiar there, and in an instant he was transported back to his family's RV. A flood of memories coursed through him—his father bringing the ornament back to him, he and his brothers all silently choosing the items that reminded them of him once he was gone, the pride he'd felt when Ash McGuyver had glued it to the hood of his Space Runner before they flew out against the asteroid storm and the pain of having to leave it behind when he and Hot Dog escaped.

He couldn't help but hold it close to his chest.

"Please, accept this as my apology," Elijah said. He glanced at Ricardo. "I wish I had something for you, too."

"You're back," Ricardo said. "That's enough."

"Apology for what?" Benny asked.

Elijah shook his head. "For my own hubris. I know you haven't forgotten the events that occurred at the resort. My time as Tull's prisoner may have been brief, but it felt much longer than it was. I had plenty of hours in the dark to think hard about everything I've done in my life—of what I've become." He shook his head. "I think you and your friends were right. At some point, after spending so much time away from Earth, I forgot what it meant to be human." He turned to Ricardo. "And what's worse, I passed that on to others around me. Those who looked up to me."

"*Look* up to you," Ricardo corrected.

"Which, given these past few days of reflection, is perhaps even more proof of my failures." He took a step forward, beckoning Ricardo to come closer. Then he placed a hand on each of the boys' shoulders. "I couldn't be prouder of the things you've done in my absence. The things you've accomplished in such a short time . . . I'm only beginning to see how blind I've been. It is . . . *difficult* to admit this. But we'll find a way to overcome these obstacles. I'm sure of it. Not because I'm here to help you now, but because you— and all the others who have helped you—are still fighting. That was always the point of the EW-SCAB. To bring the best, bravest minds on the planet together. In that, at least, I believe I was successful."

Ricardo nodded. Benny gripped the hood ornament tighter.

"Now," Elijah said with a grin, "I want full reports on how the Star Runners and Chevelle handled. I never got to test out that muscle car, you know." He winked at Benny. "And Ricardo told me you rode the Galaxicle? What was I thinking when I designed that? *And* you let the Lincoln boy drive you? If I ever needed more proof that you're a brave soul . . ."

"He's actually a pretty good pilot," Benny said. "Not to mention a great shot."

Ricardo sighed. "I hate to admit it, but he's right."

Elijah laughed a little. "More surprises at every curve of the track," he murmured.

"Elijah!" Pinky shouted, materializing in the doorway.

Her eyes were wide, her normally tight bun of blond hair slightly askew. All three of the people inside the room jumped.

"What's wrong?" Elijah asked, voice full of concern.

"We need you on the bridge," she said. "It all happened so fast. Ramona upgraded the satellite uplink, and Trevone realized the full capabilities . . ."

"What are you saying?" Ricardo asked. "What's going on?"

"We're in contact with the Lunar Taj. Ramona thinks it's possible for us to hack the servers that New Apollo has taken over." She smiled in a way that looked almost mischievous to Benny. "Care to see what we can find out about this superweapon?"

"I travel faster without you," Pinky said. _And then_ she disappeared, her imperceptible nanoprojectors soaring through the halls.

Benny, Ricardo, and Elijah stood frozen for one beat before all three of them darted through the doorway. Benny shoved the hood ornament into his space suit pocket as he burst into the hall.

"Dr. Bale probably has control of everything at the Taj right now," Benny said.

"You said you were able to overcome his reprogramming before, correct?" Elijah said as they raced through the ship. "I don't remember him being the best coder."

"Not us," Benny said. "Ramona."

"And that was by plugging her HoloTek directly into Pinky's core servers," Ricardo said.

"Ramona Robinson," Elijah muttered. "Programming

genius from Wales. Pinky complained about her *several* times while we were still at the Taj." He smirked. "I guess she had good reason to."

By the time they got to the bridge, Ramona, Trevone, and Pinky were standing around the hologram that showed the ship's course to the asteroid belt. They were speaking to each other at a rapid-fire rate, but most everything Benny could make out went way over his head. Vala and Griida stood near the Alpha Maraudi terminal, Hot Dog and Drue nearby; all of them looked *quite* confused.

"She's speaking in robot again," Drue said.

Hot Dog's eyes were bulging. "I've never seen someone's fingers move so fast over a HoloTek. It's like she's possessed." She shook her head. "And I thought *I* was good at messaging."

Ricardo passed his HoloTek off to Elijah and then he and Benny joined the others.

"Can you catch me up?" Elijah asked as he came to a stop between Ramona and Trevone.

"Before, I didn't think we'd have enough bandwidth to launch an assault on the Taj," Trevone said. "But Ramona drastically improved our abilities to communicate with the satellite she launched."

"Told you guys I'm always working on this thing," she said, nodding to her HoloTek.

"I'm patching you into the satellite connection now,"

Pinky said to Elijah. "They're already assessing Dr. Bale's security measures, looking for ways to bypass them. I'm following along as they work, investigating on my own but . . . Well, if I knew about weaknesses in the Taj's servers I would have fixed them while I was still there."

"Yeah," Trevone said. "Same."

Elijah glanced at the older HoloTek strapped to Ramona's forearm. "You're using that ancient thing?" he asked. "Someone get her a newer model."

"I would trust her on this one," Pinky said. "You do realize that's what she used to undermine my systems previously. Right under my nose." She frowned. "*Both* our noses."

"Oh. Right."

Elijah narrowed his eyes and tapped on his own screen, fingers flying.

Off to the side, Drue leaned in to Benny and Hot Dog. "I feel like we're watching some kind of very nerdy fight take place."

"Yeah," Benny said. "But one that could help us keep humanity alive."

Drue scoffed. "Hey, I didn't say it wasn't exciting. I just wish I had any idea what was going on. My experience with trying to 'bypass security' measures pretty much ends with using facial recognition to unlock one of my old nanny's HoloTeks while she was sleeping."

"You are such a creep." Hot Dog sighed.

"I've been studying the way the Alpha Maraudi create these holographic projections," Pinky said, taking a step closer to the miniature version of the solar system floating in front of them. "Give me a second, and I *should* be able to port what's happening on your screens to this projection so everyone can—"

The hologram of the flight path suddenly changed into a massive wall of scrolling text.

"Awesome," Drue said. "Nice work, Pinks. Now we can see . . . whatever that is."

"Um," the AI said, "that wasn't me."

"Should've said something sooner, hologhost," Ramona said with a smirk. "That's a level-one job."

"How did you . . ." The AI was at a loss for words.

"I was doing max research earlier. Earth systems. ET systems. It's all coding."

Griida barked across the bridge just as Jasmine darted through the doorway, running to the hologram. She stopped short a few feet away.

"Oh, wow," she said slowly. "I think this is . . . *way* out of my realm of knowledge."

Ramona took in a deep breath, and then made one long, explosion noise that eventually faded to nothing.

"Uh, any idea what's going on?" Hot Dog asked, looking around at everyone who wasn't engaged in what was apparently fast becoming all-out computer warfare.

"The Taj servers are programmed to immediately delete and overwrite any foreign code that's introduced and not approved by Elijah," Trevone explained. "Or Dr. Bale, in this case, since he's taken over. To make matters worse, the firewalls are practically impossible to penetrate. If an unauthorized user shows up, they're immediately kicked out."

"Don't you have some sort of override, Elijah?" Benny asked. "What was it back when you made Pinky take over our SRs and fly us back to the Taj?"

"Detroit?" Hot Dog asked.

Pinky grimaced at the word.

"It's not working," Elijah said. "If I were there and in my office, I could enter the override directly, but I can't do anything from here."

"No faith," Ramona muttered. "Watch and learn, newb."

Elijah just stared at her, his mouth gaping. Then he turned to the hologram. "Wha . . . ?" he managed to say before rubbing one eye. "I don't even know what part of the system you're in right now."

"Uh, yeah, I'm a little lost here, too," Trevone said.

"She found a back door into the maintenance controls," Pinky said. "She just caused every working toilet in the Taj to flush and every faucet to turn on. The H2O tanks are emptying faster than they can be refilled."

"That's . . . a lot of wasted water," Benny said quietly.

"It gets recycled," Elijah whispered softly, instinctively, his gaze going back and forth between Ramona and the various databases, registries, and strings of code that fluttered across the air in front of them.

The AI narrowed her eyes, focusing on the hologram. "That's triggered an emergency response from the central computers . . ."

" . . . which grants temporary admin privileges to a handful of high-ranking employees but . . ." Elijah continued.

"Ramona," Pinky asked flatly, "why do you know Max Étoile's username and password?"

"Meh." She shrugged. "He was a troll."

A new screen popped up, covered in what looked to Benny like a wall of nonsensical numbers and file names.

"Can I do anything to help?" Elijah asked.

"Mute yourself," Ramona said. "Also, soda."

Elijah just blinked.

"I'm on it," Drue said, sprinting for the hallway. "Soda's running low, but I hid a bunch in my sleeping tube." He looked over his shoulder. "Don't do anything cool without me!"

And then he was gone.

Benny glanced at Hot Dog. "I didn't know a HoloTek could do anything other than play games and videos and things like that."

"Seriously. How is Pinky just made up of numbers? It's crazy." Hot Dog shook her head, dumbfounded.

"How is *the entire world* running on this stuff?" Benny asked. "I mean, I know we didn't have much tech in the caravan—and numbers and me never really got along all that well—but at least solar power I understood. Heck, even *fossil fuels* made some kind of sense to me."

Trevone squinted at the hologram. "Is that . . ."

"The server where backup data and communications are stored," Elijah finished.

"And that's helpful . . . ?" Benny asked.

Trevone smirked. "Every message that's sent to or from a HoloTek at the Taj goes through that server and gets logged."

"Meaning everything sent to or from Dr. Bale in the last few days!" Jasmine said.

"Not just that. If we're lucky, a backup of his entire HoloTek drive will be there."

Pinky's eyes went wide. "The system knows you're in. It's going to kick you out."

Ramona popped her tongue. "Hold on," she said. And then one arm shot to the side, tapping on the HoloTek Elijah still held in his hands.

"What are you—"

"*Mute,*" the girl said again. Then she went back to her own datapad.

Pinky smirked. "She just tried to reboot the entire server from an unauthorized account using Ricardo's HoloTek."

"Well, obviously that didn't work," Hot Dog said.

"No." Trevone grinned. "But it forced all of the system's security to focus on booting out the foreign user. Buying her a few seconds."

Elijah grunted, tapping on the blank screen of his HoloTek. "This is completely wiped. It's dead."

"That's a *really* aggressive program," Benny said.

"Thanks," Trevone said. "It was my idea."

In front of them, the strands of code suddenly froze. Then, the entire hologram blinked out of existence.

"What just happened?" Vala asked, taking two long strides forward. "What have you done to my ship? Griida?"

The other alien turned to his terminal and started swiping at the floating lights above it. There was a flash, and then once again the hologram displayed their trajectory, mapping a route to the asteroid belt.

Ramona let out a long breath, as if she'd been holding it the entire time. Then she shook her head. "Satellite's wiped. Just a normal Star Runner now. Useless." She clicked her tongue again. "Shame."

"So . . . that's it?" Benny asked, all excitement and hope beginning to fade. "We're locked out now? And we don't even have a satellite for communication? We could have used that to contact Earth or something."

Ricardo stomped away from the others, his fingers gripping his short brown hair as he let loose a frustrated groan.

"Cool it, beast," Ramona said, tapping on her HoloTek. "My downstreams are ultrafast."

The central hologram changed once again. This time, it showed countless folder icons.

"You . . . downloaded the entire content of the backup server?" Trevone asked, his voice full of awe.

"Psh, of course not," Ramona said. "Just most of it."

"The files are certainly encrypted," Elijah said. But before Ramona could say anything, he was already backtracking. "I know, I know. That likely means nothing to you."

"I needed Ramona to outthink me in order to get into the server," Pinky said, taking a step toward the hologram. "But these folder encryptions were done by *people*." She raised a hand and narrowed her eyes, and in front of them, files began to pop up everywhere—blueprints, communiqués, maps. She smiled a little. "Humans have always been so bad at creating passwords. And some of them are so embarrassing."

"That's my girl," Elijah said, flashing a wide grin.

"I am no one's 'girl,' Elijah," the AI said. "I'm the most sophisticated computer program ever developed."

Drue ran back in, breathing heavily, a couple of cans in

his arms and a stack of energy bars in one hand. "What'd I miss?"

Ramona walked over to him, grabbed a soda. "Just saved you guys again." She popped the tab, slurping the initial fizz. "Nothing new." She took a swig. "I think I need a nap. Systems overworked. Holo-assistant can take control. Wake me if you need anything."

And then she headed off the bridge.

"There must be thousands of folders," Jasmine said.

"And who knows how many files and subfolders inside them," Trevone added.

"I'm going through everything as quickly as I can," Pinky said, staring into space, at nothing in particular. "There's so much. Blueprints. Memos. Messages. Logging keywords now. Sorting libraries."

"Try searching 'New Apollo' maybe?" Benny suggested.

"That search resulted in twenty-two thousand four hundred and ninety-two hits. And climbing. We have backups of every HoloTek in the Taj, but the directories are corrupted. I can't tell what file came from what datapad."

Benny slouched a little. "Oh."

"How many of them are designs or blueprints?" Jasmine asked.

"I'm still calculating. My processing power is limited, but . . ." The AI sighed. "Trust me when I say it's a lot."

"I don't guess any of them are named 'superweapon' or 'alien killer' or anything like that," Hot dog said.

"Unfortunately not. The designs are designated only by numbers."

Trevone shook his head. "That does us no good."

Elijah pulled on the tip of his short reddish beard. "Focus on communications within the last three days."

"Bale didn't seem to be one for recorded messages of any kind," Pinky said.

"But my dad was," Drue said, hurrying over to her side. "He had a file and a report on everything."

Pinky's eyes seemed to glaze over a bit, and then suddenly her head jolted.

"What is it?" Elijah asked.

"Give me a moment. Verifying today's date according to Taj time. Cross-referencing . . ." She stopped. "Oh, no."

"What?" Benny and Ricardo asked at the same time.

The hologram in front of them shifted again, this time displaying a series of documents with official-looking seals on the header.

Pinky turned to them. "These are communications concerning the vessel that will carry Dr. Bale's superweapon to the Alpha Maraudi home world. A ship they're calling the *Orion*."

"Tell us everything," Ricardo said. "Where is it now?"

Pinky pursed her lips. "I don't know."

"There must be a project number or name for the ship," Elijah said.

"All I can find is the code name," Pinky said. "There's no telling which of the numbered designs corresponds to it. I'm checking for more files mentioning it by name and—ah." And then her face fell. "Here. A message to Earth from the Taj. Sent from Dr. Bale's assistant on his behalf just a few hours ago. It's an order to prep the *Orion* for launch."

"So it exists," Trevone said. "It's not just a concept. They built it."

"When is it taking off?" Benny asked.

Pinky's face grew grim. "If all goes as scheduled, it will leave Earth's atmosphere and retrieve the Dr. Bale's super-weapon from the dark side tomorrow."

"Is there anything else from my dad?" Drue asked. "About the armistice? The temporary peace?"

"I'm sorry," Pinky said, "but there have been no correspondences from your father since before the meeting on Io. That I can find, at least."

A horrible quiet fell over the bridge as they took in this information.

"Does it say anything about where the weapon is hidden?" Benny asked.

"Not that I can find, but I'm still searching," Pinky said. "There's just . . . so much data."

"If we don't head back now, we'll miss our chance to

stop them from loading up the weapon," Jasmine said. "We'll have to chase them through space, toward the Alpha Maraudi home world."

"We don't know how fast this *Orion* ship can go," Trevone said. "It could be able to outrun us. Even in Star Runners." He rubbed the bridge of his nose. "We're going into this completely blind."

From the other side of the room, Griida spoke a few words in the alien tongue.

"No, plot a new course for us," Vala said. "We're not going to the asteroid field after all."

Benny stared at the hologram, the designs for the *Orion* flashing back to the forefront.

"The commander's right," he said balling his hands into fists. "If this ship is coming, we're going to be there to stop it. We're going back to the Moon."

20.

"Once we spot the ship," Benny said, "all we have to do is follow it to find the weapon, right?"

"Technically," Jasmine said, not looking up from her HoloTek, to which Pinky had ported all the stolen files. "But we have no idea what form the weapon is in, or how they plan on getting it into the ship." She frowned. "Or what the ship might even look like. Ramona downloaded hundreds of different conceptual designs. We have no idea which one is the *Orion*."

"Most of these are Dr. Bale's work for sure," Trevone said, swiping through his HoloTek. "It's difficult to make heads or tails of them."

"The point is, for all we know this ship could have shielding like the Grand Dome—also Dr. Bale's design," Jasmine continued. "And you better believe he's ready to counteract another Maraudi rock attack after what happened at the Taj."

"Let's just ram them with the mother ship," Drue said. "*That* should do the trick."

Hot Dog shrugged "That's . . . actually not a terrible idea."

They stood in a small circle on the bridge as Pinky continued to look for anything useful among the files Ramona had managed to download, Elijah helping her by skimming any documents or designs that merited a second look. Kira had come to the deck, and together with Ricardo, they were standing by Elijah, ready to aid him in any way. Meanwhile, Griida and Vala plotted the quickest route for them to get back to the Moon undetected—by both New Apollo forces *and* Tull's ship, assuming the two sides hadn't mostly destroyed each other back on Io.

The rest of them were left to look over the blueprints and other stolen files, searching for anything that might lead them to the weapon.

Benny felt some comfort in the fact that they were headed back home—or at least home-ish. Finally. But that would mean nothing if they couldn't get there in time to stop this superweapon, and so far they'd come up with nothing.

"We have to assume that the *Orion* is heavily armed," Jasmine said.

"True," Trevone agreed. "And not just with soldiers and Space Runners equipped with plasma guns. It's probably got its own weapons."

"Some of these blueprints are so weird," Hot Dog said as she turned her HoloTek to a new angle, raising both her eyebrows. "I think these are deep sleep cryochambers." She looked up at the rest of them. "If I ever, for any reason, think it's a good idea to freeze myself and wake up on the other side of the universe a million years from now, please tell me that I'm crazy." She swiped to the next blueprint.

"I dunno," Benny said. "Think of how far video games and flight sims will have advanced by them. Think of the *hyperdrives*."

Hot Dog paused, taking this under consideration. "You know, you're right. I take back everything I just said."

Drue let out a yelp, like he'd just been stung by something. He held up his datapad to show it off. "This ship is basically a giant ball, and the entire back half is made up of nothing but hyperdrives. It's some kind of light-speed space sphere!"

Trevone glanced at the schematics. "The aerodynamics leave much to be desired if you're attempting to reach light speed."

"That's cooler than whatever this is," Hot Dog said, frowning down at her HoloTek. "It's basically just an empty titanium coffin with a massive hyperdrive on the back. Why is that even in here with all these crazy ships?"

Jasmine and Trevone both perked up.

"Did you say titanium?" Jasmine asked.

"Well, yeah," Hot Dog said, holding out her HoloTek. "See for yourselves."

They hurried to her side so quickly that Hot Dog actually looked frightened for a split second.

"Whoa. Here," she said, shoving the datapad into Jasmine's hands. "You can have it."

Behind them, Elijah turned away from the hologram, his interest piqued by how excited the two of them seemed.

"Is titanium . . . a clue?" Benny asked.

Drue shrugged. "It's super strong and used in a bunch of Space Runner designs because it's really light."

"Titanium was often used to shield electronics from radiation in space before Elijah developed environmental shielding," Trevone said. "If the superweapon of Dr. Bale's has delicate targeting systems and they intend to travel through uncharted galaxies. . ."

"Then this could be what it's being housed in as an added precaution," Jasmine said. "Look at the specs on this hyperdrive. It's way overpowered."

"Right," Trevone said. "Which means the *Orion* could launch this without getting close to the Alpha Maraudi planet. If it's holding the actual weapon, this casing likely just breaks apart when it's within range of Calam. Like how old rockets used to fall off of spaceships once they were used up."

"I haven't seen any other designs like this. Have you?"

Trevone shook his head.

Benny shrugged. "Okay. So, that's something we know now. But how does it help?"

"Clever, clever," Elijah said, beckoning Jasmine and Trevone over. He looked at the HoloTek for a few seconds. "Pinky, pull up this design. Cross-reference any numbers or names associated with this blueprint against the rest of the files."

"Analyzing now," Pinky said. "Forty-two diagrams found. Scanning unknown characteristics."

As she spoke, the hologram flashed between designs, notes, and blueprints. Benny and the others gathered around. He wasn't sure what he was seeing, but it seemed important.

The blueprint of the titanium box zoomed in on what looked like locking mechanisms.

"Here," Pinky said. "These locks inside the box were designed to house something designated as EM-eleven thirty-eight."

"Search that number," Elijah said.

"I'm way ahead of you," The AI replied. "Hmmm, I've found the folder, but it's got an added layer of encryption and . . . Ah, there."

The hologram erupted with blueprints for something shaped like a thick, angular spike with five wide copper bands around it: a missile of some sort.

There, floating in front of them, were the plans for Dr. Bale's superweapon.

Elijah shook his head. "Austin, what have you done?"

After so much time wondering about this doomsday device, trying to use it to get the Alpha Maraudi and the New Apollo forces to work with them, Benny kind of couldn't believe he was looking at schematics for it.

"The more we can learn about it," Jasmine said, "the better equipped we are to stop it."

"What does it do?" Vala's voice came from behind them.

The commander walked slowly to the hologram, lifting her mask, eyes wide as they took in the object that could mean the destruction of so many of her people.

"There's a document here," Pinky said. "It sounds like the original pitch to Project New Apollo. It is *very* long. Allow me to paraphrase: This weapon is actually *several* missiles, each with its own navigational system. Once deployed into Calam's atmosphere, the weapon will break apart and strike the planet's surface in a gridlike pattern. Each segment is equipped with a device that is capable of emitting high-level electromagnetic waves on a planetary scale. Nearby *moons* would be affected. Maybe even other planets in your solar system. No wonder they're using this titanium pod as a carrier—they wouldn't want their ship to be anywhere near this. Honestly, it's overkill." The AI's voice got softer. "Without being too gruesome, suffice to say that a planet inhabited by people with metal bones would be particularly vulnerable to something like this. You're basically walking magnetic conductors. And even if your bones *could* withstand something of this nature— which I highly doubt—the radiation levels would destroy your bodies."

Vala said nothing, but her tentacles wound together into compact balls, her fingers quivering.

"How could he know all this?" Trevone asked. "It's like he's *seen* their planet."

"He has," Benny said. In his head, he was retracing their footsteps on the dark side of the Moon the day they'd first found Dr. Bale. "When we were at his camp he turned on some kind of hologram map. It looked like Alpha Maraudi tech. He showed us Calam and its suns."

"Oh, yeah," Hot Dog said. "There was something like that in the Maraudi base on the dark side, too. That hologram that Drue set off."

Benny shook his head. "He's had this information the whole time, and he just focused on how to destroy you. He didn't do a single thing to try to figure out how to save the planet."

"Neither of us did," Elijah said quietly, staring at something in the middle distance. He blinked, setting his jaw. "But that's going to change. As soon as we stop them on the Moon, we'll put all of our minds to it. We'll find a way for you to save your planet." He looked to Vala. "I swear my life on it."

But the commander did not look relieved. Benny couldn't blame her.

"Okay, so we know what this missile is made up of, right?" Hot Dog asked. "Can't we find it now?"

"No," Trevone said. "This hasn't changed anything. It's still cloaked by Dr. Bale's stealth drives, and we haven't figured out a way to track anything protected by those."

Jasmine shook her head. "I failed. I should've been able to figure them out."

"Oh, no," Hot Dog said. "You cannot blame yourself at all."

"We could really use a giant metal detector right now," Drue said.

"You're talking about hundreds of square kilometers," Pinky said.

"I wasn't being serious. Mostly."

"Well, you should be," Kira muttered, her eyes not moving from the hologram.

"Okay," Benny said, "So, we just look for the *Orion*."

"Unless it's got stealth shielding, too," Jasmine said. Her voice was getting higher pitched, her face turning red. "Maybe they can do this whole operation without ever being seen. Maybe this was all for nothing because we couldn't crack Dr. Bale's stealth drives."

"Pito's still working on them," Trevone said.

"Where are they?" Elijah asked. "I'll go look at them now. Maybe I can help."

"I guess it was too much to ask for us to be able to use his stealth to our advantage when sneaking around *and* use it to find this missile."

"Hold on . . ." Jasmine said. "We use it to find the aliens because it homes in on the distinct makeup of their bones. And the Chevelle . . ."

Benny furrowed his brow. "What about it?"

Jasmine closed her eyes and started murmuring to herself. Then, suddenly, they sprang back open, wider than before. "I'm such an idiot!" And before anyone could ask what was going on, she was running off the bridge, out into one of the hallways.

"Jazz, wait!" Benny said, starting after her—the rest of the group right behind him.

They followed her to the hangar, where they found Ash McGuyver popping dents out of the electric-green muscle car. The dust had been cleaned off the tires, which were now shiny and looked like they were made of wet goop in places where the rubber had melted and then hardened again.

"Whoa, whoa, whoa," she said as they approached. "What the heck has you fired up?"

"Good question," Ricardo said.

"Benny," Jasmine said. "Get in the car."

"Honey, this baby ain't going anywhere," Ash said.

"That doesn't matter." She turned to Benny, raising her eyebrows. "Please."

"Yeah," he said. "Of course." And then he was sliding into the passenger seat. "Uh, you want me to turn it on?"

Jasmine shook her head. "No, just the stealth drive. It's still in there, right?"

"Uh-huh." He reached forward and pressed on the red button. The Chevelle—and Benny—disappeared.

Ash whistled. "That trick never gets old."

"Fascinating," Elijah said. "So this is how Dr. Bale stayed off our grid for so long."

"Exactly," Jasmine said. "And none of your scans were able to pick him up, right?"

"That's correct," he said, reaching out and touching the invisible hood. "Though, I'll admit, I wasn't too keen on seeing him again."

Jasmine grinned. There was an energy in her that seemed ready to explode. "That's exactly how the Alpha

Maraudi stealth ships were, remember? The purple ones. We couldn't see them on any radars." She paused. "At least, none of the *Taj* radars."

Trevone took a deep breath. Then he started laughing, almost uncontrollably. "Oh my gosh, Jasmine. You're far from an idiot. You're a genius."

"Let's just hope I'm right." She shook her head. "I can't believe I didn't think of this sooner. But, then, we didn't know what to look for."

"Uhhh," Benny said from inside the car. "Am I missing something?"

"Like I said, we couldn't crack the alien stealth," Jasmine continued. She pulled out the radar they'd been using to track the Alpha Maraudi for the last few days and began tapping on it. "But Dr. Bale could. He figured out a way to scan for their bones, their ships—all kinds of things. And we have one of the radars he designed himself."

Trevone clapped once. "He gave us the tools to find this weapon."

"Well, didn't *give* us," Hot Dog said. "Drue kinda stole that radar from him."

"You're welcome," Drue said.

Benny watched as Jasmine tapped and swiped on the radar a few times. Finally, she raised her finger, pausing just above the screen's surface. She seemed to whisper something to herself, and then finally, she brought her finger down.

A little ragged breath escaped from her lips.

"Well?!" Hot Dog asked. "I have no idea what's going on, but I feel like it's something important."

Jasmine grinned as she held the radar out to them.

Benny jumped out of the car, scrambling over to his friends.

There on the screen was a blazing orange series of tubes underneath the Chevelle, despite the fact that it was still cloaked in Dr. Bale's stealth technology.

"What is it?" Benny asked.

"The titanium axels Ash installed after we busted the old ones on the dark side," Jasmine said. She smiled wider than he'd ever seen her smile before. "We can track the titanium box holding the missile, even with the stealth on. We just needed to know what to look for."

"By Halley's Comet," Elijah whispered. "You cracked it."

"No," she said. "It wasn't me. This is all Dr. Bale's handiwork. I just . . ." She trailed off.

"I'm gonna have to give you some lessons in how to take credit for things, aren't I, Jazz?" Drue asked.

"Seriously," Hot Dog agreed. "What would we do without you?"

"We know the ship is coming," Ricardo said. "We know what the weapon is. We can scan for it, find it."

"So, what's our next step?" Kira asked.

"If we can get there fast enough, we could take the weapon and run."

"We have the schematics," Trevone said. "We could figure out a way to disarm it."

"And if they try to stop us," Hot Dog said, smashing a fist into her open palm, "we fight back."

Benny looked around them, at the rows of Space Runners, prototypes—even a few of the Alpha Maraudi ships that were still docked on the far side of the hangar.

"We make a stand," he said. "We stop Project New Apollo."

He looked at Elijah West, almost instinctively. The others did, too. He stared back at them. It looked to Benny like he was trying his best not to grin. Finally, Elijah spoke.

"So, do I get to pick which car I'm driving or are they all spoken for already?"

21.

At Vala's command, Griida set the ship to fly as fast as possible toward the dark side of the Moon. While Pinky, Trevone, Jasmine, and Elijah tried to dissect the plans for the electromagnetic missile as best they could, the rest of Benny's group gathered in front of Vala's throne. Benny and Ricardo paced back and forth in front of the commander, who had remained quiet since Pinky's explanation of the weapon. Kira stood looking out into space, arms crossed over her chest.

"All this pacing is freaking me out a little," Drue whispered to Hot Dog.

She nodded, crinkling her nose. "Seriously. It's like they're VR simulations that got stuck in a loop."

"We can hear you," Ricardo said.

Hot Dog shrugged. "I wasn't trying to be quiet."

Benny ignored them. "Commander, when do you think we'll be back near the Moon?"

"Our current projections put us there shortly after this *Orion* ship is set to arrive at the Lunar Taj," Vala said. "Assuming it will have to stop there to transfer supplies or people, we should be able to make it to what you call the dark side before it does." She paused. "I assure you we're traveling as quickly as our engines will go."

"Oh, it'll definitely stop at the Taj," Benny said. "I can't imagine Dr. Bale would leave this up to anyone else. Assuming he survived Tull's attack, that's where he'll be."

"Maybe my dad will be there," Drue said. "Maybe if he sees us, we can talk to him, like we did at the meeting. We *had* an armistice. We were doing good stuff!"

"Let's hope he is," Hot Dog said, looking at Drue with sad eyes.

"Once we're close to the Moon," Benny said, "we'll have a better idea of where, exactly, this missile is. We can boot up the radar and fly straight to it."

"The mother ship is way too big a target," Jasmine said, climbing the steps to join them. She turned to the commander. "Without knowing what the *Orion* can do, I don't think it would be smart to have it close to the dark side."

"Oh, the *Orion* is totally covered in death rays," Drue said. "I mean, that's technically just a guess, but, guys, we've met Dr. Bale. The dude is crazy but he's smart when it comes to knowing how to blow things up. He'll be prepared."

"Drue is right," Ricardo said. "If his ship is built to travel across the universe, it's going to be fast *and* well armed."

"You are correct that this vessel was not designed to enter direct combat," Vala said. "We can stop at a relatively safe distance and deploy ships from there."

"How's it going, Jazz?" Benny asked, gesturing to the holographic blueprints hovering on the other side of the bridge. "Give us some good news."

Jasmine sighed. "Please don't put that responsibility on me."

"Eesh," Drue said. "Looking that great, huh?"

"*Actually,* we've learned a lot so far in terms of how the weapon itself works."

Drue crossed his arms. "And here's where things get bad."

"Don't jump ahead," Jasmine said, glaring at him. "We think we can disarm it!"

"Really?" Benny asked, a smile spreading across his face. Finally, something they could work with.

Hot Dog put an arm around her. "Way to go, Jasmine!"

Jasmine didn't return the hug.

"But . . ." Ricardo said.

Jasmine sighed. "*But,* it looks like disarming the weapon

is going to take a lot of really delicate work. And time. It's not exactly what we want to be doing when the clock is ticking and we're looking over our shoulders waiting for some kind of approaching"—she struggled to find the words—"galaxy-hopping Death Runner."

"Right," Benny said. It seemed like around him, everyone deflated again.

"I like *Death Runner*," Drue whispered after a few seconds of silence. "I mean, I would under different circumstances."

Vala stood. "Then we will take this weapon aboard my ship and flee," the commander said. "The only thing that matters is that it is out of the hands of New Apollo and far, far away from Calam, or any Alpha Maraudi innocents."

They all turned to look at Vala.

"You're sure you want to bring that thing up here?" Ricardo asked.

The commander nodded.

"Of course," she said. "I will fly this ship alone and take the missile to a dead system—or a black hole—if that is what it takes to destroy it."

"You won't have to do it by yourself," Benny said, trying to reassure her—and himself—in some way that this was doable.

"They'll come after us," Kira said.

"Probably," Jasmine said. "But I don't know how much

they'll attack us if the weapon is onboard. They need it intact. It's not the kind of thing you can just whip up in a day. Shooting at the mother ship would risk detonating it."

"Yeah," Benny said, his lips twisting—the idea was growing on him. "In a weird way, bringing that weapon to the ship is kind of like making us untouchable. Like how we wouldn't have launched a full-scale attack on Tull while Elijah was his prisoner."

"Okay, so how do we *get* it?" Ricardo asked.

Jasmine grinned. "There *is* some good news: the outside of the case is actually made up of a titanium alloy that we'll be targeting with the radar. Without getting too scientific—"

"Thank you," Benny murmured.

"—that means it's magnetic."

"Sweet!" Drue said, holding up his silver glove. "We'll just float it outta there."

"Not with that you won't," Jasmine continued. "The missile itself is the size of three Space Runners parked back to back, and that's not counting the container. It weighs a ton." She paused before adding: "I mean that figuratively, not literally. It weighs many, many tons."

"Okay," Benny said. "So, we get a bunch of people with gloves together." His eyes lit up. "Like back when we were fighting those video game robots and we had to all work as a team to pull those rocks out of the ground! No sweat."

"Those rocks were *designed* to be pulled out using teamwork," Ricardo said. "It was the whole point of the simulation. You can't apply that here."

"Plus, if the *Orion* shows up, I don't think we'll want to just be hanging out around this missile like it's a campfire, trying to get it up on to the mother ship somehow," Hot Dog said. "That's how you lose in two seconds."

"And the mother ship isn't supposed to be near the Moon anyway," Kira added.

"Okay, okay." Benny shoved his hands into his pockets. "I get it. Bad idea."

"Right idea," Jasmine said. "Wrong tech." She grinned a little and looked around, as if waiting for someone to speak. Finally, she let out a breath and widened her eyes. "Ash's oversized SR! It was *built* to tow superheavy things around."

"Yes!" Benny practically shouted. "You're right! That thing is a monster!"

"We can totally do this," Hot Dog said. "It's like capture the flag except, you know . . . the flag is a civilization-destroying superweapon."

Benny started pacing again. "We'll take the core Moon Platoon and the Pit crew down—the rest of the EW-SCAB-ers will just be in the way or, worse, in danger."

"What about Dr. Bale taking control of our SRs?" Ricardo asked.

"Ramona seemed pretty confident after the last attack that she could counter a hijacking," Jasmine said. "I think I'd be more help up here. Ramona can cover the comms, and I'll keep track of the radars."

Benny nodded. "Perfect, we're counting on you, Jazz. We'll snag the missile, fly back up here, and *bam*. We're outta there. No more superweapon." He turned to Vala. "You can send word back to Calam that not only is the weapon gone, but a bunch of *humans* helped you get it. Then"—he took a deep breath—"we'll work on saving your planet. And ours."

"Imagine Dr. Bale's face when he rolls up to grab his precious electro rocket of doom and finds out there's nothing there," Drue said with a smirk.

"We will aid you in this mission," Vala said. "Pito has long protested that he be allowed to fly into battle. I am certain he will be thrilled at the opportunity. Should something happen and your vehicles fall out of your control, our ships will remain in play." The commander lifted her chin a bit higher. "I will fly with you as well."

"Are you sure?" Benny asked, a little taken aback. "What if they need you back here or something?"

Vala raised her mask. "This is the fate of my people, Benny Love of Earth. I cannot sit by and leave it to the hands of others, no matter how capable they have proven to be in the past. No more than you can sit by and rely on others from your planet to protect humanity."

"But, if something happens to you—"

"Griida is more than capable of flying the ship. He knows what this means for the Alpha Maraudi. I trust in his abilities enough to leave him in charge." The commander brought several gold-tipped tentacles before Benny's face. "Besides, this weapon will likely be buried, yes? I can unearth this object of devastation if you will transport it for us."

"That would be . . . superhelpful, actually." Jasmine said.

"Then it is agreed," Vala said.

"I can't wait to fly out with you!" an alien voice shouted from behind them. Zee hopped up the steps, coming to a stop beside Vala and Benny, leaning on the throne. He crossed his arms and tentacles. "Our people will talk about this day for generations to come!"

Vala's eyes narrowed for a moment, and then she turned to Zee, keeping her mask off. "You know that is not possible, young one. You have been placed in more danger than ever should have been allowed already."

"That isn't fair," the little alien said. "I'm just as . . . as . . ." He groaned in frustration and then switched into the alien language.

Benny stood there while the two Alpha Maraudi spoke back and forth to each other in increasingly inharmonious tones, until it sounded like they were competing orchestras, both badly out of tune. The way they were positioned, he had a front row seat to their argument, feeling more and more awkward the longer it went on. Finally, he took a few slow steps backward and turned, ready to suggest to the others that they maybe go somewhere else to talk.

Only to find that everyone else had already skulked away and were relaying the new developments to Elijah.

He caught Hot Dog's eye. She shrugged in apology.

Behind him, Vala's tone seemed to change and grow quieter. Benny heard Zee gasp, and then the kid was running off the bridge.

Vala wheezed something of a whisper, her shoulders slumping.

Benny had no idea what to say or do. He was still standing there, trapped between wanting to leave and wanting to make sure nothing was wrong. Eventually, the latter won out.

"Um," he said carefully. "Is everything okay?"

"Yes," Vala said. "I simply worry about him."

"Well, whatever you said at the end seemed to get the job done."

Vala hesitated, and then let out a long breath. "I spoke the names of those who you would call his parents. Those who died when Tull's life mate attempted to stop the expanding star." The commander's tentacles drooped, hanging to the middle of her back. "We do not speak the names of our dead without warrant. To invoke them is painful, but is one of the most meaningful things that we can do."

"Oh," Benny said. "Sure."

He couldn't help but think of Justin and Alejandro back on Earth. After their father died, they spoke of him often, but almost never in a way that was meant to punish or hurt one of the Love boys. It seemed almost forbidden. Benny could count on one hand the number of times he'd ever had to say something like "Dad wouldn't have wanted you doing that"—and all but one of those occasions was directed at Justin, the older of his two brothers.

What were they doing now? he wondered.

"I think I get that," Benny said. "Sort of."

Vala nodded, but seemed distracted as she pulled the mask back down over her face.

"You should get some rest," the commander said. "All of you. It is still many hours to your Moon, and we must all be in our best conditions for the trial to come."

And with that, Vala descended the steps, leaving Benny alone in front of her throne, still thinking about his family so far away on Earth.

22.

Benny did sleep, eventually, worn out by the exhila-
ration and strain of the day combined with the strangeness
of not having a sun and rotating planet to tell him when
it was time to go to bed—something he definitely had not
gotten used to. In his sleeping tube, he tossed and turned,
dreaming of possible triumphs and, without fail, horrible
intergalactic disasters.

By the time he sat up, sure that he would be getting no
more rest, they were nearing the Moon.

"I was just about to wake you," Pinky said, standing in
front of the wall of circular alcoves in the sleeping chamber.

"I'm up," Benny said through a yawn, stretching his
aching muscles. "Ready to try to stop a secret weapon from
killing a bajillion aliens and then having any remaining
aliens blow up Earth."

"Breakfast first." She nodded to the tube above him.

"I'll leave Drue to you. Get him up for me, will you?"

She disappeared before he could protest.

After they were all awake, they congregated once more on the bridge of the ship, which was beginning to feel something like a home away from home to Benny. There was little else they could do in the way of planning, and so, not wanting to simply sit around, the Moon Platoon told jokes and recounted some of their adventures while downing whatever food they'd scrounged from the mess hall.

There was a strange feeling in the room that Benny couldn't shake, like all of them were secretly afraid that something would go wrong very soon—that this might be the last time they all gathered on the bridge, or anywhere, together. Which made complete sense to Benny. There was so much riding on this. How could they not be worried?

Benny was still so restless from the nightmares and general anxiety about what lay ahead of them that he wanted a few minutes alone to collect his thoughts. And so, he excused himself and decided to walk the halls a little. He wasn't sure where his feet were taking him until they were on the gravel in the great garden. It was humid inside, the air thick with scents he didn't recognize. For all he knew, they might have been smells that most people on Earth would have been able to name, or at least had the words to describe. The Drylands had not given him much of a vocabulary for such things, though.

He shuffled down one of the brightly colored paths, not thinking much about anything—or at least trying not to. Eventually he came to the focal point of the chamber, the milky opal mushroom cap dripping gold.

Elijah West stood in front of it.

The man turned his head slightly when he heard the crunch of Benny's boots behind him.

"Benny Love," he said.

"Oh. Sorry. I didn't realize you were here. I'll let you—"

"No, no," Elijah insisted. "By all means. Join me."

And so he did, the two of them staring at the gossamer rainbow of wonders around them in silence, listening to the steady drips of moisture coming from throughout the garden.

"Have you ever seen anything like this?" Benny asked eventually.

"Never," Elijah admitted. "I didn't even know the ship had this kind of oasis in it. Have you spent much time here? I'm sure it must be quite something for you, given your background."

"Well, this is where we cut through to get to the bridge when we broke in," Benny said. "And . . ." He shook his head.

"What?"

"Nothing. This is where Commander Vala took me to talk to her when we were first aboard. Just the two of us."

Benny laughed a little. "I was kind of terrified. I don't think I realized just *how* terrified at the time, but I was."

"You like the commander?" Elijah asked.

"She's been really good to us."

"That wasn't my question."

The response surprised Benny a little, only because it reminded him of Hot Dog's line of questioning just a few days before, when they had no idea what they were getting themselves into, not really, or how things would go with Vala and the rest of her crew. Before he'd stood on moons two planets away from his own.

"I do," he finally said. He shrugged. "And I trust her. Anyone Tull wants to kill is probably on our side, I think. And believe me when I say his pilots were *definitely* trying to blow up your Chevelle when I was driving her around."

Elijah nodded, and seemed to roll this around in his head for a few moments. "The only Alpha Maraudi I'd ever met in person until Tull and his guards dragged me out of the hangar were those Austin—*Dr. Bale* and I stumbled across in the secret base. All I knew of their kind was what we pieced together through the things they left behind. Tools. A few holograms. Those exploding asteroids. You can guess how strange it was to meet Vala. Or *Zee*. I never considered what their children would be like. Never thought of their planet's flora and fauna . . ." He trailed off, letting his eyes wander through the garden. "I would say something like this is worth trying to save. That *people* like this are worth it."

"Yeah," Benny said, and he couldn't help but smile a little. "Me, too."

There was a click somewhere above them, and then Vala's voice came through on a sort of intercom system.

"As far as our sensors can tell, we've avoided detection by any human or Alpha Maraudi forces," she said. "Jasmine has used the scanner to locate the weapon site. We're nearing a suitable spot for the mother ship to wait while we work. Time is scarce. Meet in the hangar."

Benny let out a long breath and then started down the path toward the door. "I guess we should go."

"Benny . . ." Elijah said.

The boy stopped and turned to him.

"Earlier, when I was talking to you and Ricardo . . ." Elijah paused. "What I wanted to thank you for was having the courage to stand up to me back at the Taj. Even now, there's a difference in the way you look at me compared to the way basically every other person in my life has for years. The Pit Crew, I think, still believes I'm infallible, despite all evidence to the contrary. I wasn't sure how to phrase that in front of Ricardo without making it sound like I was reprimanding him. The Pit Crew is so loyal, so devoted. And that's my fault. I love them. But what you and your friends have done . . . I can't begin to repay you."

Benny stared at him for a few long beats.

"A Mustang-red Space Runner," he finally said.

"Pardon?" Elijah asked.

"A Mustang-red Space Runner and a top-of-the-line gaming system," Benny continued. "That's for Hot Dog. For *starters*." He shook his head. "I don't know what the rest of them will want, but you can bet Drue is going to make you wish you'd never met him."

Elijah laughed once. "Done. Anything. What about you?"

"Once I'm back with my family and Earth is safe?" Benny asked. He shrugged. "I'm sure I'll think of something."

Benny found his friends and the Pit Crew already gathered in the hangar along with Ash McGuyver and Pinky. Pito and Vala inspected a few of the purple Alpha Maraudi ships near the entrance. Benny and Elijah joined the rest of the humans.

"How're we looking, Jazz?" Benny asked.

She held up the scanner. "The weapon is buried near the center of the Jules Verne crater."

"Ah." Elijah stroked his beard. "Of course it is."

"I've already uploaded the coordinates to Space Runner mainframes," Pinky said. "And Griida's . . . done whatever the alien equivalent of that is."

"Jules Verne?" Drue asked. "Why does that sound familiar? Was she a celebrity or something? A two-D movie star?"

"*He* was an author," Elijah said. "Nineteenth century. Fantastic adventures."

"Sure. Right." And then, something sparked in Drue's eyes. "Hey, *we* should get spots on the Moon named after us. I'm a space hero! People should be burying their secret weapons in the Lincoln crater!"

Benny glanced at Elijah. "You have the first thing on his list now."

Elijah just smiled and shook his head.

"They were about to divvy up cars," Ash McGuyver said, wiping her hands on her sides. She pulled a pair of big, gold-rimmed sunglasses out of the pocket of her coveralls and handed them to Elijah. "Found these floating around in some of the stuff we brought up from the garage. Thought you might want 'em."

Elijah's face lit up. "I love this pair," he said, sliding the frames on top of his head, into the nest of his auburn hair. "You are too good to me, Ash."

"Remember that. Now, what'll you be driving, boss?"

He shrugged. "I figured I'd take that mammoth over there," he said, pointing to Ash's oversized SR—the car that would be dragging the missile back to the mother ship.

Ash shook her head. "Never thought I'd see the day

you picked the slowest thing on the floor, but with circumstances what they are, I guess it makes sense. I'll get her ready for you."

She hurried away as Kira started toward a white SR.

"I'll take my car," she said. "Obviously."

"Mine's still in the garage back home," Trevone said. "Or at least, I hope it is. One of the training SRs with a laser mount will do fine, though. In case we need to carve into anything."

"Star Runner" is all Ricardo said.

Hot Dog turned to Drue. "You want the other one? I had a good run with her already."

Drue looked at the gold speed demon for a few moments and then let out a long sigh, shaking his head. "I can't believe I'm saying this, but no." He turned slightly, eyeing the weaponized Space Runner Ricardo had driven back from Io. "I'll drive my dad's car."

Benny raised his gold glove and made a fist. "I'm piloting one of the Alpha Maraudi ships."

Everyone turned to look at him, a vacuum of silence settling over them.

"Uh, Benny, maybe—" Hot Dog started finally.

"Absolutely not," Pinky interrupted. "First of all, I can't—"

"Guys," Benny said, holding his palms out in front of him. "It was a joke. I'll take one of the laser SRs, too."

"Phew." Hot Dog sighed. "I did *not* wanna have to watch you crash and burn in that thing on, like, one of the most important days of our lives."

Drue leaned in close to him. "But seriously," he said quietly, "you think we could take one of those alien ships out with that glove?"

"If everything goes as planned today," Benny said, "maybe we'll find out."

Pito and Vala walked over to them, fastening collars around their necks that would let them communicate with the group once they were in space.

"Elijah West," Pito said. It looked to Benny as if the gold covering most of his head had been polished very recently. "I am Pito. We have not yet met, but I have looked at many of your designs with great interest over the years." He held his palm out. "I believe this is customary in your culture?"

"A pleasure," Elijah said, shaking the alien's four-fingered hand.

"Were it not for the stakes before us, I would be thrilled right now. It has been cycles since I have flown with any purpose." The alien paused, his single tentacle snaking around his neck. "But you will find that I am highly capable."

"Once we return," Vala said, "Pito can tell you everything we know about our expanding star."

Elijah raised both his eyebrows. "I look forward to it."

"Commander," Jasmine said, stepping forward and

holding out Dr. Bale's radar. "You'll need this if you're going to dig out that weapon. It's only so precise from up here, but it will lead you straight to the missile once you're closer to the surface." She paused. "It's the only one we have, so . . ."

Vala took it, nodding to her. "I will bring it back as it is now." She looked to the others. "We should be going with haste. Are you ready?"

"Just say the word," Benny said.

Vala stared at him.

"Whenever you are," Hot Dog clarified.

The commander bowed slightly to them. "Then let us be on our way. If you'll follow me, I'll open the wall for you." She glanced at Jasmine. "I suggest you leave the room before that happens."

"That's our cue," Jasmine said. "Ash. Ramona. Let's head to the bridge."

"Don't crash," Ramona said. "Major bummer."

Pinky took a look around at them. "Be careful, everyone. I'm so proud of you." Her eyes lingered on Elijah. "And if I see so much as one unnecessarily flashy move . . ."

"I'll be good," he said. "I promise."

As those staying behind on the mother ship left the hangar, Benny spotted Zee in the corner. The alien walked up to Vala slowly, saying things Benny couldn't hear and handing over an object he couldn't make out at first. And then he realized what it was: the shiny red ball. Vala placed it in her tentacles and then drew Zee in close for a quick embrace, whispering something to him. The alien child hesitated for a moment, and then was gone. The entry to the hangar closed behind him.

Benny slid into one of the laser-mounted Space Runners painted with Mustang-red stripes. He settled in as best he could, and then pulled his father's silver hood ornament out of his space suit pocket, placing it in one of the cup holders so that it was looking at him, watching over him. If something went wrong and he had to abandon his car, at least this way he'd be able to grab it easily.

"Are we ready?" Vala asked over the comms.

And when they all said yes, the purple ship rose above them, slowly drifting to the edge of the hangar. The entirety of the hull wall retracted in seconds, and one by one they took off, soaring out into the unfathomable vastness of space. Benny was the second to last, in front of Elijah; and once he was out of the hangar he caught his first glimpse of the Moon in days and, behind it, the spinning ball he called home. As they came into view, he could barely breathe.

Benny kept his eyes on Earth the entire flight. At top speeds, it was a fairly short trip to the dark side for the nine pilots—or maybe he just lost track of time as he stared at his home planet. Either way, eventually it was blotted out by the Moon and his focus shifted to the crater-covered sea of gray.

"Seems like ages since I've been home," Elijah said over the comms. "How I've missed this sight."

"Jazz, how are we looking?" Benny asked.

"So far so good," she said. "I can't tell what's happening at the Taj or on the other side, but I don't see anything on the mother ship's radar."

"Let's hope it stays that way," Ricardo said.

Vala came over the comms. "Pito and I could try to excavate the weapon from our crafts, but it will be faster if we land and feel the ground and rock itself."

"I'm happy doing this as fast as possible," Benny said. "Anyone else?"

"Faster the better," Elijah said. "It'll only take a few seconds for me to latch on to the case once it's above ground, but I'll be slow afterward. It's a lot of mass to tow."

"We'll cover you," Ricardo assured him.

Hot Dog groaned. "Ugh. I was always so bad at protection missions in games."

"Comforting," Kira said flatly.

"No one worry," Drue said. "I'm a great shot! I'm on top of it."

As they drew closer, the blinking spot on Benny's windshield got larger, until he could see exactly where they were going with his naked eye. The Jules Verne crater was a large one, almost one hundred and fifty kilometers across, dotted with a few even deeper pockmarks within. It was darker than the surrounding area, a steely gray pool below them.

"All right," Jasmine said over the comms as they began their descents to the surface. "If Vala and Pito are landing, I suggest Elijah head down with them and the rest of you six make a circle a hundred meters above the surface. That'll give them some breathing room."

"You got it, Jazz," Benny said.

"On me," Ricardo barked, the commanding tone he'd always taken when ordering the Mustangs around suddenly back in his voice.

They followed the leader of the Pit Crew, spacing themselves out as evenly as possible, forming a ring above the site where the electromagnetic missile was buried. The two alien ships hovered just over the ground as Vala and Pito jumped out onto the surface, shining red masks covering their faces. The commander held Dr. Bale's scanner, bounding in long strides across the Moon, slowing down once she got a lock on where the weapon was and how far below it was buried.

"Ah," Pito said. "What a relief that *this* moon is not covered in ice. Ganymede was a nightmare to dig into. A pity we had to leave it behind after we'd put so much work into it."

"We are here," Vala said. "The missile is far below us. It will take a little time. Pito. Let us begin."

"As you wish, commander."

From his spot in the Space Runner, it was difficult for Benny to see exactly what was happening at first. The two Alpha Maraudi stood facing each other several yards apart. A few of Vala's tentacles flipped forward as Pito removed something dark from his pocket and placed it on the ground. Both of them got to their knees, and Benny could just make out a few flashes of gold as their tentacles and palms touched the basalt bottom of the crater.

"What the heck are they—" Drue started.

"Shhhh," Kira chided him.

At first, it seemed as though nothing was happening. And then Benny could see two circles of alien rock growing to the size of dinner plates in front of each of them—they had *planted* the strange minerals that they could control and were now using them to mine, as though the minerals themselves were alive, rooting into the surface of the Moon. The ground cracked around them. Excess debris spit out of the new rifts that formed, settling into haphazard piles. It looked to Benny as if the entire surface of the crater was shaking beneath them. All the while, Vala and Pito remained absolutely motionless, completely focused on the task at hand.

"By the glory of the Milky Way . . ." Elijah murmured.

Benny couldn't help but agree.

We're doing it, he thought.

Which was when everything went wrong.

There was a beeping in Benny's space suit collar—the kind that only ever sounded when he was connected to a new comm system.

"That's weird . . ." he murmured.

And then Dr. Bale's voice came out of the speakers near Benny's ears.

"I don't know how you found it," the man sneered, "but you're wasting your time."

Benny flinched and gripped his flight yoke so hard that his knuckles all cracked.

"Where is he?" Ricardo shouted.

"I don't know!" Jasmine said of the comms. "Nearby, maybe? He's using his stealth."

The only radar they had that was capable of seeing through Bale's holographic camouflage was down in the crater with Vala. The ground continued to shake under her and Pito as they mined deeper, Moon rock burbling to the surface, piling up around them. All the gold on Pito's head appeared to be glowing.

"Where's my dad?" Drue shouted. "Let us talk to him. We had a deal. An armistice!"

"Is that little Drue the third?" Dr. Bale asked. "Unfortunately, Senator Lincoln was seriously injured in the fight against the Alpha Maraudi on Io. He's resting comfortably in a coma back at the Taj's infirmary."

Benny could hear Drue's angry breath in his ear.

"As such," Dr. Bale continued, "I am now in control of Project New Apollo."

"It's not too late to rethink this, Austin," Elijah said. "Trust me. You don't want to use this weapon."

"Elijah," Dr. Bale spat, hatred dripping from every syllable. "Of course you're still alive. Like some kind of interstellar cockroach. That's fine. *Good*, even. I want you to see what I've created, what *we* could have done together if you only had the vision."

A gunmetal gray ship unlike any Benny had ever seen

appeared in the distance, shooting toward them. It was shaped like a thick, blunt arrowhead, with an aerodynamic front that sloped up over a large window looking into some sort of bridge.

The *Orion*.

"Holy whoa," Benny whispered.

"I figured that thing was gonna be big, but this is ridiculous," Hot Dog said. "It's like half the size of the mother ship!"

"Not quite," Pinky said. Figures filled the windshield as she analyzed the vessel. "I'm picking up huge amounts of energy at the rear."

"We're so close," Vala said. Benny glanced down—both of the aliens were still on their knees. "We've reached the weapon."

"Then we try to buy some time," Ricardo said.

"You are interfering with Project New Apollo, and therefore the future of every human being in existence," Dr. Bale said, his tone taking an authoritative air. "Troops, you know your orders. Secure the weapon site."

And then, one by one, Benny could see dozens of weaponized New Apollo Space Runners floating in the distance behind the *Orion* as their stealth drives disengaged.

"You're outnumbered!" Jasmine shouted.

"We can *see* that," Kira spat.

"We need"—Vala croaked, straining to talk—"just a little more time."

"You heard her," Ricardo said. "Whatever happens, don't let them near the crater."

"Be *careful*," Elijah said.

"Don't worry," Hot Dog replied. "We're getting good at this."

Her Star Runner shot forward toward the massive ship, a blaze of gold against the black backdrop of space.

Benny chased after her before he had a chance to even think about what he was doing, the others following suit.

"So, do we have a plan, or . . . ?" Benny asked.

"Yeah," Drue said. "We're winging it."

"Ramona," Trevone said. "Can you cut Bale out? We don't want him hearing what we're saying."

"Done," Ramona said. "Max security."

"Drue," Ricardo said, "stay back and protect the others."

"But—"

"You're our best shot, right?"

"Oh," Drue said. "Of course. Count on me."

"Pinky's found designs of the *Orion* based on our scans," Jasmine said. "It looks like there are two huge cannons on either side. Watch out for—"

A bolt of gold energy as thick as a Space Runner shot

from the ship. Hot Dog reacted in a split second, her car diving and the shot missing her by what looked like inches.

"I see one of them," Hot Dog yelled. "Uh, maybe someone with an actual laser or something could work on that? I'm kind of relying on speed here. I'll try to distract, you know, the gazillion smaller cars."

"I'm on it," Trevone said, speeding forward.

"I'll go after the other one," Benny said.

He leaned into his flight yoke as he approached the *Orion*, crossing above a clear window that looked into the bridge where he could just make out the silhouette of a human figure. The surface of the craft was a matte carbon color, making it easy for him to spot the cannon on the side—it was glowing gold, as though it were charging up.

Benny gritted his teeth and pushed forward, pressing on the button that fired the mining laser attached to the front of his Space Runner. After a few tries, he managed to blast the cannon, holding down the trigger, hitting it with a steady stream of focused energy.

But nothing happened.

"This thing's got major shielding," he said, flying toward the back of the ship, ready to make another pass.

"I know," Trevone said. "I hit it dead on several times and didn't scratch it."

As Benny's Space Runner looped around, he caught sight of the back of the *Orion* for the first time. It was a flat, rectangular surface at least five hundred feet tall, covered in alternating yellow triangles that spanned the full height of the ship. They burned so brightly that Benny almost had to look away.

Hot Dog must have been seeing the same thing. "Those can't be hyperdrives, right?"

"I'm afraid they are," Trevone said. "Or at least, something *like* hyperdrives."

"Ughhh," Drue groaned. "I'm missing it."

The *Orion* slowed down as it approached Vala. Meanwhile, the fleet of New Apollo Space Runners seemed to speed up, until they were almost upon Benny and the others.

"All right," Ricardo said. "Let's show these guys what it means to be on the Pit Crew. Kira! Remember the mobility practices we used to do? Follow my lead."

"*Hai!*" she said.

Ricardo and Kira shot forward, meeting the oncoming wave of weaponized cars head on. They avoided the golden bolts fired at them with an ease that Benny couldn't imagine, their speeds only increasing as they flew. When they finally reached the front line, the two Pit Crew members suddenly dove toward one another, their crafts almost touching. And then they were weaving in and out of the rows of enemy cars, looping past them, hardly anything but blurs.

"Y'all don't get all the fun!" Hot Dog shouted as her Star Runner shot forward, cutting off several of the enemy vehicles just like Benny had watched her do back on Io.

The New Apollo pilots seemed totally unprepared for such an unorthodox, weaponless assault, and tried to veer out of the way of the expert pilots' paths, crashing into one another, breaking formation. One of them fired, aiming at Hot Dog. But she was long gone by the time the bolt shot through the hull of one of the other weaponized SRs, which then careened out into open space.

"Guys, those cannons are gathering a *lot* of energy," Jasmine said. "Based on the position, the one on the port side could easily take out Vala and Pito."

"No," Benny said. "Not Vala and Pito. He wants *Elijah*."

"Maybe all of them," Trevone said.

"Any big ideas, Trevone?" Benny asked, as he circled back, shooting at the cannon again. But it was no use: he wasn't getting through with his weak laser.

"How 'bout any big ideas, *Drue*," Drue said. "Benny, trade places with me."

"But—"

"I'm doing what you guys wanted!" Drue continued. "I'm protecting everyone! Let me take a shot at it."

"Fine," Benny said as he changed his course and headed back toward Elijah. He passed Drue's car along the way. Watching in the rearview mirror, it looked like Drue was about to fly directly into the port-side cannon.

"Wait!" Benny shouted. "What are you doing?"

"I've got this!" his friend yelled.

Drue's weaponized SR sped faster, headed straight for the glowing, oversized weapon that looked like it could go off at any moment. Benny held his breath, his chest seizing, terrified that his friend was going to crash against the *Orion* in order to save them.

But instead of flying into the cannon, Drue began firing at the weapon with the plasma bolts Dr. Bale had designed, diving at the last second and twisting his father's Space Runner around so that the cannon was pummeled from every side as he flew in an arcing loop.

"Woo-hoo!" Drue shouted. The mining lasers Benny and Trevone had tried to use against the *Orion*'s weaponry had been useless, but the gold beams shooting from Senator Lincoln's car ripped through cannon. And then, in a huge burst of energy, it exploded, rocking the *Orion* and sending Drue's car spinning away from them at incredible speeds.

"Drue!" Benny shouted.

"I'm fine," Drue said. He paused. "Did you see that?! I was amazing!"

Benny couldn't help but grin. "Nice shooting. And fly-ing."

"Learned it from Hot Dog."

"You'll have to thank me for that if we survive," she said.

Benny turned his focus back to Pito and Vala. He had just enough time to breathe a sigh of relief before bolts of energy rained down on the middle of the Jules Verne crater.

While the rest of the Moon Platoon and Pit Crew had their attention on the *Orion* and the fleet behind it, a single New Apollo ship had snuck past them, its stealth shielding gone now that it was attacking.

Dust filled the crater. Benny gunned his hyperdrive, trying to see what had happened as the debris began to clear. Where was Elijah? Vala? Pito?

Then he spotted it—Ash's tank of an SR was on the ground.

"Elijah?!" Benny yelled.

There was a coughing on the comms. "I'm here. But . . ." Benny watched as the door to the oversized SR was kicked open, Elijah West spilling out onto the surface of the Moon. "This tow truck is dead."

Benny suddenly felt cold, like all the blood had drained from his body.

Vala was sprawled across the ground, already picking herself back up. Pito was on his back on the other side of the crater, apparently blown away by the blast. He was trying to get up, but even if he got back to the weapon site, they had no way of getting the missile to the ship now. And with no hope of diffusing it in the middle of a battlefield, Benny wasn't sure what they were supposed to do.

The New Apollo Space Runner looped around, coming in for another pass, heading back toward Vala and Elijah.

Benny knew he'd only get one chance at this, and he couldn't risk blowing it. His Space Runner surged forward, his finger over the trigger of his laser. As soon as the enemy was in his sights, he fired.

But he missed. The other SR dove out of the way, close to the ground, dodging.

No, he thought. No, no, no.

And then, out of nowhere, another laser blast shot across the crater, striking the side of the New Apollo car. It pitched forward, its hood catching the surface of the Moon, which caused it to cartwheel across the basalt before skidding to a stop upside down hundreds of yards away from Vala and Elijah.

A silver Space Runner Benny couldn't account for shot past him.

"Take that, you . . ." an alien voice said. "Fidgets? Idioms?"

A human girl groaned. "*Idiots,*" she said.

Benny recognized the voice. It was Iyabo. And . . .

"Zee?!" Vala shouted. "What do you think you're doing?"

"Protecting our people," the alien said. "*And* you."

"*Iyabo?*" Benny asked.

"You know it," Iyabo said. "Can't believe you guys left

319

me behind on the ship. Some of us are *good* at this sorta thing if you'll remember. Plus, this little squid baby in my passenger seat was starting to get really annoying. I half came out here just to shut 'im up."

"I told you not to call me that!" Zee shouted.

"Look," Iyabo said, "I got you a comm collar and stole an SR. I'll call you what I want."

"Ooo! Up there! Let's shoot that one next!"

Benny watched as a dozen new Space Runners from the mother ship joined the fight above them. It wasn't much, but it helped their numbers at least. Still, the New Apollo forces were overwhelming them, even as Iyabo's ship shot off to help.

Vala was calling out over the comms in her alien language as Benny landed beside her and Elijah. He was sure the commander was yelling at Zee, but the alien kid either wasn't responding or had turned off his comms.

"What do we do?" Benny asked, jumping out of his car.

Elijah looked dumbfounded. "I . . . I don't know."

Vala's tentacles were whipping frantically. "We have reached the missile," she said. She kept looking from the ground back to the ships above them, searching for Zee. "It's surrounded by our rock now. Is there another of these towing trucks?"

"No," Elijah said. "That was it. And if we bring it up

now, it'll just be easier for the *Orion* to pick up. We can't move it ourselves."

Benny stared at the glowing alien stone at his feet, imagining it wrapped around the missile casing so far down below them.

"Then maybe we don't bring it to the surface," he said, an idea starting to form.

"What do you mean?" Vala asked.

Benny turned to the two of them. "Maybe we bury it more."

Elijah smiled. "So deep that they can't get it. That could work."

"Straight into the underground city, even."

"That—" Vala started. She paused. "Yes." And then she repeated the word, a hint of relief in her voice. "Yes. It can be done."

"Hold on," Elijah said. He suddenly looked very concerned. "The last time I saw a bunch of alien rock up here, it was prone to *exploding* easily. Aren't we just setting a fuse if we do this? One stray laser blast and a chunk of the Moon is gone."

"Not all our minerals are alike," Vala said. "Their properties are vast. This rock is safe. It will protect." She reached a tentacle out and placed it on Elijah's shoulder. "You have my word."

Elijah looked to Benny for a moment and then back to the commander. "Okay."

Vala nodded. And then, she hesitated, glancing to the far end of the crater.

"Pito's strength was draining even before the attack," the commander said, turning to focus on Benny. "If we do this, I need your help."

Benny stared up at Vala in confusion for a second before realizing what she meant. He looked down at his golden glove and then back up at her.

"Whoa, whoa," he said. "I have no idea how to use this thing. Mostly I just destroy stuff with it!"

Vala pulled the top half of her red mask off with two tentacles, staring down at Benny with three eyes.

"Trust me, Benny Love of Earth," the commander said. "You can do this. You *must* do this. For my people. And for yours."

Benny swallowed hard—he wished so badly that he could look up now and see Earth above him. But he knew it was there, on the other side of the Moon. Still spinning.

For now.

Finally, he nodded. "Let's do it."

Vala motioned for him to follow, and then they were both kneeling on the ground around one of the circles of glowing Alpha Maraudi mineral. The commander placed two gold-tipped tentacles on top of it. Benny put his gloved hand on the other side. The key seemed to vibrate, growing warmer.

"Clear your mind of anything but what you feel under your hand," Vala said.

He shut his eyes for a second and took a deep breath, trying to do as instructed. When he opened them again, he found that Vala's bottom two eyes were closed, but the blue one on top was still wide open, staring at him.

"Now," Vala said. "Focus."

The commander's eye began to burn, the intensity seeming to grow with every second, until it was all Benny could look at, all he could see, the blinding light coming from her head completely enveloping him. He cried out as the key started to burn—not with heat but with energy, as though Benny suddenly had a comet full of power in his palm.

And then, all at once, it was as if he could *feel* the rock below him, the rivers of light that coursed through the Alpha Maraudi mineral that had been planted in the ground—and the weapon container that it surrounded. As he focused, he pushed the energy he felt in his hand out, until he could sense that the rock below them was pulsing, growing, shooting farther and farther into the Moon.

But it wasn't just underground. As the alien stone continued to dig deeper, it also spread over the surface, all around them, echoes of glowing light roiling through it and causing the crater to look as though it were being covered in some sort of cosmic thunderstorm.

People were yelling in Benny's helmet—Trevone was shot down, the wing of Hot Dog's Star Runner had been hit and she was losing control—but he could barely register the meaning behind the words.

The more energy he poured into the glove, the more he felt like he was slipping away, losing control, until just at the moment when he thought he might disappear into Vala's glowing eye forever, something exploded between them. Suddenly, he could see again, all his senses flooding back in one overwhelming burst.

Vala fell to the ground hard, eyes closed, her tentacles splayed limply around her head. The glowing red ball rolled away, and Benny instinctively grabbed it as it came to a stop in front of him, shoving it into his pocket.

"Vala!" he shouted, trying to lurch forward, but in doing so, he realized he could barely keep himself upright.

"She's breathing," Elijah said. "I think. I don't know. Benny—"

The alien radar was still in one of Vala's hands, and Benny crawled over to it, scrambling to see what they had done.

Dr. Bale's superweapon was so far beneath the surface of the Moon that it barely even registered anymore.

Benny collapsed, rolling over onto his back.

"Are you okay?" Elijah asked, at his side in an instant. "Benny, talk to me."

Benny looked up. The *Orion* was above them now. Its remaining cannon was charging up. One shot and they'd be gone.

Would Dr. Bale risk shooting them? Did he know how far underground the weapon was? Could he still retrieve it?

Had they made any difference at all?

"How strong do you think this rock is?" Benny asked.

Elijah shook his head. "I just hope Vala was telling the truth when she said it wouldn't explode." He tugged at Benny, trying to get him to his feet. "Come on. We have to get you out of here."

But, suddenly, Benny had an idea. Elijah's fear from earlier. Dr. Bale's collection of asteroids. All the tests they'd done on how to blow them up.

He shook off Elijah's grip. "Ramona," he said through heavy breaths, "patch me in to Dr. Bale."

"Epic troll is on the line," she said over the comms.

"Dr. Bale?" Benny asked.

"Have you called to plead for your life?" Dr. Bale asked. "Or for the lives of these monsters you have decided to betray your species for?"

Benny shook his head a little, exhaustion threatening to take him over. He didn't want to talk or negotiate. He just wanted to end this here while he could.

"You're right, doctor. I am a traitor. I've sided with the aliens against you."

"Whatever you just tried was futile," Dr. Bale said. "Nothing has changed. I will carve that weapon out of the side of the Moon and take it from you."

"No, you won't," Benny said. "Are you forgetting what happens to alien rock when it's shot? Think hard. One stray laser or blast—one downed Space Runner—would blow this whole crater *and* your weapon up. Think of what that would do to the Moon. Think of what that would do to *Earth*."

Elijah stared at him as he spoke, shaking his head, pointing to Vala. The commander had *just* given her word that this wasn't the case.

But as Benny finished talking, he winked at Elijah, and he seemed to understand.

The rock was harmless. But Dr. Bale didn't know that.

"You fools," Dr. Bale said. "Do you have any idea how dangerous—"

Benny took a deep breath and let out one of the explosion noises Ramona liked to make. "If I were you, I'd call off your goons and maybe stop firing your weapons anywhere near this crater."

There was silence on the comms for a long time. Finally, Dr. Bale spoke again. "Cease firing, you idiots," he yelled to his troops. "You'll kill us all. Retreat."

Elijah stared at Benny, his head shaking slightly.

"You won't get away with this," Dr. Bale said.

A smile crept across Benny's face as he rolled his head toward Elijah.

"Can you handle the rest?" he asked. "I think I need a nap."

Benny woke up in a room made of smooth, glowing stone that he'd never seen before, on a bed that had grown out of the floor. He was groggy, not really sure he wasn't dreaming. His body felt so heavy that he could barely move anything but his head. All he wanted to do was go back to sleep, to rest until his brothers woke him by jumping on his bed and begging him to get up. Or until his grandmother poked his side, telling him he needed to have breakfast.

Or his father tousled his hair, warning that he was missing the best hours of the day.

He almost did fall back asleep, but as he turned his head, something glittered in his peripheral vision. On the table beside him—among several pouches of food and water— sat a golden glove and a silver hood ornament.

In a single jolt he was awake, eyes wide, trying to sit up

in bed as everything that had just happened on the Moon began to flood his mind.

"Whoa, whoa," Elijah said from a chair near the foot of his bed. "Take it easy. You've been through a lot."

"Wha . . . ?" Benny started. "Whe . . ."

Elijah pulled out a HoloTek and tapped on it. "Let me just tell Pinky you're awake. She was very worried about—"

Before he could finish, the AI appeared beside Benny's bed, causing him to jump a little.

"How do you feel?" she asked. "Where does it hurt? We've run some scans and you don't appear to be injured, but trust your body. What do you need? What can I get you?"

"Um . . ." Benny said, looking around. "Where am I? How long have I been asleep?"

"The sick bay on Vala's ship," Elijah said, standing. "And not that long. Just a few hours since we got back. Whatever you and the commander did down there completely wiped you out."

"The commander . . ." Benny whispered, slowly starting to remember. "Vala! Is she—?"

"Okay," Pinky said. "We think. Pito has been taking care of her." The AI bit her lip. "The commander expended a lot of energy in a way that frankly I don't understand. It may take some time for her to recover. Zee is with her now.

329

He's hardly left her bedside."

"The kid is growing on me," Elijah said. "Especially after saving my butt."

"Oh!" Pinky exclaimed, perking up a bit. "I should tell the others you're up."

And then she blinked out of existence.

Benny just stared at Elijah. "What happened back there?"

Elijah shrugged. "You saved the day, kid. Quick thinking with that bluff. I think Dr. Bale might have wet his pants. *I* probably would have if I hadn't heard Vala promise it wasn't exploding rock we were all standing on." He got quieter. "And even then, I wasn't one hundred percent sure we weren't all going to blow up." He grinned at Benny. "Don't worry. I took some samples and tested the mineral. The commander was telling the truth."

Benny shook his head, trying to figure out where to begin. "What about Dr. Bale?"

Elijah shook his head. "I demanded that he surrender the *Orion* and all his ships to us. Which he refused. And then, he and his entire fleet just . . . left. I think he was so worried about being caught up in the hypothetical blast that all he cared about in that moment was saving his own skin and his toys. We tracked him as far as we could, but we lost him eventually. He's a madman, but he *is* a genius."

Elijah sighed. "Those ships are *fast*. I can't wait to pore over the blueprints." He seemed lost in thought for a beat before shaking his head. "Anyway, he was headed into deeper space, not toward Earth. And, if he thinks there's a ton of volatile alien rock surrounding his superweapon, I don't think he's going to be too keen on trying to mine it out." He paused. "Hopefully."

Benny nodded. That was at least one thing he had an answer to.

"Everyone else made it back okay?" And then fear seized his guts. "I remember something on the comms. Trevone was shot down? Or Hot Dog?"

"Everyone's fine," Elijah assured him. "More or less. There were some bumps and bruises and . . ." He got quiet. "Maybe a concussion or two." Then he plastered a grin on his face. "But for the most part, A-OK. Trevone's not even here right now. He and the rest of the Pit Crew went to scout out the resort and see how many people are left there."

Benny opened his mouth, but Elijah kept talking. "Don't worry. They're scanning from far away and not engaging if they see anyone." Creases formed on the man's forehead. "They'd better bring back pictures like I asked."

"Why didn't you go yourself?" Benny asked.

Elijah looked away for a second and then back at Benny. "I had to make sure you were okay, didn't I?"

Before Benny could even begin to figure out how to respond to that, Hot Dog and Drue burst through the doorway.

"Benny!" Hot Dog shouted.

"Nice of you to rejoin the living, man," Drue said with a smirk that quickly grew into a full-fledged smile.

"How are you?"

"You look like a zombie."

"I'm okay," Benny said. "Just really tired."

Hot Dog tossed her hair back as she sighed in relief, and Benny noticed a bandage near the top of her forehead.

"Whoa, are you okay?" he asked.

"Oh, this?" she asked. "It's nothing. My head just smashed against the window a little when I accidentally got too close to one of those enemy SRs."

"That . . . sounds like a normal day," Benny said.

"It's weird, right?" Drue asked. "It's like she's indestructible."

"Please don't jinx me like that," Hot Dog said. "Also, my Star Runner got shot twice. I mean, just the wings, but still." She turned to Elijah. "Really smart, useless decorations, by the way. Those cars run on hyperdrives! They don't *need* wings. Not to mention the fact that all the shiny gold paint makes them incredibly easy to target."

"My cars were never meant to be flown into a battle, period," Elijah said. "Plus, those are prototypes."

"I'm *fine* by the way," Drue said to Benny.

"Yeah, well, you did spend half the fight spinning around in space," Hot Dog said, looking at her nails.

"Hey! I blew up that cannon! I'm collecting *so many* medals that my space suit is going to be too heavy to wear. Just as soon as I'm back on Earth and can get them made."

"Wait, where are Jazz and Ramona?" Benny asked.

"Jazz got superexcited about something she found when she was looking at the design of Dr. Bale's weapon," Hot Dog said. "Pinky went to grab her. I think she's down in Pito's lab."

"And Ramona sends her best," Drue said. "I think. She said something about hoping your system didn't get defragged? I don't think she's much of a stop-in-and-see-a-sick-friend kind of person, if you know what I mean."

Benny nodded. "Yeah. I do." He pushed his hands against the bed, trying to sit up straighter. "Okay. So, the weapon is safely stuck in the middle of the Moon and every-one's alive. That's good. Now . . . we just have to deal with the Alpha Maraudi." Benny shrugged. "No big."

"If possible," Elijah said, "I wouldn't mind going back to the Taj. It makes a fine base of operations, and if Senator Lincoln was telling the truth, most of Vala's crew is there. I'm sure the commander would like to have them back." Elijah bobbed his head to one side. "Also, I miss it."

"I'm down for that," Drue said. "And, you know. My

dad's there." He took a deep breath. "We're so close by. I should make sure he's okay."

"*And* we can talk to Earth from the resort," Hot Dog said. "That's useful. We have no idea what's been going on back home."

"Definitely," Benny said. "Oh, man. My family must be so worried about me."

Elijah nodded. "You'll get the first call. You've earned it."

Benny smiled. "Let's do it, then. As soon as Ricardo and the rest are back and tell us what's going on there. We've survived aliens and the New Apollo forces a few times. We can totally take back the Taj."

A shadow appeared in the doorway across the room as Pito walked in. His once-shiny gold plating was smudged and dented in a few places.

"If I may have a moment," he said.

"You're not hurt, are you?" Benny asked. "That was a heck of a blast."

"I've been through much worse," Pito said. His voice was grim, lips pulled tight across his face. Something was wrong.

"What is it?" Elijah asked, obviously noticing.

"Is Vala . . . ?" Benny started.

"The commander remains unconscious," Pito said. "I believe she will make a full recovery. I just do not know when." The scientist hesitated. "We have received a message from Calam."

Silence fell over the room.

"I am unsure of what Tull told our leaders, exactly, but they seem to believe Vala has been completely manipulated by the children from Earth. And with the commander unable to defend herself right now . . ." He trailed off, and then sighed. "Tull has been given full permission to attack Earth again. It will take some time, given the state of his ship, but he will no doubt begin making more asteroids. At the very least. I would not be surprised if reinforcements are called in as well."

"No!" Benny said. "That's not . . . But we stopped the weapon! That was supposed to show that we can work together."

"Your home world is being cautious," Elijah said. He clenched his jaw, shaking his head. "I can't say I blame them."

"Hey, we beat this ET twice already!" Hot Dog said. "What's a third time?"

"Yeah," Drue agreed. "Plus, if we can go back to the Taj . . ." His head whipped around to Elijah. "Tell me you've got crazy-secret stuff there we've never even dreamed of. Things that weren't in your prototype files!"

"Tull is prepared for us now, though," Benny said, worry starting to settle in his chest. "He didn't know about our lasers the first time. Or our electromagnetic gloves when we busted Elijah out. But there'll be no surprising him now."

"That's not true," a voice came from the doorway. Jasmine stood there, a smile painted across her face. "Remember what Dr. Bale said on Io? With science, anything is possible."

Benny's face scrunched in confusion for a moment before slowly relaxing.

"Jazz," he said. And then he grinned. "What've you got for us?"

Don't miss these books by
JERAMEY KRAATZ!

"A blockbuster mix of thrills, adrenaline, and lead characters who are as clever as they are courageous."

—Soman Chainani, *New York Times* bestselling author of *The School for Good and Evil*

HARPER
An Imprint of HarperCollinsPublishers

www.harpercollinschildrens.com